"for Mischief done"

Jan Schenk Grosskopf

Andres & Blanton
Niantic, Connecticut

"for Mischief done"

Published by Andres & Blanton
Niantic, Connecticut

ISBN 978-0-9830318-2-6

1. Hannah Occuish – 1786. 2. American Revolution - Fiction.
3. Women's History – Fiction. 4. True Crime - United States.
5. New England – History – Fiction. 6. Indians of North America – History – Fiction. 7. African Americans – History – Fiction.

Printed in the United States of America

www.andresblanton.com

10 9 8 7 6 5 4 3 2 1

In loving memory of

Earl L. Grosskopf, Jr.

Acknowledgements

My warmest thanks to:

My parents, Edward and Virginia Schenk; my children, Craig Grosskopf, Myung Franz, and Kerry Grosskopf; my nieces, Kara and Jessica Schenk; my nephew, Andrew Schenk; and life-long friends, Lorraine Xirinachs Fratus, Arleen Xirinachs Brown, and Lydia Wescott Dolan, for always believing in me.

Susie Scheyder for inspired editing, insightful comments, and a wicked sense of humor.

Professors Richard D. Brown, Christopher Collier, Cornelia Hughes Dayton, Karen Ordahl Kupperman, Kent Newmeyer, Anita Walker, Alan Ward, and Lisa Wilson.

Mark Jones, Head Archivist at the Connecticut State Library and his wonderful staff for their invaluable assistance during the many, many happy hours I spent in the archives.

Kim Gero for research assistance.

Timm and Jules Balunis, Jamie Baxter, Sandy Clarke, Michele and Eric Dittner, Kat Kliphon, Jisue Kwon, Ingrid Lefholz, Joanne McCue, Karen Mullins, Janet Olivas, Jacob Scheyder, Tiffany Silva, Andy and Martha Sorenson, Erin Stanley, Verna Swann, and Chris Wood.

"for Mischief done"

Author's Note

Although glimpses into the thought processes of the characters and most of the dialogue in this book are fictionalized, the persons, places, and events are historical. I based my interpretation of the characters on contemporary public and private records. Since these sources contain very little information about the minor characters, those actors represent attitudes and conditions of the period, thus providing a richer historical context while furthering the narrative.

⁂

"We cannot understand the meaning of this moment in our culture's life apart from some knowledge of the story that has preceded it. Cultural phenomena are not static and frozen bundles of meaning. They carry momentum. They came from somewhere, and they are going somewhere, and we can't be wise about where they are likely to be going if we are ignorant about the trajectories they are fulfilling."

Ken Myers, Mars Hill

Andres & Blanton

Prologue

Morning, New London-Norwich Turnpike, Quaker Hill, Connecticut, July 21, 1786

Squinting against the morning sun, Colonel Jeremiah Halsey waded through the lush thigh-high grass and wild flowers on the north side of the Norwich-New London Turnpike and climbed the steep embankment of the sunken road. He stopped beside what appeared to be a heap of discarded rags and pushed aside the tall green blades. A cloud of swollen flies buzzed up into his face. Halsey stumbled backwards with an oath, swatting at the loathsome swarm with both hands. When the air cleared, he leaned forward and cautiously parted the grass.

The Colonel jerked violently aside, spewing vomit. For a full minute, he half-crouched, hands braced on one knee, gagging and choking as he gasped for air. When his racing heart finally slowed, Halsey fumbled a handkerchief out of a jacket pocket. Holding the pristine white cloth to his mouth, he turned toward the road and stared at a small book splayed open on the hard-packed dirt. The book's crisp pages fluttered gaily back and forth in the gentle, shifting summer breeze.

Chapter One

Evening, The Red Lion Inn, New London Town, July 21, 1786

Pushing the hair from her perspiring forehead with the back of one hand, Molly Coit forked a piece of meat from a large roast turning on the weighted iron spit suspended over the deep granite hearth, and put it into her mouth.

Chewing appreciatively, she unlocked a large chest and counted out flatware into a basket. "Go up and get the chamber ready," said Molly, handing the heavy basket to Lizzy. "Let Bess put out the good linen, but you mind my silver and pewter."

As the maids disappeared up the back stairs with full hands, Molly went into the common room and drew two ales. Balancing the dripping tankards with a practiced hand, she walked briskly across the broad central hallway to the side dining room. She found Mr. Stephen Hempstead and Sheriff William Richards huddled at the far corner table, their backs to the hall door.

"What time do you want supper served in the private chamber?" Molly looked at Richards, even though she knew that he did not sit on the Grand Jury.

"Better go ahead and start carrying the food upstairs," Richards decided. "Most of the jurors should be here soon." He shook his head ruefully and gestured toward the door. "Guess we can sit here a while longer. Maybe no one will notice us."

"What are the odds?" Molly snorted derisively.

Richards smiled wryly. "We'll carry these up with us now."

Grinning, Molly dried her hands with her apron. "You know the way."

* * *

Richards and Hempstead climbed the familiar narrow back stairs, Richards setting his pace to Hempstead's limp. They went into the private chamber and set their drinks on the long polished cherrywood table. Within minutes, Colonel Halsey and the doctor came through the doorway, the red-faced maids close on their heels. Bess squeezed a laden tray to the side of Molly's roast, in the place of honor on the large sideboard. She flicked aside a white linen cloth, revealing a large china tureen and a stack of blue china bowls. Lizzy carefully arranged a carving set next to the roast and put the large silver ladle by the tureen. Wordlessly, the women hurried out of the room, leaving the men to help themselves.

"Hot, even for July," Colonel Halsey offered, pulling back a chair.

His three companions murmured polite agreement.

"Might rain, though."

No one bothered to respond.

Finally, Colonel Halsey moved his plate aside, reached down into the leather pouch by his feet, and pulled out several large rolls of drafting paper. He spread the pages out on the table.

"These are the plans for my new ship."

Everyone dropped his fork and leaned forward gratefully.

Richards studied the pages thoughtfully. "That design looks pretty light."

Hempstead nodded. "It does."

"Well, it might seem so," Halsey temporized.

The doctor chuckled. "That ship looks like it will float on air, instead of water, Halsey." He shook his head. "You're wasting your money."

"Just wait and see," the Colonel advised, smiling.

During the ensuing good-natured debate regarding the art of ship design, Grand Jurors trickled into the chamber. They milled around the room, chatting about inconsequential matters as they helped themselves from platters and dishes, constantly replenished by Lizzy and Bess. When the clink of metal on china finally subsided, the maids discretely slipped out of the chamber, closing the door behind them. A well-dressed grey-haired man in his mid-fifties stood up and looked down the table.

"Colonel?"

Chapter Two

Evening, Private Chamber, The Red Lion Inn, July 21, 1786

Colonel Halsey took a small leather-bound book for notes out of his pocket, handed it to the foreman, and settled back in his chair with the air of a man prepared to endure a long, unpleasant evening. He barely even noticed Molly come in and begin removing the dirty dinner plates.

The Grand Jury Foreman opened the book as he sat down and quickly skimmed the first few pages. When he finished reading, the foreman cleared his throat abruptly, and began to read the contents aloud in a taut voice.

"On the morning of July 21, 1786, I, along with Sheriff William Richards and Mr. Stephen Hempstead, conducted an investigation . . ."

The jurors leaned forward as one.

About half an hour later, the foreman closed Halsey's book and laid it on the table. Then, peering over the top of his gold spectacles, he looked around the table expectantly. None of the usually talkative group ventured a word.

The foreman peeled the spectacles off his face with one hand, folded the arms thoughtfully, and laid them on top of the Colonel's book for notes. He rubbed his eyes, then looked at Halsey. "A Bolles has been murdered."

"Yes," Halsey acknowledged in a dry, neutral tone.

"You're quite sure that it is murder? Of course it is," the foreman answered himself before Halsey could respond. "The evidence is quite clear."

"We couldn't believe it either, at first," Richards commented.

Hempstead nodded. "We've come to the Grand Jury for guidance." He ran a hand over his face. "None of us has ever been called out to investigate a cold-blooded murder."

"That's true enough." Richards turned to address Colonel Halsey. "When was the last homicide in New London County?"

Halsey shrugged. "I don't know. I can't remember one. We've had a few manslaughters, but pre-meditated murder . . . Not in my lifetime," Halsey paused. "Until today, that is."

"You traveled south down the Norwich-New London Turnpike this morning," the foreman prompted the Colonel.

"Yes. I had a meeting at the shipyard this afternoon, and it being such a pleasant morning, I decided to ride down rather than come by boat."

Halsey described how, about nine o'clock that morning, something lying in the hard-packed dirt turnpike caught his eye as he came over the slope to Bolles Cove. Curious, he spurred his horse to a trot. As he rode down the hill, the small fluttering blur coalesced into a book, lying on its spine, the soft, warm wind fingering its unsullied pages. Surprised to see a valuable possession abandoned in the dust, the Colonel twisted in the saddle, searching for the negligent owner. As he scanned the verge on the north side of the road, he noticed something lying close to a tumbled-down section of the stone wall that separated the narrow sunken road from the Widow Rogers' garden.

The bundle turned out to be a corpse, sprawled in a bed of glistening red grass. It lay face down, long disheveled hair streaming over its back. A large stone from the ruined wall rested on the back of the caved-in head. Smaller stones were strewn over and round the body.

Halsey methodically walked the Grand Jury through a detailed description of the body and the scene of the crime, refusing to let his words re-conjure the horror of watching flies light on the battered head and walk to and fro, feasting on sticky blood and serum. Whenever his words called forth too vivid a memory, the Colonel shifted in his chair and looked down to consult his notes.

"I could discern finger marks coming up around the back of

the victim's neck. The victim couldn't have been dead long." Halsey cleared his throat. "I didn't move the body until later, after Sheriff Richards and Mr. Hempstead arrived to begin the formal investigation. At that point, we turned the corpse over and found more marks on the throat."

"You say the victim had not been dead long when you first happened by?" asked the foreman.

"No," Halsey shook his head. "Judging by the condition of the body, perhaps only a matter of minutes before I came over the rise above the Widow Rogers' lot. I checked for a pulse . . ." Halsey unconsciously pulled out his soiled handkerchief to wipe his clean hands, then realizing his mistake, hastily shoved it back into his pocket.

"Was that the death blow?" the foreman winced as he turned to the doctor. "The injury to the skull?"

"Maybe. We'll never know for sure. I believe the murderer probably doesn't even know. He was in an absolute frenzy and inflicted so many wounds . . . The investigators found a book and a small stone, smeared with blood and hair, in the road, so we assume that murderer and victim struggled on the turnpike. During the struggle, the victim sustained at least several blows about the head with the small rock. The finger marks and bruises around the neck indicate strangling; either in the road or after the body was dragged to the verge, where he threw the stone wall down on the body. Thank God, the throttling probably rendered the victim unconscious before the murderer held the large rock directly over the head and dropped it."

The doctor paused, then continued, "The body also had massive bruising on the torso, several fractured bones, and a broken back."

The jurors stared at the doctor in stunned silence as he sipped from the glass Molly handed him. Finally, a juror recovered his voice. "Why?"

"What do you mean?" asked the foreman.

"Why would anyone kill Eunice Bolles, a six-year-old child?"

The doctor shrugged in an eloquent gesture of mingled anger and bewilderment.

"Does someone have a grudge against her parents?"

"When we questioned the Bolles, they couldn't think of any-one," answered Halsey. "And even if the parents do have an ene-my, who among us would take such horrible revenge against a child? A stranger did this, someone passing through, or from one of the ships."

The juror hesitated momentarily. "Did he rape her?" he asked.

"No," said the doctor. "I found no evidence that he violated her, and the Widow Rogers and Rachel Rogers didn't find any, either. We thought it best for them to wash and compose the body before we let the parents see it."

"Perhaps he intended to rape her," suggested Hempstead, "but panicked and killed the child when she resisted."

Richards shook his head doubtfully. "It's possible, Stephen, but a large boy or a man could easily grab a defenseless six-year-old girl and carry her into the woods. Why struggle on a public road and risk being caught? And why leave the corpse where it would be so easily found? The murderer must have known that Eunice would be missed fairly quickly. Why not hide the body in the woods, or throw it in the river, and give himself more time to get away? Leaving it on the side of the road makes me think he wanted her found as soon as possible."

Halsey nodded his head. "That's exactly what he intended. He wanted to make it appear that the child tried to climb the stone wall and it collapsed on her by accident."

"But who would believe that Eunice, instead of going directly to school, took a notion to scramble up a steep road embankment and attempt to scale a high stone wall at the top? If she wanted to go to the Widow's, all she had to do was walk down the road twenty feet and go up into the front yard. How could the murder-er possibly think that anyone would fall for such a preposterous ruse?"

Richards shook his head again. "A desperate man."

The Foreman looked down at the notebook. "You found the Widow Mary Rogers at home just after you discovered the body, and you spoke to her first." He looked up at the Colonel.

"Yes, Eunice lay by her garden wall, and I went up to the house right after I found the body. Naturally, I questioned the Widow," Halsey's clipped tone betrayed irritation, "and Mrs. Ichabod Rogers gave us very little information."

Chapter Three

Evening, Private Chamber, The Red Lion Inn, July 21, 1786

Richards clamped a hand over his mouth, horrified by a sudden urge to smile at Halsey's exasperation, knowing how much the Colonel - like Richards and every other official in town for the last hundred years - disliked having anything to do with the tempestuous Rogers/Bolles clan. Their notorious ancestors, religious dissenters John Rogers and his friend, John Bolles, had spent decades disrupting the peace until 1721, when Rogers died from smallpox contracted during a faith healing session.

Now-a-days, scores of the huge extended family perched on ancestral lands in Quaker Hill and expended their seemingly boundless energy hauling each other in and out of court. Only a small handful of the family adhered to Rogers' unusual religious beliefs. Mary Rogers, widow of Rogers' grandson Ichabod Rogers, was one of the few.

"The Widow Rogers told us that she saw and heard nothing," Halsey continued. He turned to look at Richards. "Later on, when we questioned the victim's father, James Bolles . . ."

"Which of the many James Bolles would that be?" The foreman raised his eyebrows satirically.

Halsey turned back. "Which? Let me see, this James is married to Eunice Strickland; they live near Bolles Cove."

The foreman rested an elbow on the table and turned his palm up theatrically. Richards stepped in to answer. "James Bolles, the war veteran."

"Oh, yes, of course," responded the foreman hastily, a respectful expression replacing the smirk. "We all know the veteran James Bolles and his service."

Halsey continued. "Mr. Bolles said that they sent Eunice off to the dame's school this morning, as usual. The next thing they knew, Stephen Hempstead appeared at their kitchen door to tell them Eunice had been found murdered.

"The Widow Rogers claimed that she hadn't heard anything or seen anybody this morning," Halsey repeated. "We finally got information when we questioned Hannah, the Widow's eleven-year-old mulatto[1] servant. The girl told us that when she went out to draw water from the well in the front yard this morning, she saw four boys in the road throwing rocks. A few minutes later, she heard the stone wall fall. Very soon afterwards, she heard Colonel Halsey knocking on the door."

"Did the girl see Eunice Bolles?" asked the foreman.

"She said that she hadn't seen Eunice at all this morning," answered Halsey thoughtfully.

"You stayed with the body while the Sheriff and Mr. Hempstead searched for physical evidence of the boys."

"Pardon, I'm sorry," Colonel Halsey looked up.

"You waited by the body . . ."

"Oh, yes. I did. To make sure that no one meddled with it while they searched the woods and we waited for the doctor."

The Foreman looked to Richards. "Sheriff?"

"We didn't find any sign of the boys, nor did we find anyone else who had seen them."

A middle-aged juror leaned toward Richards. "Will, are you entirely sure that you conducted a thorough search of the area? Could you have accidentally overlooked a section of the woods?"

"I don't see how. Mr. Hempstead and I scoured the turnpike verges and side roads a mile in either direction and even went up the side roads a quarter mile or so."

"If there had been any evidence that anyone at all had been in the woods," Hempstead added in confident tones, "the Sheriff and I would have found it. Tracking four boys blundering about, throwing rocks, would be much easier than tracking game. Since we know that they did not go into the woods, they either had to escape by fleeing north toward Norwich or south toward New London. If they went north, they would have had to go by the Colonel. If the boys went south, they would have had to pass by several farmers out in their fields and local people traveling on the road. So, no matter which way they went, someone would have seen them. No one did."

Frowning, the foreman turned to Halsey. "Colonel, do you think the mulatto girl is reliable? Could she be mistaken?"

"She seemed frightened - understandable considering the circumstances - and confused about details, but Hannah insisted that she had seen four boys. I . . ."

A juror at the opposite end of table grunted contemptuously and crossed his arms over his chest. "Confused! More likely, she's lying. If she didn't do it herself, she knows who did and won't identify the murderer."

All heads, Molly's included, swiveled toward the speaker.

"Mr. Tinker, are you suggesting that a child of eleven - even an Indian - could do such a thing?"

"I am saying just that, Mr. Foreman. This girl attacked and beat Mary Fish six years ago at Poquonnock Bridge in Groton."

"Mary Fish? Oh, yes. So, this girl, Hannah, is the same child who attacked Captain Fish's daughter . . . But, Mr. Tinker, if memory serves, Hannah Sharper didn't act alone. An older boy, her brother, I believe, instigated the attack; and, in any case, the Sharpers didn't kill Mary Fish."

"Not from lack of trying."

"What did the authorities do with Hannah and her brother?"

"The Town Selectmen bound the boy out to one of the Packers."

"Of course, they did," said the foreman, voice tinged with impatience. "The proper thing to do. And Hannah. What did they do with her?"

"Nothing."

Tinker surveyed the room, obviously relishing the effect his answer had on the Grand Jury.

One of the younger jurors finally broke the heavy silence. "Why didn't they do something?"

"Her mother spirited Hannah away from Groton, and the town dropped its case against her."

"How did she get to Quaker Hill?"

"I don't know," Tinker replied. "Does it matter? She's here."

"Sheriff, you know the neighborhood better than most of us. What do you know about her?" asked the foreman.

Richards bit off the exasperated retort that almost jumped out of his mouth. Just because he happened to inherit property in Quaker Hill, everyone expected him to know all the ins and outs of the zealots' tangled lives. Since boyhood, Richards had made a point of not being associated with any of the Rogerenes, and he always emphasized that what he knew about the Quaker Hill Rogerenes and their business came from serving many warrants in the neighborhood and arresting them on various charges. Now, the foreman's pointed question forced the Sheriff to reveal in front of the entire Grand Jury that in this instance, he did happen to know something about a notorious Rogerene household.

"Although the child lives with the Widow Rogers, she isn't her slave. Mrs. Rogers told us the girl's surname is Occuish . . ."

"Occuish!" the foreman turned to Mr. Tinker. "I thought that you said that this child is the Sharper girl."

"She is," Tinker replied. "I guess the Rogerenes hoped to conceal her identity as Mary Fish's attacker by using her grandfather's name." Tinker's mouth twisted. "Not that it is much use to her to be known as Jacob Occuish's niece."

Several jurors murmured agreement with Tinker as the foreman gave his attention back to Richards.

"So you say she is not a slave, Mr. Richards. Then she is a bound girl, of course."

Richards sighed. "I don't believe so."

"That's odd," said the foreman. "A young Indian girl, without parents, who is not bound out to a master?"

"It is unusual," agreed Richards, "but the Widow told us that she took Hannah as a favor."

"How did an Occuish end up in Quaker Hill near the Mohegan Reservation?" Stephen Hempstead asked. "Her grandfather is a Nehantic. If she isn't indentured, why isn't she with her own family in Niantic? Do you know, Will?"

"I don't know much about it, and I have to admit I haven't given Hannah Occuish any thought, until today," Richards answered. "I only know that Sarah Occuish left Hannah with Mrs. Rogers about four or five years ago, while I was away fighting, and she never came back for her. Exactly how or why she chose the Widow Rogers, I can't say. Since I've never served a warrant on Mrs. Rogers from the Occuish or Sharper families or from a master or even from the Groton authorities demanding Hannah's return, I assume that the girl is not bound out to anyone else - at least not to anyone who wants her back - and that her parents or relatives and the Groton selectmen approve of her situation."

"What about her brother?" asked Hempstead. "Where is he?"

"I don't know anything about him, Stephen. I haven't ever seen him. All I know is that he isn't in New London, so he's probably over the water in Groton, with his master." Richards drummed his fingers thoughtfully on the table. "Perhaps we should go back to Mrs. Rogers' in the morning and question Hannah again. By then, she may be calm enough to give us a clearer account of what she saw and heard. It would also be a good idea to find out if her brother has been in the vicinity recently."

"Are you saying that the brother may have committed the murder? Why would he want to kill Eunice Bolles?" asked Hempstead.

Halsey spoke up. "Charles may have come to visit his sister and saw an opportunity to commit another robbery. Only this time, things got even more out of hand, and he accidentally killed Eunice. Then he tried to make it look as if the wall fell on her when she tried to climb over it."

The foreman nodded. "Yes. The attacks on Mary Fish and Eunice Bolles are too much alike. We need to know if Charles Sharper was in the vicinity of Quaker Hill today."

Chapter Four

Late Evening, The Red Lion Inn, July 21, 1786

Molly tossed her wet cleaning rag on top of the tray of dirty dishes, and went down the back stairs to the kitchen.

"Are they all gone, then, ma'am?"

"Yes. Lizzy, gather up the silver and pewter, and bring it down to me. Bess, call in James to bring the trays downstairs for you. Mind now, take care with my good linen. When you've all finished, feed James - and yourselves. No use letting my good roasts dry out."

Early Morning, The Red Lion Inn, September 6, 1781

Molly was only thirteen years old when Benedict Arnold sailed a British fleet into the Thames River and caught New London sleeping. Enemy ships hadn't been spotted in Long Island Sound since England sent its fleet south over a year before. Just as soon as the last British sail disappeared over the horizon, New London's privateers slithered back into the cold waters and went on the prowl. Month after month, the Americans wreaked havoc on English shipping without fear of reprisal. His Majesty's land and sea forces were too busy at Yorktown to worry about New London, or so the Americans believed. By the time the town realized its danger that September morning, the British ships were in the harbor.

General Arnold, a native of Norwich up the river, dispatched two divisions ashore. One landed in north New London and moved south toward the Parade, where defiant townspeople had once burned tea rather than pay tax on it. The British marched along the river bank, lighting their own bonfire along the waterfront. Small detachments of soldiers probed the town for hidden caches of prize goods and torched privateers' houses, pointed out to them by helpful local spies.

While the British advanced toward the heart of town, New London scrambled. Messengers raced through the countryside to raise the militia; sailors rushed to the harbor and desperately tried to get their ships up the river to Norwich, where the British ships could not follow. Women and children - and more than a few able-bodied men - scurried about, throwing together bundles of valuables and food.

As frightened people hurried past the Red Lion to escape the advancing British, Molly ran to the small sick room next to the kitchen and dropped to her knees by the bed.

"Father, wake up, wake up!" Molly urged, gently shaking Captain Coit's arm, then shaking a bit harder. "Oh, please, wake up! The British have landed!"

Seeing that Captain Coit had fallen into a coma, Molly sat back on her heels. She gripped her father's dry hand with her sweaty ones, occasionally letting go to wipe a wet palm on her apron or brush away tears of mingled grief and fear.

A commotion in front of the Red Lion drew Molly to the window. She cautiously pushed the curtain aside and jerked back at the sight of enemy soldiers swarming through the gate, glowing torches in their hands. After a second of befuddled horror, she realized that the soldiers intended to burn the Red Lion.

Without thinking, Molly ran out into the front hall, pushed open the front door, and sailed out into the confusion. She dodged through the British troops, stepping over muskets and knapsacks, stopping to pull on the soldiers' arms and plead with them to spare the inn. Although several looked vaguely apologetic, most of them shook her off without a glance; except one. When this soldier felt her hand, he turned and shoved Molly roughly to the ground, swearing angrily in a pure New London accent. She sprawled in the dirt, mouth opened in surprise, staring up at the familiar face. This man was a New Londoner, born and bred! His sister ran a small tavern just up Court Street; his brother-in-law fought with the American Army.

Molly had seen this Tory before. He had been on his knees in this very spot, surrounded by a small, hectoring mob, his face flickering in and out of the shadows cast by the flaming torches held aloft in the hands of angry neighbors. Although a few people attempted to reason with the mob, shouts for a tarring and feathering drowned out cooler voices. Someone broke from the faceless crowd, disappeared into the darkness, and came running back with a small barrel and a pillow. Hands reached out and took them. Two men tightened their grip on the prisoner, pressing his knees into the hard ground. A third knocked the bung out of the barrel and upended it over the helpless, frightened man. He cursed and twisted as the sticky tar slowly ran down over his head, into his eyes and over his bare shoulders and torso. A knife blade flashed in the firelight, and feathers exploded into the air. Someone shook the pillow over the man's head. Stray feathers floated lightly in the fire-lit night breeze as the crowd ran a fence rail between the Tory's knees and forced him to straddle the splintery wood. Four men lifted the rail to their shoulders and began to trot down Main Street toward the Parade, purposefully bouncing the rail, their victim desperately clinging with both hands, eyes squeezed shut, face grotesque with dripping tar. The jeering throng surged behind.

"Stay home, lass," father had said, putting a restraining arm on Molly's shoulder. "Nothing I could do to stop it, but I'll not have you going along with them."

"But, Father, he's a Tory . . ."

"Yes, and I'd shoot him in a battle, a fair fight. I won't be part of this, and neither will you be."

Now, the man stood in the front yard of the Red Lion, dressed in Tory colors, a torch in his hand.

Spying more flashes of Tory uniforms swirling around her,

Molly abandoned any notion of appealing to the soldiers for mercy. Jumping to her feet, she looked wildly about, searching for the officer in charge, praying that he wouldn't be an American. She finally spied a man in red uniform on horseback. Breath ragged, Molly dashed through the teeming soldiers and grabbed one of the officer's stirrups before anyone noticed her. The startled horse threw up his head, and backed abruptly. Caught off guard, the British officer reined in, shouting at Molly to let go and get away. Instead, she tightened her grip as the horse whickered and danced, almost pulling her off of her feet.

When the officer regained control of his mount, Molly looked up, fingers gripping the stirrup for dear life. Praying that he wouldn't slash her face with his whip, she pleaded with the officer to have mercy on the Red Lion. Without bothering to look down, the British officer coldly informed Molly that he had specific orders to destroy all Patriot lairs. Frantically, Molly explained that if he didn't call off his men, he would be responsible for burning a sick old man in his bed.

The officer looked down at Molly's anxious young face. He hesitated briefly, then remarked that everyone knew Americans were notorious liars. Molly shook her head, swearing that she was not lying, begging him to go see her father. Turning angrily in his saddle, the officer curtly ordered a soldier inside to look for a sick man. A few minutes later, the soldier ran out to report that he found an old man asleep in a small back room, looking too ill to leave his bed. The officer glanced down at Molly again and then twisted around to look down at the harbor.

"I'll spare your inn, along with the Widow's Row behind you, but it will likely catch when the area around here goes up with the rest," he said, pointing toward the north. "I suggest you get your father out of the inn."

Molly turned to the north and gasped. Everything along the riverbank - houses, sheds, fishing boats, rope walks, wharves, warehouses, ships - was on fire. Roiling clouds of black smoke billowed into the sky about a mile away; nearer by, the smoke had not risen as high - yet. Molly looked toward the Parade and river bank. The public buildings, houses, sheds, and crammed warehouses in that congested area would ignite in a flash and burn for hours.

The picture of her father lying helplessly in his bed flashed through Molly's mind. She realized that for the first time in her life, she was completely alone.

Although it galled her, Molly had the presence of mind to thank the officer before hurrying to her father's bedside. Captain Coit slept so deeply, he did not know that British soldiers were in his yard. Molly went to the window, and watched the enemy soldiers form up to march toward the Parade. While she studied their receding backs, her shocked mind a dull blank, a British soldier came around from the back of the house, her tin drinking dipper held to his lips. Seeing his comrades marching away without him, the soldier slung the dipper to the ground and ran to catch up. The sun glinted off the bright dipper, rocking to and fro in the dusty road.

Chapter Five

Late Morning, The Red Lion Inn, September 6, 1781

Molly dashed out of the sick room and ran through the inn, shouting for the two maidservants to gather buckets, tubs - anything that would hold water - and for the stableman and boy to drag the ladder out of the barn. As they leaned the ladder against the front of the inn, curls of smoke began to rise above the Parade. In what seemed like minutes, billows of black, choking smoke belched skyward and flames began to shoot up through the thick, dark clouds, broadcasting glowing cinders into the air.

Molly froze, her fingers curled around the side of the wooden ladder, watching the sea wind carry the smoke and cinders toward the Red Lion. Tearing her gaze away, Molly resolutely turned her back to the Parade and pushed the ladder firmly into place. The stableman squeezed by her and shinnied up the ladder, the stable boy behind him. Molly climbed the first few rungs to pass a full bucket of water upwards, and went back down for another while the boy toted the sloshing bucket up to the stableman.

Hour after hour, the three women hefted endless gallons of water. One of the maids carried pans of water from the well in back to pour on the dry grass along the road in front of the inn. Molly and the other woman staggered from the well to the ladder, hauling sloshing iron-bound, wooden buckets. Almost as soon as the women and boy handed the water up to the stableman, he poured it on the roof, dropped the empty container to the ground, and reached his hand down for the next. The small group worked methodically, dousing the roof section by section, stopping only to move the ladder as necessary. After they worked their way around the house, they began the whole process over again - and then a third time.

While Molly and her servants fought to save the Red Lion, terrified women and children ran frantically up Main Street, heading for the safety of the countryside. The vastly outnumbered militia ranged through town, skirmishing with the enemy. Stephen Hempstead and twenty-three men managed to get to Fort Trumbull, a three-walled structure facing the river, swivel the cannons, and fire on the advancing British. Seeing they could never hope to hold the small fort, the Americans quickly spiked the cannons, jumped into three boats, and pulled for Groton across the river. As they threaded through the enemy fleet, the British seized one boatload of Americans, but the rest made it to Fort Griswold in time for the battle there.

A huge explosion of gunpowder rocked the ground under Molly's feet. The stores and houses on lower Bank Street, just blocks from the Red Lion, burst into flame and rained down intermittent cinder showers on the few dwellings standing between the Parade and the Red Lion. Wisps of smoke began to rise from their roofs. Gazing across the large vacant lot that stood between the Red Lion and the smoldering houses, Molly burst into frustrated tears; she could have saved the inn if only the wind hadn't been against her. Wiping her cheeks with the back of one hand, she threw down her bucket and went into the inn to collect family valuables and figure out how to move her father.

Not five minutes later, the excited stableman ran inside and practically dragged her by the arm out into the yard. He gestured toward the smoking downtown.

"Look!" he shouted. "The winds have shifted!"

Molly's eyes followed the stableman's pointing finger. The fires down at the Parade and harbor burned a bit lower, and the wind was pushing the smoke and cinders from the smaller fires across the street out toward the water. Most encouraging of all for the Red Lion, the devouring fire on Bank Street had begun to race southward along the shore, away from the Red Lion, where it would drown in the cove.

Molly snatched up her bucket. As they worked, the sound of cannon and musket fire traveled over the river from Fort Griswold on Groton Heights. Even though all of them had relatives and friends at the fort, no one dared to stop and watch the battle unfolding between shifting clouds of gun and cannon smoke. One of the maids, whose brothers and sweetheart were in the fight, sobbed as she stumbled back and forth between the well and the ladder.

When the hellish flames around them finally burned to embers, the women dropped their buckets and pan and literally fell in their tracks. The stableman and boy climbed drunkenly down the ladder on rubbery legs and collapsed by the bottom rung. As the twilight deepened and the stars came out, mistress and servants sprawled in the yard, too exhausted to register the pain radiating from bleeding, blistered hands and feet. When they finally gathered the strength to sit up, they stared through red, smarting eyes at the sooty, tear-streaked faces of their companions and marveled at the filthy tatters, liberally dotted with cinder burns, that barely covered their bodies.

When they finally managed to stagger to their feet, Molly and her servants gazed around, mouths agape, unable to comprehend the devastation surrounding them. They had awakened that morning in a busy, wealthy seaport. Now, piles of collapsed timber and rubble glowed and smoked in the cool night air, and the smell of fiery destruction overwhelmed the salt breeze. All of the buildings along the waterfront and the Parade and large swaths of the town lay in ruins. Down at the harbor, gentle waves lapped charred wharf pilings and pushed bobbing debris to and fro in the oily waters. But the Red Lion serenely faced the destruction, its larders and cellars bursting, the animals safe in the barn and the coop.

While the people at the Red Lion wolfed cold beef and spider bread with trembling hands, Arnold's men piled thirty-five bleeding, thirsty Patriots, including Stephen Hempstead with a smashed leg, on the floor of the Avery house, down by the river in Groton, and left them to their fate. After prodding thirty prisoners of war onto His Majesty's ships, the British sailed away. Eighty-five New Londoners lay dead on the ground.

Morning, The Red Lion Inn, September 7, 1781

Creaking wagon wheels and loud voices dragged Molly from the depths of exhausted slumber the morning after New London burned. She sat up in bed, dazed and bewildered, looking stupidly around the room. When she realized that the noise came from outside, her heart skipped a beat. Molly threw the warm sheets aside, leapt out of bed, and ran barefoot to the window. Without thinking, she pushed up the sash and leaned out of the window to gawk at the ragged parade of weary refugees clogging the street below.

Dozens of families returned to smoldering ruins. Those fortunate enough to find intact houses and barns did not expect to find much left in them, and for once, reality lived up to expectations. Hastily secreted pewter and silver plate had disappeared, along with any livestock and household goods the owners hadn't been able to cart away. The houses on the outskirts of town came through untouched, but only because the British didn't have time to plunder them.

By mid-afternoon, a horde of anxious homeless people poured into the Red Lion, begging for food and shelter and promising to pay later. Molly squeezed in as many as possible, and for several days, people and their belongings stuffed the inn from garret to cellar. Outside, horses and cows spilled out of the stable and barn into the yard and lot, which were choked with carts, wagons, and carriages of all descriptions. Excited dogs and children darted among the tangled legs and wheels; the dogs snarling and nipping one another, the children shrieking with hysterical laughter. Sooty specters wafted into the stable yard, carrying whatever they had managed to salvage, and then stood, wondering what to do with their rescued things. The weighted well arm seemed to be in perpetual motion; the creak of its pivoted joint an oddly soothing background accompaniment to the uneven human din that lasted from dawn till well after dark.

By the end of the month all of the refugees, except a destitute widow with several small children and an old woman, had gone to homes with friends and family. Town officials and their sons, harassed by problems of their own, could not see to the old woman or the widow and orphans. Too many leading citizens had been killed or captured, and more than a few of the ones left were wounded or had lost their own homes.

Molly refused to turn poor women and children out onto the streets. She and her father gave the mother a job and a room in the garret, and let the elderly woman have a comfortable bed in the warm kitchen. The family lived and worked at the Red Lion until a new husband and father took them to his farm. The elderly lady left the Red Lion in her coffin, Molly following behind and crying tears of real grief on the way to the graveyard.

Captain Coit died a few years later and left his daughter the inn. Although the Red Lion demanded her every waking moment, Molly reveled in the work, and, unlike far too many women of her acquaintance, she did not chafe under a husband's authority. Instead, Molly ran her business to her own liking, and picked her own company. Although the common room continued to be a place of masculine conviviality, the inn's pristine reputation for orderliness and well-dressed victuals brought respectable women to the dining room. And as Molly's New London recovered from Arnold's raid and began to thrive again, she prospered with it.

Chapter Six

Early Morning, Quaker Hill, July 22, 1786

Sheriff Richards and Colonel Halsey reined their horses to a stop at the top of the rise overlooking Bolles Cove. They sat in companionable silence in the shade of a large oak, admiring the peaceful view of Mrs. Rogers' house at the head of the cove below them. When Hempstead rode up and joined them, the investigators put light spurs to their horses' flanks and trotted down the hill into the Widow's yard.

As the three investigators approached the house, Mrs. Rogers opened the front door and stood, hand resting on the door latch, watching them dismount and pull their bridle reins through the iron ring on the granite hitching post in the front yard. Mrs. Rachel Rogers, Widow Rogers' kinswoman and neighbor, came up behind the Widow and peered over her shoulder. Neither spoke or called out a greeting. Although he barely registered it at the time, Richards later remembered noticing an apprehensive expression flicker across Widow Rogers' face as they walked toward her.

Halsey took off his hat. "Good morning, Mrs. Rogers," he said to the Widow. "And to you Mrs. Rogers."

"Good morning," Rachel said over the Widow's shoulder.

"Widow Rogers, we have some more questions."

"I can't help you," the Widow said, clasping her hands in front of her. "I've told you all that I know."

"If we could come inside and speak to your servant girl."

"Hannah? Why do you need to talk to her again?" Mrs. Rog-

26

ers' eyes narrowed suspiciously. "What did she tell you yesterday?"

"I'm not at liberty to say during the investigation. If we could come inside . . ."

"Well, come in then." The Widow grudgingly pushed the door fully open and led the way to the front room. "Sit down. I'll go find Hannah."

"If you don't mind, I have some questions I'd like to ask before we see Hannah."

Mrs. Rogers stopped at the door and turned around to face the Colonel, one hand lightly gripping the doorframe.

Halsey gestured for Rachel Rogers to come into the room. He took out his notebook. "How did Hannah come to live with you?" he asked, looking at the Widow Rogers.

"Sarah Occuish brought Hannah to Quaker Hill about five or six years ago and asked me to mind the child for a spell, which I did, though she was too young to be of much use to me. Sarah came back a few weeks later and told me she wanted to go up north to visit her kin. She thought that if she could get away from alcohol, she might have a chance of curing herself, but she didn't want to take Hannah along. She thought that traveling so far through the woods on foot would be too much for the child. I agreed to keep Hannah, but only until she came back."

"When was the last time you heard from Sarah?" The Colonel looked up from his notebook, pencil poised. The Widow shook her head. "I've heard nothing from Hannah's mother since the day she left."

"Not even through friends or family?"

"Nothing," the Widow repeated, mouth tight.

"Has Hannah troubled you?" Hempstead asked, his tone polite.

The Widow flinched slightly, and her fingers tightened on the wooden doorframe. "How do you mean, Mr. Hempstead? I don't understand what you mean to ask of me."

"Mrs. Rogers," Colonel Halsey smoothly interjected, "We know that you have provided well for this abandoned girl, but she came to you a difficult child, or so we have heard."

"Heard? What do you mean?" the Widow repeated, looking at each of the men in turn, her face guarded. "I don't know what you've been told about Hannah . . . or me."

When no one moved to enlighten her, the Widow continued. "Well, yes, Colonel, you might say Hannah is sometimes a handful. For months after Sarah left, the child cried all the time for her mother, but she finally stopped asking about Sarah after a while. Then . . ." The Widow sighed before briskly continuing. "Hannah doesn't always obey as well as she should, and some of the neighborhood children are unkind to her."

"Unkind?" Halsey glanced at the Sheriff, as if for confirmation. Richards looked away.

"I seem to remember something about Hannah attacking another child when she lived in Groton," Hempstead remarked, almost offhandedly.

"She did, years ago." The Widow paused. "But she was only five years old at the time, and her older brother instigated a quarrel with Mary Fish. It was all his doing."

"You say some of the neighborhood children are unkind to her. Does she get along with those who aren't mean?"

"Get along? Mostly she does. It's true that Hannah has argued with children in the neighborhood, but she has never used force against them." The Widow turned in her chair. "Isn't that true, Rachel?"

"I can't say that it is, Mary," answered Rachel.

"What do you mean? How can you say that?"

"Hannah has bullied and hit other children."

"Just children's arguments that don't mean anything."

Rachel Rogers took a deep breath. "Mary, everyone knows that Hannah stole the smaller children's strawberries and threatened to give Eunice a whipping for telling on her."

"Oh, that was all talk," the Widow said dismissively. "Hannah was angry at the time. She didn't really mean it. Besides . . ."

"Hannah threatened Eunice Bolles? Why didn't you mention this fact to us yesterday, Mrs. Rogers?" the Colonel demanded.

"I didn't think it was important. I tell you, it didn't mean anything."

"When did Hannah make these threats?"

"Tell them the whole story, Mary," Rachel urged. "You gave Hannah a whipping for it."

The Widow Rogers let go of the doorframe. Looking suddenly old and tired, she came into the room and sat down.

"Several weeks ago, my granddaughter, Mary - she and Eunice are - were - playmates, went berrying in the woods with some of the other children from the neighborhood. Not long after they left, Eunice and Mary came to me crying. When I asked them what was the matter, the girls told me that Hannah had snatched all of their strawberries and eaten them. When I went to see about it, I found out that Hannah had taken the berries, just as the girls claimed. I gave Hannah a whipping and put her to work, away from the other children."

Rachel took up the story. "The next day, Hannah stopped Mary and Eunice on their way home from school and told Eunice that she owed her a whipping for tattling, and vowed to pay it to her right quick." Rachel made a face. "It's not the first time Hannah has caused trouble. She intimidates the younger children, and even some of the bigger ones. They're all afraid of her."

Surprised, Halsey looked over to Richards as if he expected the Sheriff to say something, but Richards only shrugged.

"Is it true?" the Colonel asked the Widow. "Have there been problems with Hannah for some time?"

Mrs. Rogers sat quietly, staring into the distance, seemingly lost in thought.

"Mrs. Rogers? Is it true that Hannah is a bully?"

The Widow jumped slightly and refocused on the Colonel. "Yes," she admitted slowly. "I suppose that she does argue with other children on occasion, but mostly all she does is make idle threats. She's not capable of actually hurting anyone."

"Mary Fish might disagree," Rachel replied acidly.

The Widow snorted. "That was years ago."

Rachel stood up impatiently, somewhat regretting her candor, especially in front of Mrs. Rogers, a kinswoman. If the investigators wanted more details, they would have to question the neighbors, some of whom would be more than happy to describe Hannah's unruly behavior. They would also be happy to voice their anger at Mrs. Rogers for keeping Hannah. The child's presence had been a point of contention in Quaker Hill for years.

Seeing that pressing for more information would be a waste of time, Halsey thanked Rachel Rogers and asked the Widow to fetch Hannah. Mrs. Rogers reappeared so quickly with the child in tow, Richards suspected Hannah had been eavesdropping in the hall.

The child balked at the threshold, but her mistress grabbed her by the arm and yanked her through the doorway. She put her hand on Hannah's back and pushed her into the room. "Get in there." Arching her shoulders and whimpering, the girl staggered forward, then immediately scuttled backwards until she bumped into the Widow.

Suppressing a frown, Halsey gestured to Hannah. "Come over here, Hannah," he said gently. "There's nothing to be afraid of."

The girl crept forward cautiously and stood in front of the Colonel, wringing her hands.

"We only want to ask you some questions about yesterday."

Halsey's gentle manner had no effect. Hannah mumbled muddled, contradictory answers, or nervously shrugged her shoulders to every question put to her, wringing her hands all the while. Finally, the Colonel told her that she could go.

As the girl's footsteps faded quickly down the hallway, Halsey asked the Widow if they could borrow the room for a private consultation. Shrugging in unconscious imitation of Hannah, Mrs. Rogers went out, pulling the door closed behind her.

Halsey shook his head. "Much as I hate to agree with Tinker, he is right to suspect the girl."

"Maybe," Richards conceded. "I'm not convinced that Hannah actually committed the murder, but I do think that she may have seen who did, or at least knows something that she is afraid to tell us. And I'm not sure that I believe her when she says that she hasn't laid eyes on her brother since she left Groton five years ago."

"She did it, Will," Hempstead said. "No one else has ever seen the brother around here, let alone recently. Of all the people we questioned yesterday, only she claims to have seen four boys, but we didn't find any evidence to support her story. What we did find out is that Hannah threatened to whip Eunice, and within weeks, Eunice is lying on the side of the road beaten to death.

"All of that added to the fact that the similarity between this murder and the attack on Mary Fish is too remarkable to be a coincidence. I think we should take her in."

Richards shook his head. "This isn't Ireland. I can't take a person into custody without any hard evidence against them, Stephen. Nobody saw Hannah with Eunice yesterday morning, or even in the road by herself. We didn't see any bloodstains on her clothes or shoes when we were questioning her yesterday."

"True enough, but we can't risk leaving her here while we continue the investigation. If we don't take Hannah with us today, she will likely run away. Besides, Rachel Rogers already told us that everyone in Quaker Hill knows that Hannah Occuish threatened Eunice Bolles last week. It wouldn't surprise me if some of the neighbors decided to take matters into their own hands."

Richards sighed. "I know."

"Well, then, I don't see what else . . ."

"And remember, Sheriff," the Colonel looked up from the open notebook on his lap. "When the search party returned from scouring the woods yesterday, we saw Hannah doing the wash in the back yard."

"That's so," said Richards. "I had forgotten. She was out back by the well, kneeling alongside an overturned washtub, wringing out wet clothes."

"Maybe she was washing blood-splattered clothes," suggested Hempstead. "If Hannah stood behind the wall to drop the large stone on Eunice's head, she could have come away clean, except for the blood she got on her hands and clothes during the struggle."

"Or perhaps Hannah was just doing the week's laundry," Richards pointed out.

"Yes," Hempstead conceded. "If we ask, the Widow might tell us that she gave Hannah wash to do, but that doesn't mean that Hannah couldn't have sneaked her bloodstained dress and apron into the pile. And even if her mistress didn't tell Hannah to wash clothes, the girl could say that she decided on her own to do them."

"So, we would be back where we started," Richards said. "I guess we should start by asking Mrs. Rogers if she told Hannah to do the laundry."

Halsey shook his head. "Let's not get tangled up in another long session with the Widow that probably won't get us anywhere." He leaned forward. "I think that it would be better to take Hannah to the Bolles' house and have her look at Eunice's body."

Chapter Seven

Late Morning, The Bolles' House, Quaker Hill, July 22, 1786

The investigators, Hannah riding double behind Richards, rode around a curve in the road and simultaneously pulled up short. While their horses snorted and stamped, the men stared in open-mouthed amazement at the Bolles' house and yard. Scattered knots of somber-faced men, dressed in their Sunday best, idled in the garden, smoking and talking quietly. A large group of men and women clustered on the front porch, spilled down the front steps, and trickled out into the front yard. Small packs of young children dashed around the lot and barn, playing games of tag and hide and seek, laughing and calling out to one another, their preoccupied parents apparently oblivious to the disrespectful din.

Shifting uncomfortably in the saddle, Richards wondered why he suddenly felt on edge. Large groups of people had never bothered him before. He had grown up as part of a crowd, and as an adult lived and moved in a congested world. As a child, he, like everyone else he knew, shared a sleeping chamber with several children and adults. Whenever company came to stay, as often happened, he and the other children slept on pallets scattered throughout the house. He particularly liked to put his bed by the kitchen fireplace during the winter. When an especially large group of family and friends visited, Richards and the other boys and young men threw quilts over the hay and slept in the barn. During the war, he huddled with comrades around small campfires, and tossed and turned in cramped huts and tents, gingerly stepping over prone bodies when he had to go out at night. Every day he socialized elbow-to-elbow in jam-packed, busy taverns and made his way through bustling streets. When traveling long distances, Richards squeezed into cramped coaches and shared a bed with complete strangers in tiny ship's cabins and small rooms at ordinaries.

This felt different. Glancing apprehensively at one another, the stunned investigators rode slowly forward. As they threaded their way through the crowd, a tired-faced woman came from around the back of the large farmhouse, shouting irascibly at the excited children to be quiet.

"Oh!" Hannah's arms tightened reflexively around Richards' waist.

Although a number of well-known acquaintances called out greetings, Richards and his companions noticed that a surprising number of faces did not look at all familiar. Strangers or not, most of the people gathered around the front door recognized the official nature of the visit, and several men stepped forward to untie their horses and lead them away, leaving the hitching rail empty. The Sheriff and his companions dismounted and threw their horses' reins over the rail and walked toward the door, Hannah in tow. The crowd on the steps and porch washed back, opening a pathway for them.

An almost palpable oppressiveness enveloped Richards as soon as he stepped over the Bolles' threshold. He quickly dismissed his feelings, attributing them to being in a house of mourning, but then reconsidered. He'd been to many wakes without ever having felt this odd sensation. Although the extraordinary manner of Eunice's death made the loss especially wrenching for her family, even the tragic senselessness of the child's death did not entirely explain the strange air in the house. Standing in the hall, surrounded by the haggard, red-eyed faces of the grief-stricken clan and breathing in their sorrow, Richards began to feel angry at the people outside.

Turning to close the door, Richards remembered the persistent flies swarming around Eunice, darting down to feast on her blood while the doctor, swatting them away with curses, carried out his examination. The strangers outside reminded him of the insatiable flies. He felt outraged by the sudden insight. Mourners should be a source of comfort to a bereaved family, and their numbers should be, in the case of the death of a child Eunice's age, a testament to the extensive kin and friendship connections of her family. This multitude, many of them obviously total strangers to the Bolles, offered no solace. Their presence distressed Eunice's kin while they struggled to make sense out of her death. Neither her parents nor anyone else could possibly have the faintest idea about how to incorporate so many people - supposing the family even cared to try - into the traditional customs that gave meaning to death and mourning.

This crowd came not to comfort, but to seek . . .

Diversion, Richards thought as he waited in the hallway with Halsey and Hempstead. *These people want to go home with something sensational to tell their friends and neighbors. And they are determined to get it, even if it means trespassing on the Bolles' grief and trapping Eunice's family in their own house.*

The mob's callous willingness to hold the grieving family hostage to its base quest for novelty and excitement made the Sheriff's hands quiver with anger as he watched Alexander Rogers slowly come down the stairs.

When Rogers stepped onto the hall floor, Hempstead respectfully pulled him aside to ask in a low voice if they could speak privately to James Bolles.

"I'll fetch him. He and Mrs. Bolles are sitting with Eunice." Rogers paused. "Better go into the back room. Come with me, I'll show you, and then get James."

As they followed Rogers into the small room, he turned to speak, but shut his mouth in surprise when he saw Hannah walking behind Richards. He stared fixedly at her for a few seconds, started to say something, but closed his mouth again, his face hard. When he finally spoke, Rogers kept his voice calm, but Richards could see it cost Rogers something to control his anger.

"I suppose that I can guess why you brought her, so I'm not asking any questions that you won't answer anyway. But I will say that I don't think it would be wise for Mrs. Bolles to see that girl in this house."

Alexander Rogers ran a thumb back and forth along his jaw, thinking. His hand dropped to the side. "Mrs. Bolles can't eat or sleep, and she can't stop crying," he said, looking at the Colonel. "She refused to eat or lie down all day yesterday, and insisted on sitting up with Eunice all night. She's still by the coffin as we speak. If this continues much longer, Mrs. Bolles will collapse and likely never recover her health. I'm going to suggest to James that it would be wise to slip his wife a dose of laudanum and take her upstairs to sleep for a few hours before the funeral."

"Funeral?" said Halsey, surprised. He'd never heard of a family holding such a brief wake.

"Yes, they plan to bury her later this afternoon, even though she's been dead for barely a day. There's no chance at all that she is in a trance, and the heat . . . Well, anyway, it's not good for Eunice's mother to see her like that. And I hope," he added bitterly, "that once Eunice is in the ground, those strangers outside might go home and leave us to grieve in peace."

Richards nodded sympathetically. "We'll wait here, Alex."

The three men sat down on the chairs pushed up against the wall to make room at night for the folded pallet that someone had shoved into a corner that morning. After hesitating a few seconds, Hannah perched on the edge of the bulky pallet and leaned forward to rest her elbows on her legs, hands dangling between her knees.

A stab of pity twisted Richards' heart when James Bolles walked through the door a half hour later. Although the Sheriff had attended the wakes and funerals of many children over the years, he had never seen a father in such a condition. Although Bolles looked no more disheveled than other bereaved fathers, the expression on his face bespoke an almost unbearable anguish.

At a loss for words, Halsey put a sympathetic hand on Bolles' shoulder.

"James, I am sorry to intrude," Richards said, "but we can't postpone our business."

Bolles acted as if he had not heard the Sheriff. "I can't console her. No matter what I say or do, it does her no good. I'm afraid she will go mad with grief. Thank God, she's finally asleep."

Richards glanced at the Colonel and Hempstead, silently pleading for help, but they cut their eyes away. The Sheriff tried again.

"James, I hate to ask, but we need to see Eunice, alone."

"You need to see Eunice alone," Bolles repeated dully. "Why? What for?" He looked at each in turn. "You examined her yesterday and saw the extent of her injuries. Surely there is nothing more to learn about her . . ." Bolles wiped a wrinkled, crumbled handkerchief across his wet forehead. "Her wounds," he choked.

"Yes, but it would help our investigation if we could see Eunice one more time."

Bolles stared at Halsey until Hannah's nervous fidgeting caught his attention.

"What . . . what is she doing here?" he asked confusedly, looking down at Hannah and then back up at the Sheriff.

"Ah, she is helping with . . . that is, she has information . . ."

"She has information? What do you mean? What does she know about it?"

Richards shifted uneasily and looked away. Comprehension flamed in Bolles' eyes. "You brought her here because you think she killed Eunice!"

Bolles moved toward Hannah, but Hempstead and Richards moved forward quickly to politely, but firmly, block Bolles' path. Hannah scuttled backwards away from the angry father and crashed into the wall. She jerked forward with a small cry. Richards reached out and grabbed Hannah's arm to keep her from falling.

"She's here to help us in the investigation, James," Halsey assured him, voice low and soothing. "We don't know who killed your daughter."

"Help you? How can she help you?"

"There are some questions about particulars discovered during the investigation."

James looked bewildered. "Particulars? You've discovered some important information or evidence?"

Richards stepped closer to Mr. Bolles. "We aren't sure, James, how some of our discoveries are related, and we would like to see Eunice for a few minutes, alone, if we may, sir. It will help us in our inquiries."

Bolles searched the Sheriff's face. "You think that maybe she killed Eunice, or at least that she knows who did; maybe even helped him," he amended, his expression and voice strangely calm. "That's the only reason why you would bring Hannah Occuish to this house today."

"Yes," said Richards, feeling that he owed the grieving father the truth. "We believe it's one or the other."

Chapter Eight

Late Morning, The Bolles' House, Quaker Hill, July 22, 1786

A light breeze stirred the thin veil of cheesecloth draped over the coffin to keep insects off of Eunice's body. The sight put Richards in mind of stories - everyone had heard them - about mourners thinking that the rippling was caused by the body taking a breath. For a few brief seconds, the bereaved rejoiced, convinced their loved one had come out of a trance. Once in a very great while, a body actually did shock onlookers by sitting up in the coffin.

As Richards peered through the gloom at Eunice, Hempstead went over to the windows and pushed the curtains aside. The unforgiving July sunshine poured into the room; every detail of the battered corpse sprang into view.

Richards clamped a hand over his mouth. *This body will give no one such a start,* he thought grimly, *no matter how much the cloth ripples above that ruined face.*

Looking down at the mangled body, Richards felt oddly embarrassed, as if he had accidentally interrupted someone engaged in a private act. It occurred to him that, irrespective of the heat and crowd, the family was wise to lay this battered corpse to eternal rest as quickly as possible.

"Hannah, come here and look at Eunice," the Colonel said.

The girl shook her head "no" and edged towards the door away from the Colonel. Hempstead grabbed her arm, and pulled her over to the side of the coffin. The three men surrounded the child, trapping her.

"Hannah, you must look at Eunice," said Halsey.

Hannah kept her eyes fastened on the floorboards, refusing to raise them to the corpse.

Richards squatted down and craned his neck to see into the girl's down-turned face.

"Hannah, you must look."

Shaking her head, Hannah turned her face to him instead of to Eunice. For a fleeting second, Richards had the impression that she knew him, but he didn't understand how that could be possible. They had never been within ten feet of each other until the investigation of Eunice's murder, and had certainly never spoken before then.

"You have to look at Eunice," he repeated in a neutral tone.

Hannah glanced over Richards' shoulder into the coffin, and quickly looked away.

"Do you know what happened to Eunice?" He waited a moment. "You know something you haven't told us, don't you?"

The fear drained from Hannah's face, and a remote, detached expression dropped down over her features. She nodded.

"Do you know who did this to her?"

Hannah nodded again.

"Who did it?" he said, hoping, wishing that she would tell him that she had happened to see a stranger kill Eunice, but had been too afraid to speak up the day before.

"Who did it?" Richards repeated.

"I did."

"You did it?" The dull thudding of his heart pounded in Richards' ears.

Hannah nodded.

"You . . . you beat Eunice to death?"

"Yes."

"Was someone else there? Did someone help you?"

"No."

"You're telling us that you killed Eunice by yourself?"

The girl nodded.

Richards took a deep breath. "Why, Hannah? Why would you do such an awful thing?"

"She deserved a whipping!" Hannah's face contorted with fear and rage. "I wanted to make her pay for the one she caused me."

"How did she cause you a whipping?"

"Because of the strawberries."

"The straw . . . you killed her for the whipping Mrs. Rogers gave you for taking Mary's and Eunice's strawberries?"

"Yes."

Richards stood up.

"Surely," Halsey interjected, "you had other provocations . . . you had other reasons . . ." He faltered, unable to imagine anything a six-year-old could have done to spark such anger.

"She got me in trouble! She told on me, and my mistress got so angry she gave me a terrible whipping."

"You didn't mean to kill Eunice, did you?"

Hannah shook her head. "Not at first, but then I thought that I better."

The three investigators stared, open-mouthed. Richards recovered the power of speech first.

"When did you decide to kill her?"

"After I hit her on the head, she fell down and I choked her. I knew that she would wake up and run home to tell on me, and then my mistress would give me another whipping. Another whipping! I couldn't let her tell!" Hannah slapped tears from her face. "I thought she might still be breathing, so I dropped the rock on her head to make sure she was dead."

"You dropped the rock . . . to make sure she was dead . . ." Halsey groped for the chair at the head of the coffin and pulled it over to him. He sat down, feeling all of his fifty-odd years and wishing himself anywhere else but in this room questioning this child.

Hannah burst into tears. "I promise I'll never do it again, if you'll only forgive me. I promise. I promise! Please forgive me. I won't do it again, I won't, I promise!"

Halsey studied the girl warily until she stopped crying. "You admit that you killed Eunice?"

"Yes," Hannah said, voice dull.

"And you did this in retaliation for her telling on you?"

"Sir?"

"You gave her a whipping, because she caused you one?"

Hannah nodded.

Halsey took out his book for notes and a pencil. "Tell us from the beginning exactly what happened."

Her voice an indifferent monotone, Hannah said that after Mrs. Rogers whipped her, she found Eunice playing with her friends and promised to pay her back for tattling to the Widow.

"How did you manage to catch Eunice Bolles alone?"

"It was easy." Hannah shrugged. "I watched for her to go past the house on her way to school. She was by herself yesterday."

Hannah explained that she had been hauling a bucket of water when she spied Eunice down by the cove. Knowing that she had to act quickly before someone else came along, Hannah rushed into the house, carefully eased the door open as quietly as possible, and set the pail of water in the front hall. Then she rushed back into the yard, scooped up a small rock on the run, and held it down by her side, concealed in the folds of her skirt.

Clutching a bit of colorful patchwork in the other hand, Hannah dodged across the garden, climbed over the wall, and ran down the hill, holding out the cloth and calling for Eunice to wait. She slowed down when she came to the road and walked toward Eunice, still holding out the cloth, urging her to come closer for a look at it. The unsuspecting six-year-old child walked over, her eyes captivated by the bright patchwork. Hannah stepped forward and hit the preoccupied girl with the rock. Stunned, Eunice reeled backwards, and dropped her schoolbook in the road. Hannah went after her and struck again. Eunice began screaming.

Enraged and desperate to silence Eunice, Hannah lost control of herself; she hit the girl over and over, ignoring her pleas for mercy. Dazed, Eunice staggered and fell in the road. Hannah threw herself down on top of Eunice and dug her fingers into her neck. She squeezed as tight as she could until Eunice stopped struggling. When Hannah realized what she'd done, she panicked. In a frenzy, Hannah dragged Eunice's body over to the stone wall.

Then she pushed the stones down toward the road, hoping to make it appear that the wall had fallen on Eunice when she tried to climb over it. Worried that Eunice might not be dead, she picked up a large stone. Standing with the wall between herself and Eunice, Hannah held it directly over the girl's head and dropped it. She paused for a split second to look down at the body, and saw that Eunice had to be dead. As she turned toward the house, she heard a horse walking down the road. A few seconds later, the horse broke into a trot.

Hannah sprinted around the house and leaned against the clapboards, trembling and trying to catch her breath. In what seemed like seconds, but must have been at least five minutes, she heard Colonel Halsey pounding on the front door. Hannah peeked carefully around the corner and watched the Colonel and Mrs. Rogers hurrying out to the road. After they disappeared into the low roadbed, she slipped through the back door into the kitchen, pulling at her apron strings. In her haste, Hannah accidentally pulled the ties into a knot. Frustrated, she tugged the long apron, which covered her from neck to hem, over her head, threw it into the washtub, and piled dirty clothes over it. She ran to the front hall, grabbed the bucket of water she had left by the front door and carried it back to the kitchen. She sloshed the water over the clothes, added a hand full of soap, and left the laundry to soak while she went upstairs to put on a fresh apron.

After she changed, Hannah crept into the garden and hid in the gloom under the apple trees growing along the stone wall. Although she could not see into the road unless she stood by the wall and looked down, Hannah could hear her mistress and Colonel Halsey, and then, later, Sheriff Richards and Mr. Hempstead, and gleaned enough to know that pushing the wall over on Eunice hadn't fooled anyone. After learning that the investigators planned to question everyone in the neighborhood, Hannah concocted a story about seeing four boys.

"So, you never saw four boys at all?" asked Richards.

Hannah shook her head.

"You made them up?"

"Yes."

The Colonel closed his book and put it in his pocket.

"How do we get her out of the house without James seeing us?" Mr. Hempstead asked. "We can hardly tell him right now that Hannah killed his daughter."

"I'll get Alex Rogers and see what he thinks," Richards offered.

"James is upstairs with Mrs. Bolles. If you hurry, you should be able to get out before he comes back down," Alex advised the investigators. "As soon as you're gone, I'll go upstairs and wait in the hall and keep him from coming down while you're still in sight. Otherwise, when I'm sure you are well gone, I'll fetch James out and tell him that Hannah Occuish confessed. He and I will decide when to tell Mrs. Bolles." Rogers darted an angry look at Hannah. "Just get that girl out of here."

Chapter Nine

Afternoon, The New London-Norwich Turnpike, Quaker Hill, July 22, 1786

The three investigators, with Hannah clinging to the Sheriff, rode out of the Bolles' yard at a fast trot. When the trees had swallowed up the house, the men reined their horses to a stop. Richards looked back to make sure that no one had followed them. "Should we go back to the Widow's?"

Halsey shook his head. "No reason to, that I can see. Mrs. Rogers told us herself that she doesn't have an indenture agreement for Hannah, so she's not the child's legal guardian. Besides, we couldn't trust her to watch Hannah."

"Then whom do we notify? Who are her guardians?" Hempstead asked, shifting in the saddle as his horse stamped a hind foot and flicked flies with his tail. "Hannah's parents haven't been seen or heard of in years, and the rest of the family hasn't claimed her."

"She's at least an abandoned child, perhaps even an orphan. Either way, after she attacked Mary Fish in Groton, the Groton Selectmen became responsible for Hannah," the Colonel replied with evident relief. "If we take her on the ferry to Groton now, they can hold her until the Justice of the Peace returns from Hartford."

"I don't think we'd better do that, Colonel." Richards looked thoughtful. "Groton didn't pursue the case against Hannah, and the New London authorities didn't object when Sarah brought her here or when she left her with the Widow."

"How could we have, assuming we even knew Hannah had

come to Quaker Hill?" Hempstead demanded, his face flushing pink. "We had enough to do, trying to keep body and soul together after Arnold's raid! The town burned, and so many dead or wounded. They pulled me half dead from the Avery's house, and I lay sick abed for months . . ."

"All true, Stephen," admitted Richards. "I'm not casting blame on anyone. We all know that New London and Groton were both in dire straits. All I *am* saying is that I believe that allowing Hannah to live in New London - for whatever reason - during the past five years makes her a legal resident of the town."

Richards ran a hand across his jaw. "It follows that the New London town fathers are responsible for her."

Halsey and Hempstead stared at Richards, clearly appalled by the idea.

"You . . . you're probably right, Sheriff," faltered Halsey. "But what do we do with her now - tonight?"

"Take her to Ebenezer Douglas."

"I thought you were worried about not having a warrant," Hempstead commented, wincing as he took a foot out of the stirrup and stretched out his leg. "How can we take her to the ja . . ."

"Hannah will be safe with Ebenezer Douglas and his wife," Richards broke in. "A nice room and a bed, no chores to do, and good food every day. Sounds pretty good." Richards tapped his heels on his horse's sides and started toward New London.

The three men walked their horses down the peaceful, verdant corridor. Lush fields of heavy-headed wheat undulated in the morning air, and flocks of fat sheep, a few cows mixed among them, grazed luxuriant pastures. Promising immature fruit dappled the apple and quince orchards, and bands of clucking, sleek hens roamed the turnpike verges, intently searching for bugs among the wildflowers and grasses growing along the stone walls. As they approached a large farm, a flock of vigilant geese waddled out to the road to flap and hiss at them.

Far too soon, in Richards' mind, the top of the hill above New London came into sight.

"We'll leave you here, Will," Halsey broke the silence, "and go apprise Richard Law of Hannah's confession."

Richards nodded. "Go ahead. I'll take her to Douglas."

Halsey and Hempstead drew up their reins and brought their horses half-way around. "We'll catch up with you at the Red Lion later on tonight," Hempstead promised.

Richards watched Halsey and Hempstead trot their horses southwestward, away from the river, picking up the pace as they went. After they disappeared over the rise, he took out his pocket watch and flipped it open to check the time. Surprised, he looked up at the sun for confirmation that it was already late afternoon. He shoved the watch back into his pocket, and tapped the horse's sides with his heels.

Everyone turned to gawk at Richards and Hannah riding down Main Street. Seemingly, all of them dropped the task at hand and turned to follow their Sheriff. As he came abreast of the Red Lion, Richards groaned at the sight of a large crowd surrounding the new jail house down by the river bank. Swiping an arm across his damp forehead, he rode across the Parade toward the jail, dogged all the way by his informal escort.

For the second time that day, Richards threaded his horse through a swarm of bodies, dismounted, and twined his horse's reins around a rough wooden hitching rail. Chafing under the gaze of the crowd, he lifted Hannah down from the horse and walked her across the yard, refusing to look to the right or left. The door opened as he reached for the iron latch.

Late Afternoon, The Jail House, New London, July 22, 1786

"I didn't believe it until I saw you coming," Ebenezer Douglas said when he came back into the kitchen after locking Hannah in a cell. He hung the iron key ring on the hook by the hallway, and gestured for Richards to take a seat.

"You don't mean to tell me that you already knew I was bringing Hannah Occuish to jail."

"One of the Rogers saw you take her from the Widow . . ."

"And he rushed into town to tell you, spreading the news along the way."

"That's about it, except I don't think he wasted time stopping to gabble. He headed to Greene's from here."

"No surprise in that," Richards observed sardonically. The proximity of Greene's small tavern to Timothy Green's print shop, which produced books, almanacs, pamphlets, sermon reprints, and the *Connecticut Gazette*, routinely attracted thirsty people hoping to quaff free news with bought ale.

"Greene's custom is probably three times the usual number by now," Douglas remarked. "Pretty big crowd when I was up there a while ago."

"What's the mood in town?"

Douglas considered. "I'd have to say stunned. For now."

Richards nodded. "Hard to believe a child could commit cold-blooded murder."

"Do you really believe that she did it?"

"Yes, I do. Hannah Occuish admitted to strangling and beating Eunice to death."

"So, it's all true . . . even about the girl's head?"

"You know about that? What else did you hear?"

"That Eunice Bolles had a broken arm and back."

"This *is* a rare occasion! All of the gossip is accurate." Richards rubbed his eyes. "But in this case, it would have been difficult to exaggerate the facts."

"What happens now?"

"When Justice Coit gets back, Hannah will go before him. With all of the evidence against her, she'll be arrested for suspicion of murder."

"Do you think the Grand Jury will indict a child for murder?"

"I don't know. They'll have to do something with her."

"If the Grand Jury does vote to indict her, surely it will be on a lesser charge. Probably manslaughter."

"I don't know." Richards shrugged. "Seems like strangling someone and dropping a rock on her head is an intentional act."

"Surely the Grand Jury will call it manslaughter," Douglas persisted. "Her age must be a mitigating factor. And remorse; she must be remorseful."

"I just don't know, Eb. Nothing like this has ever happened

before. Hannah told us she plotted to waylay Eunice and give her a beating over a grudge, then decided to murder her to keep her quiet about the beating. It's a clear case of pre-meditated murder, and what the Grand Jurors will make of her age, I can't tell you.

"But as for remorse - I can tell you that Hannah isn't particularly sorry about murdering Eunice. She's only sorry to be caught."

"Did she actually say that she isn't sorry for what she did?"

"She doesn't say much of anything."

"Well, then, you can't be sure."

Richards put on his hat and headed for the door. "I hope you're right."

Chapter Ten

Evening, The Red Lion Inn, July 22, 1786

"No doubt the local 'historians' will soon add another ghost to the list supposedly haunting Quaker Hill," Timothy Larrabee commented wryly, taking a sip of ale.

"Bound to do."

"What does that make now? Four?"

"Seven, counting Indian Kate and the English woman, Sarah Bramble; eight if you count Kate's babe, but it didn't die here, so I'd say seven," Sherriff Richards replied. "Five children murdered, and two adults hanged; all in Quaker Hill."

"Have you ever been waylaid by transparent forms on stormy nights in Quaker Hill?"

Richards chuckled. "Sorry, I can't say that I have. Maybe they fear I've come with a warrant in my pocket to serve them for breach of peace." Richards' face turned somber. "Embellishments aside, the stories of the Bolles and Stoddard murders are grisly enough to survive a hundred years."

Larrabee frowned. "I only know the general details. We have our own ghosts in Preston to worry about."

"Aye, most towns do," Richards replied. "But a lot of people around here took John Bolles' religious notions seriously when he claimed that God saved him from the murderer's axe to make him a prophet."

Larrabee nodded. "Anyone who survived a massacre would have to make sense of it somehow, or else go mad."

"True enough," Richards said, leaning down to rub the hard

leather on the toe of his left boot. "Bad enough for John, but for his father . . . I can't imagine how Thomas Bolles coped. He leaves a peaceful domestic scene: young mother home alone with the three children, sitting by the fire, baby cradled in her arms. Then out of nowhere, a madman bursts through the door, axe in hand, and chops the mother and two children to death."

Larrabee grimaced. "Didn't they arrest some Indians for the crime?"

"Yes, on the statements of the Indians who reported the murders. One of them said that he had gone to the Bolles to ask if they wanted to buy venison. When he got to the house, he found a small girl lying in the doorway, gasping and drowning in her own blood, and a younger boy and Zipporah Bolles inside by the fireplace, hacked to death, and a baby wallowing in his mother's gore. On the way for help, the first Indian met another, who told him that he overheard two other Indians vowing to kill Englishmen."

"When was this again?"

"Way back in 1676, during King Philip's War."

Larrabee gave a low whistle. "So, the authorities arrested the second two Indians on the word of the first two?"

"They did," said Richards. "And maybe held the first two as well, I don't know. In any case, while the Indians sat in jail, someone killed a baby up the road from the Bolles, again using an axe. The baby's sixteen-year-old half-brother, John Stoddard, said that his parents had left him alone with the child, apparently for a day or two. According to the boy, while he was working in the field he noticed two Indians sneaking out of his step-father's house. He ran to the house and found the baby hacked to death."

"Couldn't have been the same Indians in jail for the Bolles."

"No, it couldn't have, and that fact, combined with the murder of the Bolles, heightened fears of an Indian uprising. New London was in a fever pitch while the authorities conducted a full investigation - an investigation that failed to turn up evidence against the Indians. Instead, the evidence pointed to John Stoddard. Neighbors marked him as a vicious, foul-mouthed liar. One of them claimed to have seen Stoddard near the Bolles' on the day they were murdered. When authorities re-questioned

Stoddard, he broke down and said his mother and step-father had left him with the baby and had been gone a long time, and the baby wouldn't stop crying. He lost his temper and hit his brother a blow with the axe. In for a penny, in for a pound, I guess, because he then confessed to murdering the Bolles earlier, and he picked out the axe he used to kill them from several axes the investigators showed him."

Larrabee shook his head. "Tensions between family members sometimes lead to violence, but why kill a family unrelated to him?"

"Mrs. Bolles refused to let him stay in the house while her husband was away. When she turned him out, Stoddard grabbed the axe, and came back intent on murdering her. He killed the older children to keep them from identifying him, but left the baby alive. After Stoddard's arrest, the town released the Indians and sent the boy to Hartford for trial. With a confession and correct identification of the murder weapon, they couldn't do anything else but find him guilty and hang him."

"And Thomas Bolles, John's father?"

"He had two more wives, but, oddly, no more children. All of his money and property, and he had a lot of both, went to John Bolles, even though he'd joined up with John Rogers and the Rogerenes before his father's death." Richards took a sip of ale. "I wonder what an orthodox man like Mr. Bolles would say if he knew his son's group ran a good minister like Reverend Byles out of the Congregational Church right into the Anglican."

"Where does Eunice Bolles fit into the family genealogy?"

"Eunice Bolles was the great-granddaughter of the baby found lying in his mother's blood. And the Widow Rogers Hannah Occuish lives with is John Rogers' granddaughter-in-law."

Larrabee shook his head. "You couldn't make these stories up."

"That's the truth."

"My kin tell me the Widow is a Rogerene. Is that a fact?"

"Yes, and she's of the old style: no public services or prayers, not even family prayers. Those types of Rogerenes are mighty thin on the ground these days, thank God for it."

"Yes, it's a mercy," Larrabee agreed. "I know the type. I have kin in Quaker Hill."

"That's right." Richards leaned back in his chair. "I'd forgotten. One of the John Rogers' wives."

Larrabee nodded.

"The first John Rogers got land from the Indians, didn't he?"

"His father, James, bought and was given large parcels of Indian land back in the 1600s. He gave John large swaths of Quaker Hill by gift and inheritance," Larrabee said. "Not many Indians up there anymore."

"Some, but not so many as there used to be." Richards leaned down and rubbed the toe box of his left boot again.

"Maybe they've gone up north to Brothertown."

"Probably so. The ones who survived the war, that is. A lot of the good Indians from New London got killed fighting on our side." Richards sat up. "That's the way it always seems to go, the good ones get killed and the bad survive."

"Um," Larrabee paused. "What does that say about us former soldiers?" he deadpanned.

Richards stared at his friend, then burst out laughing. "I suppose nothing good."

"What about Hannah Occuish?" Larrabee tacked the conversation to safer waters. "Is the girl a heretic?"

"I don't know," Richards said, wondering how many times circumstances had forced those words from him over the last two days. "Her grandfather is Philip Occuish, the Baptist Indian minister, a well-off man. He gave both his sons property when they came of age."

"Why didn't Sarah take Hannah to her parents instead of leaving her in Quaker Hill?"

"I can't say for sure. Philip must be close to eighty now. I've heard that he's distracted[2], but that wasn't the case five years ago. I think Sarah went to Groton, because she was on bad terms with her parents. Sarah is an alcoholic, and they disapprove of drunkenness. It's no wonder that they do. Their son, Jacob, killed his wife in a drunken rage."

"I remember that case pretty well," Larrabee remarked. "The

court found Occuish guilty of manslaughter and ordered him to forfeit his land to the state, after being whipped and branded."

"Yes, but at least he escaped with his life."

"Are there other children?"

"A couple daughters and a son, Joseph. Several grandchildren," Richards answered.

"None of them wanted Hannah?"

"It wouldn't have mattered if they had. Even without considering Jacob's arrest and trial, the authorities wouldn't have turned Hannah over to the Occuishs. The town fathers would want her to live with a white family. I guess that's why they let the Widow keep the girl," Richards said, shifting uncomfortably in his chair. "I was in the army, fighting, when Sarah brought Hannah to Quaker Hill. A lot of us were," he added.

"Yes," Larrabee acknowledged, "it probably seemed like a good idea, at the time. Be that as it may, I don't imagine we'll see much of the Occuishs around town now that Hannah has been arrested, and I can't say that I blame them. People might get it into their heads to take out their resentment on Hannah's' family."

Richards nodded. "I wouldn't be surprised."

"Let's hope that the court will be as lenient with Hannah Occuish as they were with her Uncle Jacob." Larrabee drained his tankard and set it down on the table. "She's just a child after all."

"I don't know, Timothy," Richards replied. "Too much history to ignore."

Jan Schenk Grosskopf

Chapter Eleven

Evening, The Red Lion Inn, July 22, 1786

After making his goodbyes to Richards, Timothy Larrabee walked agitatedly toward the river. He went down Sparyard Street and then wandered through the maze of warehouses along the docks until a growling stomach set him in the direction of the Parade. He crossed the Parade and Main Street, skirted around the Red Lion, and startled the maids when he came into the kitchen through the back door.

"Bless me, Mr. Larrabee! Is something amiss?"

Larrabee smiled ruefully. "I came to ask if you would send a tray up to me."

"Certainly, sir. I'll have it brought right up," Lizzy promised.

After the door closed behind Bess, Larrabee pulled his small table and chair over to the garret window facing the harbor and sat down to eat. Indistinct voices from the room below mingled with the rhythmic sound of waves slapping against wooden hulls across the Parade; dusk crept over the docks and wharfs until only swaying pinpoints of light from deck lanterns betrayed the ships' positions. As he sat above the meeting, separated only by wooden planks, Larrabee began wondering how many of the men had actually been to a hanging. Probably only a few, if any. And with that thought, visions that had hounded him for almost forty years attacked again.

* * *

Happy to escape their Latin grammars, Timothy and his friends walked to Betty Shaw's hanging in high spirits. None of them feeling at all inclined to sympathize with a woman depraved enough to leave her new-born infant in the woods to starve. Five days after she abandoned it to the mercy of the July sun, insects, and predators, the smell told the investigators they had correctly followed Betty's directions to the hollow log where she had hidden her newborn. Grown men wept as they brushed leaves and bark off of the tiny rotting corpse. The memory foul in their eyes and noses, the investigators condemned Betty for murder. No matter how simple-minded she appeared, if Betty Shaw had the wherewithal to conceal her pregnancy, deliver in secrecy, and sneak away to hide the baby, she knew what she was doing when she left him in the woods to die.

Timothy and his friends managed to squirm their way to within ten feet of the low gallows; close enough to see the young woman's terrified face, and hear the squeak of the rope over the cross-beam as the hangman hoisted Shaw high into the air. Betty's legs kicked and jerked, but struggling only pulled the noose tighter. Her face mottled and her tongue protruded from her mouth. Timothy spun around and wildly pushed his way toward the back of the crowd, burst free from the pressing bodies, and ran for home. Halfway there, he fell to his knees and vomited.

Larabee shifted restlessly. He stood up, hand to his back, and walked around the room to stretch. Despite the many years between that day and this, he could not forget the sight of Betty dangling from the noose; ghastly memories that fed his aversion to capital punishment. But after years of exposure to the evils that some of his fellow citizens seemed almost routinely capable of, Larrabee had reconciled himself to the execution of cold-blooded murderers. Sane murderers, even those of the rare breed who seemed unable to have compassion for their fellow creatures, at least understood the consequences to themselves of their actions. The question of what to do with murderous incompetents, such as Betty Shaw, is what ate at him, and as for a young child committing murder . . . he hadn't ever considered the idea. Until today, there had been no call for him to do so.

In the past few years, he had wondered how to think about capital punishment during a new era - a time when former beliefs and practices should be called into question and examined. In just a few short years, Americans had transformed themselves from subjects of a monarch into free citizens of a state governed by their own elected officials. Getting rid of the King made for a different, indeed, a radically new, relationship between the individual and the state. Should that new government, elected by and constituted of citizens, execute citizens who committed the most heinous of crimes? If not, what should it do with them?

To Larrabee's mind, although all inhabitants of the state were technically citizens, the responsibilities and privileges of individual citizens depended upon other conditions. Hannah Occuish, for example, might be a citizen of the State of Connecticut; however, for her not much had changed from when she had been a subject of the King. Although she would eventually leave behind childhood, the one category of dependence experienced by everyone high or low, she would always be, in some fashion, a dependent. This reality didn't trouble Larrabee. Although a patriot who had drunk deep of Revolutionary rhetoric, he believed that non-white people and women possessed immutable characteristics that made them forever suited for dependence. Like all females, white or not, Hannah would never cast ballots for the men who would represent her in the institutions of government that fashioned the laws of her country. Although a few wild-eyed radicals advocated letting women meddle in civic matters, Larrabee couldn't imagine women going to the polls in Connecticut.

How tragic that living with Mrs. Rogers has gone so badly, he thought. At the Widow's, Hannah had been almost exactly where authorities wanted to see young free-born girls of color: working under the daily supervision of a white master or mistress until the day she was ready to go back to her family, or to a husband's house. Or, in this case, a husband might have gone to hers, if Hannah inherited from her grandfather or made a claim to reservation land. Of course, Hannah's husband would control whatever she brought to the marriage, subject to the legal and customary limitations imposed on men of color. But, that was all out of the question now. If the court should find Hannah guilty of manslaughter and allow her to live, Philip Occuish would never risk giving his granddaughter property. The state would snap it up as part of her punishment. In the unlikely event that she managed to keep an inheritance, only a fool or desperate man would marry such a notorious woman.

Larrabee began to undress for bed, reminding himself that speculating about Hannah's marriage or property was extremely precipitous, to say the least, in light of her current situation. As to her guilt - he refused to decide about that until he saw the evidence for himself. He would, however, ask Judge Law to appoint him as Hannah's counsel. It would be a thankless job. Trying an abandoned child of color for murder and deciding what to do with her afterwards would expose troubling legal and social conditions. In fact, the whole trial would be an unwelcome test of Connecticut's experimental state government - and of all of its leaders.

Chapter Twelve

The Jail House, New London, July 22, 1786

While the town gossiped, conjectured, and speculated, the current object of their curiosity sat quietly in the small gaol on the river's edge. Most criminals exhibited a range of emotions during their first day behind bars. But Hannah didn't act like most inmates. The grating of the iron key in her cell door sparked no tears. Instead of crying, she was calm and remote, apparently detached from her surroundings. Hannah didn't call out for the jailer, and whenever he looked in on her, Douglas found his prisoner staring at the wall or out of the barred window. If she happened to notice the jailer, Hannah didn't attempt to convince him of her innocence or express remorse, calculated or sincere. The girl only roused herself to provide dutiful, monosyllabic answers to direct questions.

A few hours after Richards left Hannah at the jail, Mr. Douglas had gratefully opened the front door to a middle-aged woman and her husband. This couple, and the few other townspeople who actually took the biblical commission to visit prisoners seriously, regularly called on the drunks, petty thieves, and other run-of-the-mill, unexciting prisoners who normally inhabited Douglas' jail. No matter how unattractive these criminals' persons or how uninteresting their crimes, these visitors sat in the cramped barred rooms, attempting to comfort the penitent or awaken the conscience of the hardhearted.

Apprehension flickered across Hannah's face when Mr. Douglas unlocked her door, and she warily studied the couple as they pulled chairs close to her. The couple struggled to draw Hannah out, finally admitting defeat after a painful half an hour. As they stood up to leave, the woman asked Hannah if she would like to pray with them. Hannah shrugged indifferently, but she sat through the prayers without protest and glanced briefly in their direction when they turned at the door to say goodbye.

"Is the child always so withdrawn?" the man asked Douglas when they reached the front room.

"I don't know," Douglas said, unconsciously echoing Sheriff Richards.

"Here," the jailer's wife snapped, slamming a covered tray down on the small wooden table in Hannah's cell. Mrs. Douglas stalked over to the window. Making sure not to touch the prisoner in passing, she reached through the bars, grasped the shutters, and pulled them closed against the night air, careful all the while not to even glance in Hannah's direction.

By rights the Widow Rogers should have brought the girl's meals or at least paid someone else to do it. After all, masters were responsible for their servants. But the prisoner had to eat, and someone had to feed her, so Mrs. Douglas came into Hannah's cell as a favor to her husband.

Being asked to feed the girl was bad enough, but her normally rational husband completely flabbergasted Mrs. Douglas by informing her that he did not intend to charge the town for Hannah's keep! She had stared at him in openmouthed surprise, hardly hearing his explanation that it was just as well that the Widow stayed away; that he would rather not draw attention to his infamous prisoner any more than necessary. Seeing the Widow coming and going would be sure to excite public comment, and as for submitting a bill for Hannah's expenses - he didn't care to light a firestorm of controversy. Even after she agreed to cook for Hannah, nothing Mrs. Douglas said - and she said plenty that evening - convinced her husband that it would be foolish to pay for a prisoner's food out of his own pocket.

Early Morning, The Jail House, July 23, 1786

Tired of twisting and turning, Mrs. Douglas gave up and got out of bed before dawn. Yawning, she went into the kitchen and reached into the larder cabinet for the spider bread she had set aside for breakfast. It was gone.

At daybreak, Mr. Douglas came downstairs to find his wife squatting by the stone kitchen hearth, wiping sweat from her forehead with the hem of her long apron. She tucked the apron around her knees, away from the flames, and leaned forward to rake hot coals under the tall, three-legged, cast iron frying pan. She dropped a spoon of bacon grease on the hot surface of the spider.

"No need to make a fire inside on such a morning," the jailer commented mildly.

Mrs. Douglas grunted and stood up. "And how would you have your spider bread for breakfast if I didn't? Your son ate what I put aside."

"Growing lads," Douglas murmured in the boy's defense, taking note that their beloved, but hungry, son had only a father this morning. As he watched his angry wife, the jailer cast his mind over other hot summer mornings when the spider bread had disappeared during the night. Never before, that he could remember, had his wife felt moved to stir up hot coals on account of his purloined breakfast. And if she needed a cooking fire, she had a perfectly good summer kitchen in the yard.

"It's fair hot already," Douglas observed.

"So it is. I've had occasion to notice," Mrs. Douglas replied curtly, tossing cornmeal, salt, baking powder, and milk into a pottery bowl. She cracked an egg on the edge of the bowl with a quick, impatient flip of her wrist, dropped the egg into the mixture, and stirred briskly. She stalked across the room and squatted down by the hearth. The spider hissed when the cornmeal batter hit the thin layer of dancing hot bacon grease.

Studying the resentment spelled out in his wife's every lineament, the jailer sighed. He considered going back out to finish the morning chores, leaving an unpleasant task for another time, but decided that he might as well get it over with now. Douglas didn't foresee his wife's attitude about Hannah improving in the coming days and weeks.

At first, Mrs. Douglas actually could not speak, absolutely could not form the words of protest, while her husband explained his most recent outrageous scheme. After she had given in about the food, now he wanted her, he actually had the gall to ask her, to give Hannah Occuish some of their daughter's old clothes to wear so that her own could be washed!

"You cannot mean that!"

"Well, yes, I do," he replied evenly. "I'd hoped that you would understand."

"I understand that you have lost your senses! And I can promise you, Mr. Ebenezer Douglas, that I will never live to see the day that I allow a murderer to put on my, and I might add your, child's clothes."

"Now then, Mary, would you have the girl sit naked in the cell while you . . . while her clothes are being washed?"

"Whether she sits naked or not is none of my concern. Let Mrs. Rogers bring Hannah Occuish clean clothes. The Lord knows that the girl is her responsibility. And don't think I didn't hear what you just said, Mr. Douglas, about her laundry. I have no intention of putting that girl's clothes in my wash tub. I am the wife of the town jailer, not a common washer woman!"

"No, of course not." Her husband sat down heavily, his expression already weary, and it not yet seven of the clock. "I could send for the Widow, about the food as well as the clothes. But I've already told you why I don't want to do that. People are angry, at Hannah, to be sure, but they also bitterly resent her mistress for harboring a menace, and the sight of the Widow coming to and fro in town would be like a spark to a powder keg; there'll be no way to control the explosion. It's better that the Widow Rogers stays put in Quaker Hill, out of sight, until the town cools down."

"And, as I told you, the Widow must pay someone else to do what she will not."

The jailer shook his head. "We can't get the money from her.

She doesn't answer her door; likely hiding inside, unless she's gone away." Mr. Douglas paused. "That's what I'd do, if I were she, go away for a while."

"Then go to her kinfolk. She has a surplus of them, a regular swarm of them up in Quaker Hill."

"The result will be the same whether we go to her family or to the selectmen: arguments over responsibility, which will then spill over into the town. Fruitless, senseless arguments that will pit neighbor against neighbor and kin against kin." He shook his head sorrowfully. "People are like to get as stirred up over this affair as they did over the King's taxes."

"No! This is a different matter altogether."

"The topic may be different, but the people are the same, and they are very angry . . ."

Mrs. Douglas searched her husband's tense face, the fingers of her hand slowly relaxing their death grip on her favorite horn spoon.

"I'll give her the clothes when I take in her breakfast, Ebenezer," she conceded. "But - I still don't want to look at her."

Chapter Thirteen

Mid-Morning, The Jail House, July 23, 1786

Mrs. Douglas plunked down Hannah's breakfast tray on the table. "Before you eat that, put on these and give me your dirty clothes." She slung a bundle of clothing at the child, lying stomach down on her rumpled bed. "Get out of bed, and hurry up about it."

The jailer's wife swung open the shutters and looked out the window. When it seemed by her impatient calculation that Hannah should be finished changing, Mrs. Douglas turned around to snatch up the soiled clothes. As her hand shot forward, she stopped short and watched in shock as Hannah leaned forward to pick up the underdress from the bed. The light from the window fell directly on the child's naked back.

Her back! Mrs. Douglas had never seen anything like it. The bright morning sun revealed crusted wounds hash-marking Hannah's back from her shoulders to her upper buttocks. The fresh stripes, some partially scabbed over, lay over flesh ribbed by the scars of at least one previous lashing, possibly more. Serum oozed from wounds reopened when Hannah pulled off her clothes and the adhered scabs came off with them. Mrs. Douglas watched in horror as the pinkish fluid trickled slowly down the poor girl's back.

"Who did that to you?"

Hannah turned dead eyes to her. "Did what?"

"Who lashed you so brutally, child?"

Hannah shrugged, and turned her head.

"Come here. Don't be afraid." Mrs. Douglas sat down on the chair and gestured. "Come over here, and turn around so that I can see your back."

Hannah edged forward, face suspicious, and turned around. Mrs. Douglas felt sick as she examined the weeping sores under the harsh light. The fresh injuries overlaid and hid some of the evidence of previous whippings, confirming her initial impression that Hannah had been severely whipped at least two times before.

Mrs. Douglas dipped the washrag into the cool water in Hannah's china wash bowl. She wrung the rag out and dabbed it very gently on the open wounds. The child twisted away, whimpering in pain. Mrs. Douglas got up and closed the shutters, and went to the door to let herself out. "Don't get dressed, I'll be right back."

Hannah obediently sat down, naked to the waist.

"Put something over your chest until I come back." Mrs. Douglas hurried back to the kitchen and quickly gathered fresh rags and the small earthenware pot of homemade salve kept on hand for treating burns and injuries. She put the pot and bandages into a basket, and carried it back down the hall. When she let herself into the cell, she found Hannah sitting exactly where she had left her, soiled clothing clutched to her chest, face expressionless.

After thoroughly washing Hannah's back, Mrs. Douglas dipped a clean rag into the pot and patted the medicine over the wounds. She tore the rest of the clean rags into narrow strips and wound the soft linen around Hannah's torso, loosely binding the medicated rag against the lash marks, and tied the ends of the bandages together. She gestured toward the tray.

"Sit down and eat your breakfast."

While Hannah spooned up the lukewarm porridge, Mrs. Douglas studied her.

"Now, tell me, who whipped you like that, child?"

Hannah shook her head.

"I'll wager Mrs. Rogers gave you that hiding, didn't she? No, don't look away and don't be frightened. I think that I can promise you that she'll never have the opportunity to lash you again."

For a brief moment a tiny spark of hope flamed in Hannah's eyes, completely transforming her face.

Why, she's an attractive child! Mrs. Douglas thought in surprise. Heretofore, like almost everybody else, she had found Hannah unappealing, but when stripped of her sullen, guarded demeanor, Hannah was pleasant to look at. It occurred to Mrs. Douglas that had the circumstances of her life been different, Hannah may have turned out an entirely different child.

The light burned in Hannah's eyes for a brief second, and then extinguished as experience drowned hope. The sullen pall fell back over her face.

Though no sentimentalist, it cut Mrs. Douglas to the quick to realize that Hannah classed her with the majority of the authority figures in the girl's short life - most of whom had, obviously, routinely broken their promises to her. She shuddered to think of any child growing up under the fear of the lash with no one who cared enough to protect her.

"I will keep my promise to you about the Widow, Hannah. She will never whip you again, of that you may be sure. And many another will back me up when they learn what has been done to you." She put a hand on the girl's shoulder. "Now tell me, did the Widow do this to you?"

Hannah shrugged, but did not push the hand away. "Yes."

"And what had you done to so anger your mistress?"

Hannah looked away from Mrs. Douglas. "Eunice told her that I took her strawberries."

Mrs. Douglas sat down on the bed, so that she could look into Hannah's face. "Yes, I've heard all about the strawberries, but what else did you do?"

"I took them."

"Yes, Hannah, I understand. You took Eunice's strawberries, but what else did you do?"

"What else?" Hannah was clearly puzzled by the question.

"Yes, what else did you do when you took the berries from Eunice? Surely you did something to deserve punishment . . ." Mrs. Douglas struggled to imagine what Hannah had done to deserve the type of whipping the court used to punish an adult who had committed a very serious crime; a lashing like the one given to Hannah's uncle for accidentally killing his wife.

"I took her strawberries, and I ate them," said Hannah slowly and clearly, as if talking to a slow-witted person.

"You . . . ate the strawberries . . ." Mrs. Douglas sat back in her chair. "You ate them."

Hannah nodded.

"Did you do anything else to Eunice?"

"I pushed her and Mary Rogers down and snatched their strawberries."

"And then you . . ."

"And then I ate the strawberries."

Mrs. Douglas pried information from Hannah until she believed that she had a pretty good understanding of the Widow's method of disciplining her charge. If method it could be called, seeing as the Widow apparently punished by whim.

When Mrs. Douglas saw that Hannah had nothing more to say, she gathered up the empty breakfast dishes, stuffed the bundle of dirty clothes under one arm, and went back to her kitchen. She put the dishes in one tub and the clothes in another, and went outside to pump water. She filled the large pot on the tripod in the yard and started a fire underneath it. When the water boiled, she brought the tubs outside and dipped water to fill them. While the dishes and clothes soaked, Mrs. Douglas went inside and got out a sheet of paper. She dipped her pen into the inkwell and wrote two short notes and signed them. She folded the pages in half and sealed them with wax. Letters in hand, she went to the door and called her son into the house.

"Take these messages to Mrs. Shaw and Mistress Coit. Hurry and don't dally along the way; it's important."

As the boy dashed off toward the Red Lion, Mrs. Douglas went down the cellar steps and brought up a crock of fresh, sweet butter. She cut a large slice of golden spider bread she baked that morning, sliced it in two, and spread a thick layer of rich, yellow butter on the bottom slice. She put top and bottom together, and wrapped the bread and butter in a clean napkin. Taking up the small bundle, Mrs. Douglas walked toward Hannah's cell.

Chapter Fourteen

Late Afternoon, The Jail House, July 23, 1786

Mistress Coit and Mrs. Shaw sank gratefully into Mrs. Douglas' front-room chairs while their hostess went out to the summer kitchen in the back yard to heat water for tea. Although the relentless July sun beat down outside the jail house, a steady stream of cool air flowed from the shade of a tall tree through the propped-open back door. The cool air slowly warmed, and wound up the stairs to escape out of the open garret windows. The fresh green of tree leaves filtered the sunlight streaming through the front room windows, casting shifting patterns of light and shadow on the polished floorboards and papered plaster walls.

When the tea water boiled, Mrs. Douglas carried the heavy black kettle into the kitchen and poured the hot water over the shredded leaves in the good china teapot. She put her silver strainer and her best china cups and saucers on the tray, next to the pot. She carried the tea things into the front room.

Molly Coit shook her head. "I wouldn't have believed it if I hadn't seen Hannah's back with my own eyes! How could a woman - a mother - beat a child half to death? Are you sure it was Mrs. Rogers who gave Hannah this whipping?"

"Yes," Mrs. Douglas affirmed. "I'm positive."

"And you say it was all because Hannah took strawberries from Eunice?" asked Molly.

"Yes, from Eunice and little Mary Rogers, the Widow's

granddaughter."

Molly shook her head. "And, judging by the old scars, this wasn't the first time Hannah has been lashed within an inch of her life."

"The poor child didn't seem to think it wrong, or even unusual, to be given a severe whipping for such a little thing as taking berries from another child. She only seemed upset and afraid to answer when I asked her who had punished her. She finally told me that her mistress had done the job herself, but only after I promised to protect her."

"But can we believe her?" wondered Mrs. Shaw.

"Yes, I think that we can. When Sheriff Richards gave Hannah into my husband's custody, he told him that Hannah said that she attacked Eunice for telling on her about the strawberries. My husband didn't know what to think; it all sounded so outlandish. But he did understand Mr. Richards to say that Hannah had vowed to give Eunice a whipping to make up for the one her mistress had given her over some trifle. I'm sure neither of them knew that the Widow had whipped Hannah so severely.

"But Hannah didn't really attack Eunice over the strawberries. She said that she wanted to give Eunice a beating like the one she got from the Widow."

"Fantastic . . ." Mistress Coit faltered. "No matter what Hannah did, how could anyone whip a child so brutally? And the scars . . . scars laid over scars."

Mrs. Douglas nodded. "It is unbelievable, Molly. Hannah told me that sometime last fall, the Widow handed her a crock of butter she had just finished churning, and told the child to put it in the spring house. On the way across the yard, Hannah tripped and dropped the crock. It smashed on a stone. Naturally, the butter went into the dirt, and Hannah could only save a bit of it. Mrs. Rogers flew into a rage when she found out and took the whip to Hannah. You have seen the results of that punishment under the new wounds on her back."

"An occasional whipping, justly and temperately given for serious misdeeds, these parents and masters have a right, even a duty, to give, and I don't object to such punishments," Mrs. Shaw pronounced. "But to mercilessly beat a child for any reason, especially an accidental spilling of butter - something that could happen to anyone - is wrong."

Mrs. Douglas nodded, apparently in complete agreement with all of Mrs. Shaw's opinions about corporeal punishment, but Molly kept still. No matter what almost everybody else believed, she did not hold with striking children - slave, servant, or free - regardless of the circumstances. It troubled her very little to be out of step with the rest of New London, but she also saw no need to broadcast her unusual philosophy.

"And the poor child is confused; doesn't know which way to turn to please her mistress," Mrs. Douglas continued. "The Widow Rogers overreacts to accidents like the butter and small misdeeds, but in the case of serious misbehavior, she sometimes neglects to punish Hannah at all.

"Hannah told me that when neighbors complained to the Widow that she bullied their children, Mrs. Rogers didn't punish her! Blood drawn over butter and nothing done for bullying much smaller children."

"The Widow's behavior doesn't make any sense." Molly frowned.

"My thoughts, exactly," Mrs. Douglas agreed.

"All very sad, but we can't do anything about the past," Mrs. Shaw observed.

"Yes, what do we do now? My husband tells me that he believes that once Hannah is formally arrested, the Grand Jury will have no choice but to indict her for murder."

"You mean he thinks the jury will put an eleven-year-old child on trial for her life?" Mrs. Shaw asked, nonplussed.

"Mr. Douglas said that they have no other choice. He thinks that she will go on trial in the late summer."

Molly Coit's eyes flashed. "How could Hannah be expected to learn to govern her temper when her mistress can't manage to? Hasn't Mrs. Rogers as good as taught the child to fly into a passion over trifles? A few more stripes on Hannah's back this week past, and the Widow might be the one in the cell down the hall instead of her servant."

"Certainly, we can all see the truth of what you say, Molly," Mrs. Shaw pointed out. "But as sorry as we feel for her, Hannah killed Eunice Bolles, and by a most vicious method."

"If only the Widow had sent Hannah packing back to Groton," said Mrs. Douglas.

"Groton?" Mrs. Shaw asked. "Why should Mrs. Rogers have sent Hannah back to Groton?"

"Groton had a warrant against Hannah for attacking a child in Poquonnock Bridge - Mary Fish, a white girl. Before they could deal with her over there, Sarah, Hannah's mother, brought her to Quaker Hill and left her there."

Mrs. Douglas' hand trembled slightly as she reached for a napkin. "I pray that the town has better self-control than Hannah and the Widow. My husband told me that a lot of people are angry with Mrs. Rogers for refusing to send Hannah away, and he's worried that some of them might decide to take matters into their own hands."

"Regarding Hannah, or the Widow?"

"Either one . . . both. I don't know."

"I think that everyone in town should know what we just learned." Molly's voice was steely. "It shines a different light on the murder."

"It does . . ." Mrs. Shaw tilted her head thoughtfully. "But we must alert Judge Law and the Sheriff before we let any information escape into public knowledge."

"I will tell my husband today, and ask him to go see Judge Law immediately," promised Mrs. Douglas. "Do you think that the Judge will call the women's jury to examine Hannah?"

"We are members of the women's jury and have just completed an examination," Mrs. Shaw replied.

"Yes, but Judge Law might wish to have the opinion of all the members."

"Perhaps," Mrs. Shaw smiled, "but I doubt it." The older lady paused. "No need to send Mr. Douglas to see the Judge. I will go to Richard Law's house myself right now. I'll send you each a note after I talk to him."

Mistress Coit tried not to look too pleased. She had intended for Mrs. Shaw to take it on herself to go to the Judge. Law would, as Mrs. Shaw stated, see her right away, and he would take her opinions on the case seriously.

"I'll tell the Sheriff. He usually drops by the Red Lion a couple of times a day. As soon as we know that Judge Law and Sheriff Richards are informed, well, each of us knows a friend who can be relied upon to broadcast the story almost before we have finished telling it. As a matter of fact," Molly smiled, "I will drop a word tonight, in confidence, naturally, to one or two patrons, and I guarantee you that by nine o'clock tomorrow morning, everyone in New London will be able to describe Hannah's wounds as if he had seen them himself."

"The Widow will not be able to show her face in town after tomorrow," Mrs. Douglas commented a bit apprehensively.

Molly snorted derisively. "Mrs. Rogers may skulk in Quaker Hill all of her live-long days, as far as I am concerned. It's little enough punishment for her role in this murder."

Chapter Fifteen

Late Afternoon, Richard Law's House, New London, July 23, 1786

Judge Law fulfilled all of Mrs. Shaw's expectations by putting down his pen and coming around his desk to greet her. After politely showing her to a seat, he sat down across from her.

"Mrs. Douglas called on me for advice today."

The Judge raised his eyebrows. "A woman's matter?" He smiled indulgently. "How might I help you ladies?"

"No," Mrs. Shaw replied, her face bland. "A town matter."

Law's deepening frown as he listened to Mrs. Shaw tell Hannah's story didn't surprise the elderly lady, but he did startle her when he leapt up out of his chair. Before she had time to wonder about the man's peculiar reaction, the Judge threw open his office door and called down the hall.

"Jim, find the Coroner and the Sheriff and send them to meet me at the jail," he ordered, snatching his hat from a peg. "And don't forget Stephen Hempstead. I want him there, too."

He pushed the door fully open and gestured to Mrs. Shaw to precede him. Within seconds, Law and his visibly-stunned companion were walking briskly down Main Street toward the harbor. They covered the blocks between Judge Law's house and the jail in record time, leaving staring townspeople in their wake.

* * *

Late Afternoon, The Jail House, July 23, 1786

Mrs. Douglas' eyes darted from the Judge's face to Mrs. Shaw's, her own visage a caricature of astonishment, as she stood, water dripping from the blue china platter that she held over the washtub. Law walked into the house, Mrs. Shaw close on his heels.

"Mrs. Douglas, is your husband home?"

"Uh, he's . . . he's about, somewhere, Judge. I . . ." Mrs. Douglas glanced around for a place to set down the platter.

"Please call him, if you will."

She put the platter back into the tub. "Certainly. Come in and sit down while I go for him." Drying her hands with a cloth, she hurried into the house lot, completely thrown off kilter.

Mrs. Douglas found her husband in the stable, gently running his hand along King George's tender fetlock. A small worried frown creased the jailer's face, Georgie being something of a pet. Whenever he rode the big horse, Douglas enjoyed remarking that he had gotten up that morning and put the reins on King George. Younger men respectfully trained their eyes straight ahead, lips suppressing heavy sighs at the stale joke, but Douglas' battle-scarred former comrades-in-arms always broke into loud, appreciative sniggers.

The jailer spoke at the sound of his wife's footfalls. "It's still a bit swollen, so no . . ."

Mrs. Douglas glanced distractedly at the gelding's leg. "Yes, yes, too bad. I'm sure he'll be fine in another day or two. Ebenezer, Judge Law is here to see you. He wants you to come right away."

"What's the matter?" he looked curiously at his wife as he stood up. "It's not like you to get so frazzled."

"We called on him; that is, Mrs. Shaw did on our behalf."

"She called on the Judge?" Douglas cocked his head. "On your behalf?"

After listening carefully to his wife's quick explanation, the jailer merely remarked, "Well, let's go in and see what the Judge has to say."

The Douglases found the Judge seated in their kitchen nervously tapping his foot. Mrs. Shaw, composure regained, stood by a window, studying a small group of boys gathered on the Parade. While she watched, one of the boys gestured angrily toward the jail. Urged on by his mates, the boy picked up a rock and lobbed it toward the prison. Although the missile fell far short of its target, the other boys scattered. The rock thrower hesitated, and then, seeing that he stood alone, ran after his friends. Mrs. Shaw turned away from the window.

"Good day, Ebenezer," Richard Law said to the jailer as he came through the door.

"And to you, Mr. Law. My wife tells me that you would like to see Hannah's wounds. So would I," he added. "While we're waiting for the others, the women can go ahead and prepare Hannah."

As soon as they were alone, Law thumped down his glass. "Damn me, Douglas, if what Mrs. Shaw says is true, and I don't doubt her word, that Rogers woman has put us all in a most untenable position. As I understand it, Mrs. Rogers has corrupted the child by example and terrorized her with the lash, and now we are called upon to untangle this mess."

Mr. Douglas studied the Judge's face. "Considering her history of violence before she came to the Widow, Hannah Occuish might have turned out a murderess no matter who raised her."

"That we will never know, now," Law fumed.

"Mr. Coit will be bound to issue a warrant for Hannah, but perhaps the Grand Jury will not indict because of her age," Douglas temporized, "and the case will never come to the Superior Court."

"Maybe, but I don't see how they can justify letting her go. The girl confessed to smashing Eunice Bolles' head with a stone, and everyone in town knows it. No, there is no escaping it for any of us. Sooner or later, Hannah will stand before the bar in my courtroom, and if the jurors find her guilty, I will have to sentence her."

"There is only one sentence for a capital crime: the noose."

"Precisely. Because of Mrs. Rogers' sins, I may be called upon to put a child to death."

Douglas surveyed the Superior Court Judge sympathetically. *Ah, well,* thought the jailer. *The Judge's station in life brings many enviable perquisites along with some unpleasant duties. He'll have to take the rough with the smooth, just like the rest of us.*

Evening, The Jail House, July 23, 1786

Hannah stood in her cell, stripped to the waist, a blanket draped like a large bib over her bare chest. Mrs. Shaw and Mrs. Douglas flanked the child on either side, while Mistress Coit stood behind, a hand resting on Hannah's shoulder. Each woman clamped a fist on the blanket, holding it securely in place.

Hannah trembled at the sound of the men's heavy steps coming up the hall. Molly looked down at her.

"Shush. Don't be affrighted; you're safe with me."

The door opened, and the tall figure of Mr. Douglas loomed in the doorway. The shadowy outlines of the Judge, Stephen Hempstead, Colonel Halsey, and the doctor crowded in behind him. Everyone froze for a split second; then Judge Law edged around the jailer, and the rest of the men squeezed into the room.

Judge Law nodded at Mrs. Shaw.

"Turn around, Hannah," she said. "Mind the blanket, and don't drop it."

The women stretched their arms and held the blanket in place. Hannah awkwardly turned her back to the men and her face to Molly Coit. The innkeeper bent down to catch Hannah's whisper. "Which of them is going to do it?"

"Do what, child?" Molly whispered back.

"Whip me." She looked up at Molly. "Which of them is going to whip me for what I did to Eunice?"

"No one is going to harm you," Molly promised. "These men want to see what Mrs. Rogers did to your back."

Hannah looked confused, then comprehension dawned on her face. "Oh, they want to see how long before they can whip me again. The doctor will tell them."

"What?"

"They want to see if it's been time enough to whip me. My mistress says that she does not hold with laying the lash over open wounds." Hannah paused, searching her memory for one of the Widow's dictums. "Unless there is just cause," she parroted.

"My Lord," said Molly, softly, prayerfully. "No, child, no. No one is going to whip you. The Judge wants to see how the Widow has used you."

"Here," said the doctor, picking up Hannah's candle holder. "Someone light this for me." Mrs. Douglas took the candle holder and went out. She came back with the candle and passed it to the doctor. As he lifted the candle up to cast light on Hannah's back, the child peered over one shoulder. Seeing the flame moving toward her, Hannah shrieked and tried to pull away. Startled, the doctor stepped back, almost dropping the candle.

"What the devil . . ." he sputtered, catching hold of the back of the chair.

Jostled, the women lost their grip, and the blanket slid to the floor. Molly threw her arms around Hannah, as the child lurched forward to clutch her around the waist and press her face, eyes closed, against her.

"Let me hold the candle." Mrs. Shaw reached out her hand for the light. "Here, now, Hannah don't take on so. No one is going to hurt you. I'm going to hold the light up so that the doctor can examine your injuries. No, don't move," she said firmly, as Hannah cringed away. "Let the doctor see."

Hannah buried her face in Molly's apron as the doctor bent forward and began to go over her back, inch by inch. He worked silently, occasionally gesturing for Mrs. Shaw to move the flame more advantageously or tersely asking her to hold the candle at this angle or that. When he finished conducting a thorough examination, the doctor took the candle holder and held it up to the top of Hannah's back.

"Look here," he pointed a finger to the raw upper portion of the girl's shoulders. "You can see ribbed flesh just under these open sores. They look as if they came from another whipping that appears to have been as severe as this recent one. And here," he indicated another area of damaged flesh. "This is another old wound. And over here."

The doctor looked over to Mrs. Douglas. "Have you been attending these?"

"I didn't discover them until I came for her soiled garments this morning. After I saw the wounds, I bathed her back in water, and then applied salve and bound clean rags about them." Mrs. Douglas gestured to the bandages, lying on the seat of the chair.

The doctor picked up the rags, which still looked fresh on the top, and turned them over. After looking the rags over carefully, he sniffed them.

"Good, no sign of active infection," he remarked. "Did your mistress tend to these injuries?" he asked Hannah.

Hannah kept her face turned away. "Yes, sir. She always does."

"Always does? How many times?"

Hannah shrugged.

"And what does Mrs. Rogers say about these wounds?"

"Sometimes she cries when she puts the medicine on me, and says I'm a bad girl for making her whip me."

The doctor shook his head in disgust, and then looked at Mrs. Douglas. "Put some honey on her back to stave off infection, and you might have her sit with her back in the sun a few minutes each morning when you change the bandages." He turned his attention back to Hannah. "Are you marked elsewhere?"

"Sir?"

"Did your mistress thrash you anywhere else on your body?"

Hannah nodded. "My legs."

"Will you please, Mrs. Douglas?" asked the Judge. Mrs. Douglas squatted next to Hannah, wondering why she hadn't had the wit to look at the child's legs. She rolled down Hannah's stockings. Once again, the doctor bent forward with the candle in hand; this time the flame illuminated a crisscross pattern of thin scars that covered Hannah legs, knees to ankles.

"And these marks, Hannah, how did you get them?"

"What?" Hannah stretched her neck to look down. "Oh, those," she said, obviously dismissing them as nothing. "Those are from the switch."

"Do you have any more scars or wounds, Hannah?"

The girl shook her head.

The doctor stood up, a hand bracing his back. "Are we finished here, Mrs. Shaw?"

That lady looked to Mrs. Douglas and Mistress Coit. Both nodded.

"We are," Mrs. Shaw answered for the women.

The doctor blew out the candle.

Chapter Sixteen

Late Evening, The Jail House, July 23, 1786

Mrs. Douglas proudly held a burning twig to the wicks of the sweet-scented beeswax tapers standing in her mother's silver candle holders. As the wicks caught flame, she remembered the terror of fleeing down Main Street toward Quaker Hill in September of 1781, these very candle holders held tightly to her chest.

Watching the candle flames dance, Mrs. Douglas ran her larder through her mind's eye, wondering what she had on hand to offer important guests on such short notice. Quickly divining her friend's dilemma, Molly offered to send to the Red Lion for dinner. Mrs. Douglas accepted gratefully, and sent her son to the inn with Molly's instructions.

A few moments later, the Reverend Channing arrived, stepping over the threshold into the flickering candlelight.

"I've come to see Hannah Occuish."

The young man sat down in the chair proffered by the jailer. "I spent all day yesterday and today with Mr. and Mrs. Bolles, trying to offer them comfort. As you can imagine, they are borne down by heavy grief."

A general murmur of sympathy ran through the room.

"I suppose you have heard about Hannah," said Mr. Douglas.

Mr. Channing nodded. "She was pretty much the topic of conversation at the wake, when the parents weren't in the room, of course. They say Hannah is odd, barely speaks."

"Yes," Mr. Douglas said, gesturing to the doctor. "There is that, but there is more to tell you."

Reverend Channing, an inquiring expression on his face, looked toward the doctor.

"This morning, Mrs. Douglas found serious wounds on Hannah's back. I examined her this evening, and it is clear that someone whipped her viciously with a lash very recently."

"Viciously?"

"Yes, she has open and scabbed stripes from her upper back to her lower back."

Channing's face blanched.

"There are also scars from a previous lashing - just as bad - and scars on her legs and knees from switches."

"Who abused her?"

"The Widow Rogers," the Judge said. "The wounds are shocking. Perhaps you should look for yourself."

"No," said Mr. Channing, repulsed by the idea. "It's not necessary. I believe you."

Before the doctor could reply, Lizzy and the stable boy came through the door, toting large covered baskets. Molly jumped up, gesturing for them to set their heavy loads on the table. While the servants unpacked the laden baskets, Molly and Mrs. Douglas rushed about setting the table and urged Mr. Channing to join them. He declined, explaining that he had eaten with the Bolles, and had come over to see Hannah before he went home.

"Here, you'll need this." Mrs. Douglas handed Channing a shining brass candle holder, the candle sheathed in a glass chimney to protect the flame.

Mr. Douglas plucked a large key from a wrought iron nail, and walked the young preaching candidate to Hannah's cell.

"You say that Hannah has been described to you?" the jailer asked.

"In great detail."

"Hannah is usually unresponsive if I speak to her," said Douglas, "but my wife tells me that the girl was almost talkative with her and the other women today."

The jailer unlocked the cell door and stepped aside to let the minister pass.

* * *

Hannah's eyes followed the young minister mistrustfully as he walked over to the small table and put the burning wick of his candle to hers. When the candle burned well, Channing sat down in the chair opposite Hannah's, the table between them. They began what he would later describe as the most extraordinary conversation of his life, the particulars of which he remembered in the most vivid detail.

"Hannah, do you know who I am?"

Hannah shook her head.

"I'm the Reverend Channing, from First Church. Have you ever been to First Church?"

Hannah shook her head again.

"Do you know why you're here?"

Hannah shrugged and looked away. "Because of Eunice Bolles."

"They tell me that you killed Eunice, that you lay in wait for her, choked her, and threw a wall down on her. Can that really be true? Did you do that?"

"Yes."

Channing searched Hannah's face. "Why did you attack her?"

"For getting me whipped." Hannah's face crumpled. "Please don't let them whip me again. I promise, if you forgive me, I'll never do anything like it again. Please forgive me."

"You don't mean that you want me to forgive you, you want God to forgive you, don't you?"

"God?" Hannah looked irritated. "I've never heard of him."

"Never heard of him! What do you mean? Surely, your mistress has told you about God, at least what she believes," he amended.

"I've never heard of God."

Reverend Channing started. He had expected Hannah to mouth Rogerene heresies, which ran the gamut from commonplace dissenting notions about Baptism and communion, all the way to the advocacy of polygamy, but to say she had never heard of God . . . How could anyone in New London make such an astonishing claim?

"Hannah, you must have heard about God. You read your Bible, don't you?"

"I can't read," Hannah spat.

"Can't read! Why not?"

Hannah shrugged. "I don't know."

"Mrs. Rogers reads the Bible to you, then."

"No, she doesn't read to me."

Channing's mouth fell open. When his brain finally began to function, the young minister gradually began to feel relieved that Hannah had never heard of God. Ignorance of the difference between right and wrong meant that there was still hope for Hannah, both now and eternally. Instead of laboring to uproot inculcated heresies from her heart, as he assumed that he would be doing, Channing could simply proclaim the gospel to Hannah. Once she understood that she, like all of mankind, suffered from the effects of a sinful nature inherited from Adam and Eve and that Christ had died for the transgressions of all, Hannah could repent of all her sins, including the crime of murder, and be regenerated. With the help of God, this child would be able to control her violent impulses and could eventually be restored to society.

"Hannah, would you like to know who he is?"

"Who?"

"God, your maker."

Hannah shrugged.

"Wouldn't you like to know your heavenly father?"

Hannah looked up. "I don't know where my father is. He went into the army and never came back. Mrs. Rogers says likely he's dead." Hannah's eyes filled with tears. "My father can't help me." She wiped her eyes. "I'm sorry!" Hannah clutched Channing's arm with tear-dampened hands. "I'm sorry, I won't do it again, I promise. If you forgive me, I won't do it again. Please help me."

"Quiet, Hannah, quiet. I will help you. I'll visit every day and teach you the catechism."

Disappointment washed across Hannah's face. "Oh."

"I'll come back tomorrow. We can start then." Channing picked up his candle and stood. "Good night, Hannah."

The minister looked back through the small barred window at the forlorn child as he locked the door. Only the most hardhearted man would not feel at least a glimmering of pity for the abandoned child, as well as for Eunice Bolles, lying in the dark coffin, which her grieving family had shoveled clods of dirt over just a few hours ago.

Chapter Seventeen

Late Evening, The Jail House, July 23, 1786

"Hannah will have to stay in jail while the investigation is being completed," Judge Law remarked during dinner.

"Nowhere else for her," Stephen Hempstead agreed. "Though I doubt we have much more to do, other than finish our interviews in Quaker Hill."

"Unless Hannah's wounds suppurate and she dies."

The Judge nodded. "Yes, Molly, then we'd have a case of manslaughter on our hands."

"I'd call it murder," answered Molly.

"Little fear either way," said the doctor. "Hannah Occuish has a healthy constitution and with Mrs. Douglas taking care of her, we should see the girl fully healed within a month's time."

"Shouldn't you arrest Mrs. Rogers anyway?" Molly persisted. "Isn't it a crime, beating someone that severely?"

The Judge shook his head. "A mistress is entitled to punish her servant, just as parents have the right to discipline their children as they see fit."

"Doesn't what the Widow Rogers did to Hannah go beyond the bounds of correcting chastisement, Sir?"

The Judge pursed his lip and grimaced. "Not quite."

"If the lashings the Widow gave Hannah don't outrage convention, what would?"

The Judge shifted uncomfortably. "Something unusually cruel. There was a case, before my time in New London. Back in the 1750s, if I remember correctly. A master nailed his servant's ears to a board and left the boy alone for hours. The authorities arrested the master."

"My father told me something about that," injected Stephen Hempstead. "I think it happened in Waterford."

"It did," said Mrs. Shaw. "I was a young woman at the time, and I remember the story very well. Oddly enough, that case also involved the Rogers and Sharper families."

The doctor looked surprised. "I vaguely remember hearing something about the incident, but I didn't realize the boy was a Sharper."

"Yes, Sharper, Jane True's son. A James Rogers, I don't remember which - so many of that huge clan are named James. This James Rogers took young Sharper out to the barn, stuffed the child's mouth with a corncob to keep him from screaming, and nailed the boy's ears to a wallboard. Rogers left that poor child nailed to that board for at least twelve hours. I believe someone else found him and reported Rogers. When authorities came out and saw what Rogers had done to Sharper, they arrested him for cruelty."

"Did it come to court?" Molly asked.

"Yes, the County Court heard the case. Rogers excused himself by claiming that Sharper stole money from him and was on his way to join the French . . ."

"Ah, yes, during the war with the French. A treacherous thing, attempting to aid the French and their savage allies," commented Sheriff Richards.

"Surely, the French and Indians took many English scalps during the war, and there was no love lost for those whom Rogers said that young Sharper planned to join," Mrs. Shaw admitted. "Still, the case came down to Rogers' word against Sharper's. Rogers should have turned the boy over to authorities for an investigation. What if he *had* met with French spies? Right here in the county?

"Instead, Rogers took the law into his own hands. Although the jury found Rogers not guilty, the court ordered Rogers to pay the court costs for his trial, which . . ."

"Suggests that neither the judge nor the jury really believed

Rogers' story or else, they didn't approve of what he did," interjected Judge Law. "But whether or not they believed that Sharper intended to go over to the French, the court did not condone Rogers' behavior, hence its decision not to order Sharper to pay court costs, which he could do only by serving more time with Rogers. On the other hand, even if they thought Rogers a liar, the court did not want servants to get the idea that they could run away with impunity. Imagine how many servants might have been encouraged to go over to the French during the wars. Therefore, the jury found Rogers not guilty. And since they also wanted to discourage masters from administering rough justice to their servants, they forced Rogers to pay court costs."

The Judge smiled. "A very sound decision under the circumstances."

"Yes, a good compromise for the general good of the town," Mrs. Shaw remarked. "But perhaps less satisfying to young Sharper. He may have hoped for a bit more justice after having endured half a day with his ears nailed to a board, choking on a corncob."

"Is this Sharper related to Hannah?" Mr. Douglas asked.

"He could be." Mrs. Shaw thought for a moment. "A boy in the 1750s . . . he is of an age to be her father, assuming he also went by the name Tuis or added it later. In any case, the boy Sharper is probably related to Hannah's father somehow."

Mr. Channing came into the room, blinking like someone who had stared into a bright light. He handed the key to Mr. Douglas.

"I think that I will have some dinner, Mrs. Douglas, if there is enough left."

"Certainly there is. Sit down, and I'll get you a plate."

"Well?"

Channing looked at the Judge. "Sir?"

"What do you think about Hannah Occuish?"

The minister threw up his hands. "I don't know what to think. Hannah just told me that she has never heard about God."

The Judge looked from the Sheriff to the Colonel. "Richards? Halsey? Did she tell you that, too?"

Both men shook their heads, faces mystified.

"Mrs. Shaw?"

"The topic never came up, and it wouldn't occur to us to ask. Why would we? The child lives in a nest of dissenters, who love to dispute doctrine all day long. I can see her having wrong ideas about God, but not knowing about God . . . Besides, her grandfather is a Baptist minister."

"I can believe that Hannah doesn't know about God," Molly said. "I think Sarah Occuish avoided her parents, since they didn't approve of her drinking, so the Occuishs couldn't have taught her. The Widow apparently keeps Hannah working all of the time, and she herself is a Rogerene."

"Aren't they Baptists and Quakers?" Mr. Channing asked. "Misguided they may be, but they do believe in God."

"It is confusing, especially for someone new to the town," Molly replied. "After John Rogers died decades ago, many of his followers started Baptist and Quaker churches. Mrs. Rogers is his granddaughter-in-law and is an old-style Rogerene. They don't believe in church services, and they don't have public or family prayers."

"No wonder Hannah doesn't know anything about religion," Channing said. "No church meetings, no prayers, and she can't read, so . . ."

"Can't read?" Mrs. Shaw and Molly Coit echoed in surprise.

"Not a word."

"I don't know of many females, including free-born servants and African slaves, who can't read at least a little bit," Molly remarked. "I have heard that some Indian women resist learning to read, despising it as an English practice, but Hannah comes from a literate family. Even if the Occuishs didn't value reading, Mrs. Rogers should have insisted that her young servant learn."

"Well," Judge Law said, obviously relieved. "This information changes everything." He walked over to the table and sat by the doctor, across from the Sheriff.

"Does it? How so?" Colonel Halsey inquired curiously.

"Surely you understand," the doctor turned his head, the better to see the Colonel, standing off to one side of the room. "The child does not know right from wrong and has no way to learn the difference. She certainly can't take any edifying lessons from the punishments of her unpredictable mistress. An uneducated, terrorized child cannot be held responsible for her actions."

"Maybe that's true." The Colonel's frown was skeptical. "Or perhaps seeing the lash marks on Hannah's back has made us temporarily forget Eunice Bolles' grievous wounds." He looked about the room. "Will any of us ever be able to forget the sight of that battered body? The broken limbs and back. Her smashed skull. A crushed windpipe. All of the blood . . ."

Everyone winced.

"Colonel Halsey is right." Stephen Hempstead stood up and walked over to the cold, bare hearth and turned to face the room. "Much as it pains me to say it, I don't believe ignorance and mistreatment excuse murder. If Hannah accidentally killed Eunice - the child fell and hit her head on a rock while they scuffled - then we might have reason to be lenient and charge Hannah with a lesser crime. But by her own description of what she did, Hannah Occuish committed premeditated, cold-blooded murder. Those of us who saw Eunice lying in the road have seen the result of Hannah's unleashed rage, and she is only eleven years of age. What will she be capable of at sixteen or twenty?"

No one answered.

"There is another possibility," suggested Channing, "a better possibility. No matter what you eventually decide to charge her with, Hannah must be educated about God and the commandments. Once she understands what she has done wrong, she might repent and be converted. If so, with God's help, she might be able to make good her promise to exercise self-control."

"How will we know if her conversion is sincere? And what will we do with her afterwards?" Hempstead asked.

"I am not sure about that," admitted Channing. "If we believe she is regenerated, you can charge her with assault or manslaughter, but at least she won't be on trial for her life. In any case, no decisions should be made until Hannah is catechized."

"Very true," Halsey murmured.

Chapter Eighteen

New London, Summer and Early Autumn of 1786

A steady stream of visitors began washing up to the jail house door just after dawn on Hannah's third day in jail. People crowded in the jail yard around the open window or took turns trooping down the hall to peer through the small, iron-barred hole in the cell door. The experience of strange faces materializing at the door and window took Hannah aback at first, but after a while, she reassumed her usual indifferent demeanor. Her morose countenance and occasional monosyllabic replies to the questions tossed through the bars discomfited most visitors enough to speed them on their way, feeling a bit cheated. Almost all of them had looked forward to witnessing high feelings and dramatic scenes of tearful protestations of innocence, or of guilt for that matter, and pleas for assistance, understanding . . . But instead of being held in the grip of strong sensations and emotions, Hannah sat in isolated silence. At the most, she occasionally ran a blank eye over the well-dressed ladies and men, mopping tears with fancy handkerchiefs selected for the occasion.

Despite Hannah's remote, detached attitude in her first few days in jail, people continued to jostle one another around the windows and door. Some of them even came into her cell. They crowded into the small room and stood, looking at her as she sat on her bed or in the wooden chair by the small table. At first, Hannah couldn't help wondering at their interest in her, but she didn't care enough to think about it too long.

One morning when Mrs. Douglas came back to the kitchen

with Hannah's dirty lunch dishes, Mr. Douglas wryly observed to his wife that he feared his prisoner had let down most of the people who had come to enjoy a close examination of her person. Offered so little encouragement, he opined, the stream would dry up to a trickle after everyone had a few good looks at Hannah.

As Mr. Douglas predicted, Hannah gravely disappointed the throngs swirling through the prison every day. Despite almost unceasing attention, Hannah never betrayed even the slightest interest in cultivating the crowd. Eventually the majority of townspeople gave up and found better things to do. Occasionally, parents brought their children to the jail to show them what happened to disobedient youth, but by the middle of August, only Hannah's first visitors and the Reverend Channing came to the jail every day.

Although the rest of the town no longer yearned to sit in Hannah's cell with her, they certainly enjoyed discussing her, and everyone and everything else connected to the case. Throughout the summer and into the fall, no matter what the occasion or setting, conversation inevitably came around to Hannah and the Bolles, and once there, seldom moved on to another topic any time soon. After weeks of dissecting every aspect of her life, her demeanor, her family, and her history, even the most obtuse began to suspect that the brutalities regularly visited on Hannah had wreaked more than physical damage. The thought of Hannah being wounded in spirit, as well as body, garnered her sympathy, despite what she had done.

When the conversation reached this point, however, the town could not reach a consensus. As in most problems of a vexingly complex nature, a small minority expressed polar opposite views. A few made so bold as to suggest holding an immediate trial and hanging Hannah forthwith. A brief hearing in which she could repeat her confession publicly would be edifying for everyone. Their opponents, faces aghast at what they deemed barbarism, said that she should be released, immediately, and put into the proper situation.

"And where, pray tell," the inevitable jeering question followed, "would that be?"

Over the months, no one had managed to devise a clear answer to this perplexing question. Someone would inevitably offer a half-hearted reference to the prisons and hospitals of England, knowing full well that America had no such provisions for the long-term holding of prisoners and mad people. Besides, New Londoners couldn't imagine dumping a child into a stew the like of England's institutions. It would be too cruel, no matter what crime she had committed.

The majority of people dismissed arguments to either hang Hannah immediately or to release her as a fatuous waste of time, claiming that the question of Hannah's comprehension seemed more important. But even then, anything resembling agreement quickly fell apart. Most people chalked up her unresponsive - ungrateful, others called it - attitude to an unhappy combination of her experiences and her race and urged their opponents to be of a more charitable state of mind. Indians are generally impassive, they claimed, and, under the circumstances, any child, but especially an Indian child, would naturally be withdrawn with adults. Let Hannah learn that no one will beat her, and she will respond properly to the out-held hand of friendship. After all, they said, Indians can be very loyal to those who are kind to them. This opinion elicited polite chuckles to loud hoots from the people who agreed with Mr. Tinker's negative opinion of Indians.

A few brave souls ventured to state the novel opinion that complexion had nothing at all to do with the case. They argued that people with Hannah's lack of understanding could be found among all races and nations. When goaded, they pointed to illustrative examples from the local population; people whose behavior was frequently the subject of town gossip. At this point, someone else would counter by pointing out that the examples belonged to the lower sorts. Sometimes, depending on the company, there would be a hinting reference to or outright speaking of the names of people from prominent families.

All discussion came to a sudden halt on August 22nd after a bolt of lightning killed the fifteen-year-old daughter of Thaddeus Brooks, a prominent man. Townspeople crowded into the old meeting house for Sally's funeral the following day, frightened and wondering how to interpret the unusual death. Afterwards, there were mutterings that the girl's death was a sign of God's displeasure with New London.

Late Morning, Mr. Stephen Hempstead's House, New London, September 2, 1786

The foreman of the Grand Jury stood in Hempstead's large front room seeing his own mixture of relief and apprehension reflected in the faces around him. He called the meeting to order and moved quickly to the business at hand.

"We are *not* here to review the evidence against Hannah Occuish again," he instructed. "Our investigation in July proved the truth of her confession. Mr. Joshua Coit, Justice of the Peace, has examined the prisoner, and Mr. Channing has had ample time to catechize her."

"Although I pity Hannah," Steven Hempstead began.

Mr. Tinker jumped up. "I cannot share Mr. Hempstead's sentiments for the girl." He turned to Hempstead. "I'm saving my pity for Eunice Bolles and her family."

Hempstead waited for the room to quiet down. "Our hearts wring for Eunice Bolles and her family, but pity for one doesn't preclude sympathy for the other, Mr. Tinker. But that's not the point. A murder has been done and the killer is behind bars. Now we must decide what to do with her, remembering it is her second crime of violence."

The foreman nodded. "We can't postpone our decision any longer. Sally Brook's death has unsettled the town, and the Superior Court will sit in October. Mr. Channing has been to see Hannah almost every day for over six weeks, and has explained the principles of religion to her. Our duty is to follow correct procedure in order to administer impartial justice to all concerned. We have to indict Hannah. She is, after all, entitled to a public hearing and a defense. Our only decision is whether to charge her with assault . . ."

"Assault?" An older juror put a restraining hand to Tinker's arm, forestalling his second leap from the chair. "Eunice Bolles is a rotting corpse, not an invalid recovering from injuries!"

Hempstead grimaced. "That's true. It would be a miscarriage of justice to charge anyone who beat a person to death in cold blood with assault, or even manslaughter."

Evening, The Jail House, September 2, 1786

Mr. Douglas unlocked Hannah's cell door for Sheriff Richards and moved to stand in the hall behind him. Hannah turned from the window and watched Richards unfold two sheets of heavy paper, shake them smooth, and begin reading aloud.

" *'The jurors of the state of Connecticut for the county of New London on oath present that Hannah Occuish, a mulatto girl of New London in the County of New London, not having the fear of God before her eyes but being moved and seduced by the instigation of the divil did in New London aforesaid on the twentieth-first day of July in the year of our Lord one thousand, seven hundred and eighty-six with force and arms feloniously, willfully, and of her malice aforethought make an assault in and upon the body of one Eunice Bolles, the daughter of James Bolles of said New London, being then and there in the peace of God and in said state in that the said Hannah with the same force and arms aforesaid that is to say with a stone which the said Hannah then and there had and held in her hand, did feloniously, willfully, and of her malice aforethought with great violence strike the said Eunice Bolles many heavy and mortal strokes or blows on her head and other tender parts of her body by which said strokes or blows the said Hannah then and there gave to the said Eunice Bolles many mortal wounds, bruises, and broken bones in her head, neck, arms and other parts of her body of which said mortal wounds, bruises, and broken bones the said Eunice Bolles then and there immediately died and so the jurors aforesaid on oath do say that the said Hannah Occuish in manner and form aforesaid did feloniously, willfully, and of her malice aforethought did kill and murder the said Eunice Bolles against the peace and dignity of the state of Connecticut and contrary to the form and effect of the statute law of said state in such case made and provided.' "* [3]

Richards refolded the pages and looked at Hannah's placid face. Of course, he hadn't expected her to understand all of the words, but he thought that she might react to hearing her crime described in such detail. Instead of being upset, Hannah shook her head indifferently when Sheriff Richards asked if she had any questions.

Chapter Nineteen

Morning, The Courthouse, New London, October 6, 1786

The pure sunlight, typical of a fine New England fall day, streamed through the large windows and fell in broad swaths across the crowd jammed into the second-story courtroom and vestibule and trailing down the steps and out into the front yard. Although the people standing in the vestibule couldn't see much, if anything, they could at least hear the first trial held in the new courthouse.

Outside, a large crowd stood in the yard, craning their necks hopefully toward the open second-story windows. A lucky few managed to wiggle their way to spots below the windows, and obliged the less fortunate crowded ten deep behind them with repeated snatches of conversation.

Timothy Larrabee sat at the lawyers' table, a slight frown of concentration on his face, perusing his notes. The prosecutor stood off to one side of the courtroom, conversing intently with several well-dressed men. Judge Law fidgeted and paced in the privacy of his chambers, glad to be sheltered from inquisitive stares. He hadn't felt so nervous before a trial since his first days on the bench.

Shouts from the Parade drew all eyes toward the harbor. A few minutes later, Hannah came into view, riding uphill in a small cart, seated between Sheriff Richards and Mr. Douglas. They came up Court Street at a steady pace, all three ignoring the commotion swirling around them. The crowd surrounding the courthouse parted to let Richards drive the cart around to the back entrance. Ten minutes later, the Sheriff and Hannah stepped into the bright light of the sun-lit courtroom. Richards turned the prisoner over to Larrabee.

Hannah stayed by her advocate's side. She appeared either unaware of or uninterested in the multitude of people vying to see her. All through the long day in court, the girl appeared completely disconnected from everything and everybody around her. Even the impressive sight of the robed and bewigged Judge sweeping on and off of the bench failed to rouse her notice beyond the payment of a cursory glance when, prompted by her lawyer, she obediently stood up.

Judge Law did not disappoint. To the spectators' relief, he convened court without tedious delay, completed all the preliminaries quickly, and instructed the prosecutor to proceed.

The state swore Colonel Jeremiah Halsey as its first witness against Hannah Occuish. The Colonel took his oath in clear tones, and as soon as he took his hand off of the Bible, the prosecutor asked him to tell the jury about the morning of July 21ˢ. Halsey pulled out his book for notes and, occasionally glancing down to refresh his memory or check a detail, spoke at length in the same unemotional, economical manner he had used with the Grand Jury in July.

Under the eye of a fascinated courtroom, Halsey described how he happened upon the corpse within minutes of the murder having been committed and detailed the shocking condition of Eunice's body. He reported what the Widow Rogers, Rachel, and the other witnesses had told him before the arrival of Richards and Hempstead. He told the court that Hannah claimed to have seen four boys on the morning of the murder. Colonel Halsey also recounted the investigators' conversation with Mrs. Rachel Rogers and the Widow on the day after the murder, in which they learned that Hannah had recently threatened Eunice Bolles. He also outlined the results of their interviews of Hannah's neighbors in Quaker Hill. Finally, he described the girl's response to seeing Eunice's body at the wake and testified to her subsequent confession and description of her crime.

Mr. Hempstead took the stand after Colonel Halsey stepped

down. Hempstead spent less time before the bar. He added a detailed account of the investigation of the neighborhood and local woods for the boys, and confirmed Halsey's testimony about Hannah's confession at the Bolles' house.

Despite Halsey's and Hempstead's detached, professional tones, their testimony conjured disturbing images of Eunice's body and of her shocked and grieving parents that wrung tears and moans from the spectators. But these exclamations of shock were as nothing compared to the sobs and loud groans that rose from the gallery when the doctor walked the court through a recreation of the vicious beating and a detailed explanation of Eunice's dreadful injuries. Women grew faint and tears rolled down the faces of battle-hardened men while the doctor explained the cause of the grotesque twisting of Eunice's torso as the investigators struggled to carry her body into Mrs. Rogers' house.

After the doctor stepped down, the crowd tensed in anticipation, waiting for the state to call Eunice's deeply shocked parents to give evidence. Instead of Mr. and Mrs. Bolles, however, the prosecutor called Mrs. Deborah Bolles, mother of Eunice's father, to take the stand on the family's behalf. Mrs. Bolles, her face drawn with grief and exhaustion, painted a vivid picture of her entire family's suffering. The older woman's eloquent description of her son's and daughter-in-law's anguish wrung even more tears and groans from the gallery.

Mr. Larrabee let Colonel Halsey, Stephen Hempstead, the doctor, and Mrs. Bolles step down without asking them any questions. He thought it best to have them out of the box as quickly as possible. Questioning them further would draw more attention to the lurid evidence against Hannah Occuish, while simultaneously keeping Eunice's wounds and her family's grief in the forefront of the jury's mind. He made an exception of Sheriff William Richards.

"Sheriff Richards, did Hannah at any time during her confession or, to your knowledge, during her imprisonment, express a fear of punishment?"

"Yes, Hannah exhibited great concern about that subject."

"Fear of the noose?"

"No, sir," Richards shook his head. "She has never been much worried about hanging."

"Never! Surely, she understands the penalty for cold-blooded murder."

"I don't believe she grasps the concept, or at least the notion that it could apply to her."

"Even while sitting in jail, awaiting a trial to determine her fate? How could that possibly be the case?"

Richards almost smiled. Despite the seriousness of the situation, he couldn't help secretly admiring Larrabee's theatrical technique.

"Her understanding of her dangerous circumstances is limited. When she confessed to having done murder, Hannah believed that she would be given a whipping. A severe lashing, similar to those she has been given for other misdeeds. While in jail the subject of execution has, of course, been explained to her, but apparently Hannah has relied on the opinion of friends, who have told her that she is too young to be hanged. That, and the fact that she is familiar with her uncle's case, has convinced her that she is not a fit subject for execution."

"You mention her uncle. Are you referring to Jacob Occuish?"

"Yes, Hannah knows that Jacob killed his wife, but did not hang. She also knows that he received a very severe lashing."

"Has anyone explained to her the difference between manslaughter, which the jury found her uncle guilty of, and premeditated murder?"

"Yes, of course."

"And do you believe she understands all of this, the implications of her age and the difference between her uncle's case and this?"

Richards enjoyment of Larrbee's tactics faded, and his voice grew weary. "How can she? I don't entirely understand it all myself."

Larrabee managed to conceal his surprise; he had expected

Richards to give a short negative reply. He decided to let the jury make what they would of this frank admission.

"Do you know what Hannah believes this trial to be about?"

Richards nodded. "As far as I can tell, she thinks that the jury is to decide whether or not to whip her and how many lashes to give her."

An audible gasp rippled through the courtroom. Almost as one, the spectators looked toward the prisoner, but Hannah was staring down at the floor in front of her, apparently oblivious to her own trial.

Chapter Twenty

Late Morning, The Courthouse, October 6, 1786

A succession of witnesses from Quaker Hill took the stand after Richards stepped down. Every one of them described Hannah in terms that ranged from unflattering to outright damning, and several confirmed hearing that she had threatened to give Eunice a whipping. The witnesses agreed that Hannah could not be trusted to tell the truth or to keep her hands off of things that did not belong to her. Some of them also noted that she tended to bully weaker or smaller children and, under close questioning by the prosecution, provided examples of her cruelty.

Larrabee's brief cross examination of each neighbor consisted in asking if he or she had complained to the Widow about Hannah. Several answered that yes, indeed, they had complained. When asked what had come of their complaints, the witnesses told the court that the Widow Rogers either turned a deaf ear or harshly punished the child.

After the neighbors finished testifying, the state called Mrs. Rogers as its final witness. When the Widow took the stand, she attempted to defend her former ward. The prosecutor's polite but relentless questioning, however, elicited information that confirmed the neighbors' general assessment of Hannah. Helplessly, Widow Rogers could only answer in the affirmative when asked if she had ever caught Hannah lying or stealing.

"Yes, Hannah did sometimes lie and take small items, but when I remonstrated with her, she would always be very sorry and promise not to do it again."

"Did she, nevertheless, continue to lie and steal?"

"Yes, I suppose she did, but she never took anything important or very valuable."

"And did she lie?"

"Sometimes," the Widow admitted.

"What did she lie about?"

"Oh, this and that." The Widow's eyes cut to one side. "I don't remember. Nothing important."

"Did neighbors ever complain to you that she bullied their children, Mrs. Rogers?"

Mrs. Rogers balled her hands in her lap. "Yes, one or two of the neighbors complained, and I spoke to Hannah about it. She explained that she was only defending herself after the children picked on her first. I told her that she must not take notice of teasing, that she should come home if they would not stop bothering her after she asked them to."

"Were these children who teased Hannah often younger and smaller than she?"

The Widow sighed. "I believe so, a time or two."

"And did Hannah say that she would pay Eunice Bolles back for telling on her?"

"So, I've been told. She never said so to me."

When the prosecutor indicated that he had finished questioning Widow Rogers, Timothy Larrabee strode toward the witness box and faced the Widow.

"How long has Hannah lived in Quaker Hill?"

The Widow thought for a second, "About five years, I would say."

"And has she lived that entire time with you?"

"A good part of it. I lived alone after my husband died, and Hannah has been a help, as well as some company for me."

"A help to you? Has she been a good worker?"

"Yes, she usually does as she is told and has improved in abilities as she's gotten older and bigger."

"Is she ever saucy to you?"

"Certainly not. She is a very quiet child, who doesn't often speak."

"Is Hannah bound to you?"

"No, her mother brought her over from Groton and asked us to take care of her."

"Us?"

The Widow assumed a slightly guarded manner. "We who are followers of John Rogers, my husband's grandfather, and of John Bolles."

Larrabee paused, a slightly dramatic air about him, as if he had forgotten for a second who John Rogers and John Bolles were; then he said, "Oh . . . yes. The Rogerenes."

The Widow bridled slightly. "Yes, some call all of us that. Although a plenty in Quaker Hill call themselves Rogerene Baptists or Rogerene Quakers."

"And you . . ."

"I follow my husband's tradition."

Larrabee did not ask for clarification, knowing that each juror would interpret that answer according to his own notions about the religious sect.

"Did Hannah's mother visit her often?"

"No, never since the day she went to visit her family up north."

"So Hannah has been abandoned?"

"Well . . . no . . . not exactly. Her mother realized that she was unable to care for her child."

Again Larrabee paused, knowing without glancing away from Widow Rogers' face that this line of questioning had captured the focused attention of every single person in the courtroom, except Hannah.

It's as good as a play for them, he mused for a split second. *Well, lucky for me it is, since I don't have much to build a defense on.*

"Mrs. Rogers, you have described for the court Hannah's misbehavior as sometimes lying and occasionally stealing 'small items.' Is that accurate?"

"Yes, it is."

"You've also testified that in her dealings with children in the neighborhood Hannah only retaliated after they tormented her."

"That's correct."

"Did you punish Hannah for these various misdeeds?"

"Yes, I did. I hoped that correction would help her learn to better discipline herself."

"In your attempts to teach Hannah to control her behavior, did you also teach her to read so that she might benefit from the Scriptures?"

Mrs. Rogers raised her hands and then dropped them to her lap. "I tried for a time to teach Hannah her letters, but her attention wandered and the task proved very difficult."

"You read to her, of course."

"Not for a while now."

Larrabee swept his eyes across the courtroom, then back to the Widow.

"Since you found it toilsome to instruct your servant, you gave up on her?"

"I don't know that I would say that I gave up on Hannah. It just seemed to me that she . . ." Mrs. Rogers searched for a clear explanation. "She appeared so uninterested in reading, I attributed that to her parentage and . . ."

"Do you mean her race?"

"Yes."

"Doesn't the fact that Hannah is a mulatto confer more responsibility on you in regard to her education?" Larrabee asked. "Didn't you have a responsibility - a moral, as well as a legal responsibility - to give your servant at least a rudimentary education?"

"I . . ."

"Did you take her to church so that she might hear the word of God and be thus instructed?" Larrabee interrupted.

The Widow's face took on a subtly defiant air. "No, we do not believe in church services."

Larrabee turned to look at the jury and then turned back to the Widow. "We? You are a Rogerene of the original type who eschews all divine worship services?"

"Yes, as I mentioned, I follow the undiluted precepts of John Rogers, my husband's grandfather."

"And did you instruct Hannah in these particular . . . ah, principles?"

"Indeed, I tried to."

Larrabee let that information sink in for a few seconds before asking his next question.

"Mrs. Rogers, you have told me and the jury that you corrected Hannah in the hopes that she would learn self-discipline."

"Yes, I did."

"Did you enlist corporeal punishment in your scheme to educate Hannah in self-control?"

"Do you mean to ask if I whipped her?"

"Yes. Did you?"

"If her misdeed seemed to warrant such punishment, I did."

"What did you use?"

Mrs. Rogers flinched. "Pardon?"

"What did you use to whip Hannah?"

"My hand."

"Your hand. Did you ever use a switch, a rod, or some other like object?"

The Widow looked away. "Sometimes a switch or a small rod."

"A knotted lash, perhaps?"

She lifted her head, but didn't meet Larrabee's eyes. "Yes, but only if she had done something particularly bad."

Larrabee walked over to stand in front of the jury. He stood with his back to them, facing Mrs. Rogers, as if he were sitting with the jury, examining her.

"But Mrs. Rogers, you have just testified that Hannah did her chores when bidden and that her behavior was not as base as your neighbors believe it to have been. Why, therefore, would you need to employ a switch or a rod, even a small one, when a whipping by hand would have sufficed for minor offenses such as you just described to the jury?"

"I . . . sometimes," the Widow's voice faltered, ". . . especially as she got older . . . there were a few occasions when Hannah needed sterner correction."

"And you applied such necessary correction?"

Mrs. Rogers nodded miserably. "Yes, a few times."

"Only a few? Even in light of the fact that, as you have just said, you whipped her more as she got older?"

"I whipped her if her behavior called for it. I don't remember each time . . . it can't have been very often."

"Did you, in fact, employ the lash on more than one occasion?"

Mrs. Rogers looked up quickly, then cast her eyes back down. "Yes," she answered tersely.

"Did those whippings ever leave marks upon her body?"

"A few bruises . . ."

"What about blood?"

The Widow did not answer.

"Mrs. Rogers, did your whippings ever draw blood?"

Mrs. Rogers looked haggard. "Perhaps a time or two."

"A time or two?" Larrabee glanced back at the jury, his face skeptical. "Did one of those times occur in the recent past?"

"Recently?"

"Yes, I mean this summer, in mid-July, while Hannah still lived under your governance."

"Yes, I whipped her for misbehaving around that time."

"Did you draw blood and mark her body?"

"I don't remember that I did."

"Perhaps you might need to cast back into your memory, Mrs. Rogers. Or, if you are unable to recollect, the defense will call Mrs. Douglas or Mistress Coit to testify."

The Widow sat silently for a few moments, her face twisting. Finally, she answered quietly. "Yes, the whipping drew blood."

"I'm sorry, Mrs. Rogers, but your voice is too soft. Would you please repeat your answer?"

"The whipping drew blood."

Larrabee hesitated a second, considering whether or not to force Mrs. Rogers to fully describe Hannah's injuries, but decided against it. Detailed information about the condition of Hannah's back had already circulated throughout the county and gained her sympathy. He thought it would be better to remind them why the Widow gave her those wounds.

"Hannah must have committed serious mischief to earn such punishment! What did she do, Mrs. Rogers?"

"She . . ." The Widow's voice wavered again.

"Yes, go on," Larrabee urged, his face a bland mask.

"She took . . . she stole strawberries from other children."

Larrabee gazed steadily at the witness; he turned to look at the jury, then turned back to Mrs. Rogers. "You laid open her back, drew blood with a whip over . . . strawberries?" he asked quietly, almost sorrowfully. Behind him, the entire courtroom held its collective breath, waiting for an answer that everyone already knew.

"Yes."

The courtroom breathed.

Larrabee paused a few seconds to allow the members of the jury to collect themselves, and then shifted tactics.

"Mrs. Rogers, several of your neighbors told this court that for a number of years they have complained to you repeatedly about Hannah, and that you have administered punishment . . . We will ignore, for the moment, the question of the fitness of the punishment . . . and consider the ineffectualness of your methods. What is your response to such testimony?"

"What do you mean?"

"Mrs. Rogers, today we have heard clear evidence, even from your own mouth, that your disciplining of Hannah has been a failure. Is that not so?"

Shoulders drooping, the Widow nodded dejectedly.

"Would it be correct to say that by persistently striving with Hannah yourself, by refusing to put her into better hands, you have endangered the community?"

The Widow's head jerked up. "I don't know that I have thought of it that way."

"Isn't that the point, Mrs. Rogers? That you relied solely upon your own judgment, a lone woman, and that you did not consider the ramifications of your decisions for your fellow townspeople?"

"My fellow . . . I . . ." the Widow stuttered.

Larrabee fastened a pitiless gaze upon her. "What prompted

you to such arrogance?"

The Widow stared at Larrabee, her mouth slightly ajar.

Although Larrabee wanted to fire more difficult questions at Mrs. Rogers, the animosity against her emanating from the gallery convinced him to let her go at this high point. His cross examination had succeeded in turning the spotlight away from Hannah and focusing it on Widow Rogers; but, as any good lawyer knew, diverting everyone's attention to her was a risky tactic that could easily backfire on him. As things now stood, he had capitalized on the general undercurrent of resentment against the Widow for harboring a violent child and for abusing her. The answers she had just voiced provided everyone, whether orthodox or dissenter, with more reasons to dislike her and point the finger of blame in her direction. On the other hand, even the staunch orthodox jurors, who abhorred Rogerenes and their outlandish doctrines, wouldn't care to see Larrabee continue. None of them relished the idea of embarrassing an older white woman - and a widow - in public; especially one connected to a rich and powerful family with a decided propensity for quarreling.

"Your silence is answer enough." He turned to the bench. "I have no more questions for this witness, your Honor."

As Larrabee walked toward his chair the Widow turned abruptly and hurriedly stepped out of the witness box. Before anyone realized what she had in mind, Mrs. Rogers walked quickly towards the door. She slipped adroitly through the throng in the back of the room, and vanished into the crowd outside the courthouse.

Chapter Twenty-One

Early Afternoon, The Courthouse, October 6, 1786

Judge Law lifted his gavel and ordered Sheriff Richards to bring Mrs. Rogers back. Larrabee and the prosecutor stepped forward, however, to assure the judge that neither of them intended to call her again.

"Let her go, then." Law consulted his pocket watch. "We'll hear the prosecution's final witness after we eat."

Only Judge Law, the jurors, the lawyers, and defendant left the courtroom. The mob in the gallery and the people clustered outside around the windows knew better than to desert their advantageous places. Some people sent servants to fetch lunch for them. Others relied on the generosity of their neighbors, or went hungry in order to keep their spots.

Less than an hour later, the state called Captain Fish of Groton as its final witness. The well-dressed Captain strode up to the front of the courtroom, took the oath in confident tones, and directed his answers to the jury.

"Captain Fish, did Hannah Occuish and her brother Charles attack your daughter Mary at Poquonnock Bridge in Groton in September of 1780?"

"They did."

"Would you please, sir, tell us all of the facts of this crime?"

Clearly quite happy to oblige the prosecution, the Captain spent almost half an hour painting a vivid and heartrending picture of the brutal assault, and provided a detailed account of Mary's wounds and a description of the entire family's distress and suffering. As Larrabee listened to Fish's damaging testimony against his client, the lawyer struggled not to wince whenever the spectators groaned aloud in sympathy with the witness.

"It was in September of 1780. I was in the kitchen with my wife when Mary suddenly appeared at the back door and staggered into the room. Her hair was disheveled and bloody, and her body was naked and bleeding, and at first I thought - I feared . . ."

Fish wiped a hand down his face.

"Take your time, Captain," the prosecutor urged, only too happy to give the jurors time to put themselves into the witness's place and consider how it felt to see a young girl child stumble home naked, incoherent, and dripping blood.

"Naturally, we rushed to her side, asking what happened. At first we could make no sense of Mary's speech; she was so distraught and in such a state of shock that I feared the blows to the head had deprived her of her wits. She eventually recovered herself enough to tell us that an older boy and a girl about her age accosted her on her way home from school. Mary said that Hannah stopped her in the road to show her something. While Mary was looking at some small object, a boy suddenly jumped out of the woods and attacked her. Then both of them pummeled my daughter about her face and body with their fists. One of them managed to get a hold of a large rock and strike her. Mary collapsed unconscious in the road. When she came to sometime later, she realized that Charles and Hannah had stripped her body and yanked her gold chain from around her neck. When she heard acrimonious voices, Mary realized that the young criminals who had beaten her senseless were now arguing over the spoils of their crime. While the attackers' attention was diverted, she gathered her strength and ran home."

"What followed next?"

"Mary identified two mulatto children, Charles Aves and his younger sister, Hannah Sharper, as the persons who attacked her. I immediately sent for the doctor and notified the authorities. There was an investigation, and a writ was issued for the arrest of Charles and Hannah. The sheriff went to the house of Joseph Packer to read the writ to the children's mother, Sarah Occuish."

"Were you present at that time?"

Fish shook his head. "I did not want to leave my daughter's bedside."

"So, you did not know what the authorities had done with the children," Larrabee stated rather than asked.

"No," Captain Fish's face looked grim. "I did not find out until several days after the fact that Sarah had absconded with Hannah."

"And what did you think when the details of the murder of Eunice Bolles in Quaker Hill reached Groton?"

"I immediately thought about what had happened to my daughter." Captain Fish glanced over at Hannah. "It did not at all surprise me to learn that Hannah Sharper had been arrested for the crime."

"Why?"

"As everyone now knows, the similarities between the assault on my daughter and on Eunice Bolles are unmistakable. In both cases, assailants stalked young girls whom they knew to be walking alone on their way to or from school, struck them upon the head with a stone to render them incapable of defense or flight, and then delivered a severe beating to their bodies. Only in one instance did I detect an important difference between the two crimes, and I subscribed that to Hannah's having employed an important lesson - for her, in any case - that she learned from the first incident."

The entire courtroom leaned forward with mouths agape.

The witness shifted in his chair and then stated in the same clear, deliberate tone he had used to answer all of the other questions. "She learned to make sure that her victim could never rise up and identify her."

"Thank you, Captain Fish." The prosecutor looked down at his notes. "Your witness, Mr. Larrabee," he said in a perfunctory voice.

A barely suppressed gasp of surprise drew the prosecutor's eyes up. Larrabee had gotten up from his chair and was walking toward the witness. The spectators looked at one another wonderingly. Why would Larrabee choose to cross-examine such a damning witness after having passed by the less dangerous ones?

Larrabee approached the state's witness without any sign of trepidation. The Captain's direct, if somewhat pompous and lengthy, manner of answering questions was a two-edged sword; wonderful if he gave the answer Larrabee wanted, difficult to control or stifle if he did not. Also, Larrabee thought it would be best to address Fish as the equals they were. Too obsequious a demeanor and the Captain, a man of substance and standing, would take control of the cross examination and destroy the progress Larrabee had managed to wring out of the morning session.

"Captain Fish, would you please tell us what disposition the Groton Town Selectmen made of the case against the Sharper children?"

"The Selectmen bound the eldest child, Charles, to Edward Packer, who agreed to be responsible for the boy in return for his service."

"And Hannah Sharper, now known by her mother's natal name of Occuish, what punishment or correction did she receive?"

"Nothing."

Larrabee turned to look at the jury, his face incredulous. "Nothing at all?"

Captain Fish nodded, his face sour. "That is correct. After the authorities went to Mr. Packer's house to read the writ in the hearing of the children's mother, the child disappeared with Sarah. As far as I could tell, the town made almost no attempt to locate them, and didn't pursue its case against the girl, content, I assume, with having bound the boy to Mr. Packer. Not long afterwards, I found out that Hannah's mother had spirited the child away to Quaker Hill, and while not pleased with the outcome of the case, my wife and I felt some relief in knowing that a river divided Mary from at least one of her attackers. I had to trust vigilance of Charles' master regarding the boy. To Mr. Packer's credit, we have had no more trouble from that quarter."

"And in regard to Hannah Sharper?"

"As I said, Mrs. Fish and I felt some measure of ease knowing that Hannah no longer resided in our immediate environs. Still, I felt very displeased that the Groton authorities had been so remiss as to let her go unpunished. For her own sake, as well as to promote social order, the child should have been placed in a well-regulated household where she could be trained properly while still of tender years. Perhaps if the authorities had been more diligent, we would not be gathered in this courtroom today."

"Captain Fish, it is quite understandable that you are annoyed by the failure of the Groton authorities to discipline Hannah Occuish. Did I correctly understand you to say that if they had done so, Eunice Bolles might be alive today?"

"I can only conjecture, but yes, if she had been given proper instruction, especially in religious matters, when still young enough to benefit from such attention, Hannah may have turned out differently."

"Differently?" Larrabee seemed to be considering. "Do you mean she might not have been violent?"

"Yes, possibly."

"But, as you say, of course we don't know that she would have been improved even if given the best of training."

Fish's next remark delighted Hannah's lawyer. "No, but certainly there would have been a possibility of improvement if the authorities had bound Hannah to a proper master instead of allowing her to live in a household headed by an aged, lone woman of . . . unconventional beliefs."

"Would you believe me to be correct, Captain Fish, if I stated that in allowing Sarah Occuish to secret her daughter at Quaker Hill in an unsuitable household, the Groton authorities failed in their duty to Hannah Occuish, an ignorant child, as well as failing to give justice to your poor daughter, Mary?"

"Yes, I believe that would be right." Captain Fish looked at the jury. "I have already said as much and more than once."

Yes, sir, you did, Larrabee thought jubilantly to himself, while maintaining a grave outward demeanor. *Indeed, you did.*

Chapter Twenty-Two

Late Afternoon, The Courthouse, October 6, 1786

Both sides rested their cases after Captain Fish stepped down. Before the trial ever started, Larrabee had never intended to call any witnesses for the defense, knowing that he would make his most telling points in cross-examining Sheriff Richards, the Widow, and Captain Fish. Since he had done just that, Hannah was the only other person he could have called. Although he had briefly - very briefly - considered putting her on the stand, Larrabee had decided he could not risk alienating the jury. Although the jurors had seen Hannah's detached attitude before now, the trial had given them an opportunity to study the child for hours. He hoped that the jurors interpreted her quiet demeanor at least somewhat favorably. If he allowed the state to question his client, however, Hannah's remorseless lack of sympathy for her young victim would be sure to offend men already sickened by the details of Eunice's death. Better, he thought, to let his final summation speak for Hannah.

When it came time for closing arguments, the prosecutor stood in front of the jury. He meticulously reviewed all of the physical evidence, witnesses' testimony, and Hannah's confession, reminding the jury that one could have very little doubt as to her guilt. He followed up by explaining to the jury that despite her age, Hannah's behavior established the criteria for premeditated malice aforethought.

"Though young in years, Hannah Occuish demonstrated guile well beyond her age in the commission of the crime of murder which proves her a fit subject for capital punishment. In an act of vengeful premeditation she took up and secreted a rock before she approached poor Eunice Bolles and with it struck grievous blows to her victim's head . . . And even when, as Hannah Occuish told the investigators herself, Eunice cried out for mercy, saying that she would die if Hannah did not desist in her felonious attack, the said Hannah did not desist. No. Instead she continued to strike Eunice Bolles - until that tender child of only six years - lay helpless in the road.

"Having learned, as one esteemed witness pointed out, that she must not allow her victims to identify her and thus bring down upon her such just punishment as she deserved for the lesser crime of violent assault, Hannah Occuish choked the life out of Eunice Bolles and then attempted to conceal the crime by throwing down a stone wall upon her victim's head and body."

The prosecution paused to allow mental pictures of the crime to reform in the minds of everyone within hearing.

"The prisoner then demonstrated an advanced degree of guile that one would expect from a much older criminal by making up a story about four boys.

"If the jury were to be swayed by sentiments of pity for Hannah Occuish and lay her crime to a want of years, each must be prepared to understand the dangerous message that you convey to her and to the youth of this county; the message that age will excuse crimes, even the most heinous of crimes.

"Surely each member of the jury thinks of that awe-filled day when he will stand before the final judge and must, for his soul's sake, account for his decision in this most grave matter before us. It is well that he thinks on this final judgment, for each man must consider what answer he will give if this prisoner, a confessed murderer of an innocent child, is freed. What will he say if Hannah Occuish kills again or if some other youth is emboldened by a verdict of not guilty and embarks upon a life of crime?"

Instead of standing up after the prosecutor finished, Larrabee stayed at his desk, looking over his notes, giving the jury time to realize that the prosecutor had said nothing surprising or unexpected. He hadn't told them anything new about the evidence, about Hannah, or about how to interpret the case that hadn't been said many times in the months leading up to the trial or in the courtroom. Even Fish's statement, which had the most potential to undermine Larrabee's strategy, had been mitigated by the Captain's outspoken criticism of the Groton Selectmen. Larrabee also lingered, because he wanted to whet the jury's already sharp appetite. For months, everyone had been wondering how Larrabee would be able to craft a defense based on anything more than Hannah's age. Now that they had a glimmering, the room was heavy with curiosity as the jury and spectators waited to see how Hannah's lawyer would draw the threads of his case together in the final summation.

After several minutes, Larrabee looked up from the papers in front of him and stood up. He walked over to stand in front of the jury and stayed there throughout the rest of the summation, looking the members full in the face by turn.

"It is true, gentlemen of the jury, that Hannah Occuish murdered Eunice Bolles. The evidence proves that fact, and Hannah herself told the investigators that she committed this crime. Her clumsy and transparent attempts to conceal the crime tell us even more, however. They tell us, as clearly as the spoken word, that Hannah Occuish, an eleven-year-old child, knew that she had done something very wrong and that she hoped to escape detection and punishment.

"What the evidence cannot explain to us, and what Hannah herself cannot articulate for the jury, is how she conceived of her actions and of the punishment she believed that she would receive if caught. Colonel Halsey, Sheriff Richards, and Mr. Hempstead have testified to the fact that when confronted by the sight of Eunice Bolles' battered corpse the morning after the murder, Hannah Occuish confessed to having done murder and said that if she could be forgiven she would never do such a thing again. How could she have conceived the notion that having confessed to committing the act of murder, she would be freed after offering a mere apology? And as we have discovered, gentlemen, when she learned that she must be punished, incredible as it sounds to our ears, Hannah expected to receive a severe whipping for having done murder.

"Experience, sirs, was her teacher! Experience had schooled her to expect either no punishment for serious misdeeds or to endure chastisements of a transitory nature, however severe when administered. When Hannah, probably led, as Captain Fish suggests, by her brother, attacked Mary Fish, no representative of the government took her into custody and advised her of the seriousness of her behavior. Nor did the government place her in a household where she would learn to understand that what she had done to Mary Fish was wrong and where she would be taught to govern herself. Instead, by the negligence of those responsible for her, Hannah escaped justice, thus learning that she could get away with committing the most gross acts of violence.

"During Hannah's years in Quaker Hill, Widow Rogers, as she testified herself, failed to teach Hannah to read. Think of it! Hannah, the child of an Indian mother and an African father, languished in inherited ignorance, unable to unlock the Scriptures and find the means by which to govern the passions that roiled within her breast. Her mistress gave Hannah no guidance. Whether the child committed and confessed to serious acts such as lying, theft, and bullying - acts that presaged the crime for which she answers today - or admitted to minor misbehavior, the Widow, by her own description, meted out inconsistent punishment. We have heard that Mrs. Rogers whipped the child with a rod or strap, sometimes leaving marks upon her body, for minor offenses. Often, we have heard from witnesses under oath, the Widow ignored Hannah's serious misdeeds. Even after neighbors complained to Widow Rogers about Hannah, she persisted in the same unfruitful course of correction. For five years, during which Hannah Occuish's behavior deteriorated and precious formative years were squandered, her mistress disdained to seek wiser counsel in the matter.

"What brings us here today is, therefore, the result of an unfortunate combination of inadequate governance, by both the state and Hannah's mistress, with the child's natural ignorance, sadly unameliorated by proper instruction. This unhappy, this tragic circumstance rendered Hannah incapable of learning the full import of her actions. Indeed, when she lied about murdering Eunice Bolles, she did so in hopes of avoiding the punishment of a whipping!

"Although her term of imprisonment and the assiduous attention of Reverend Channing have alerted this young child to the seriousness of her crimes, Hannah, it bears repeating, came into court today under the belief that if found guilty, she would be sentenced to a lashing.

"Now that she is come before this court and is awakened to her dire circumstances, we can be assured that soon this ignorant child will experience a softening of her heart that will invite a sincere act of conversion. After such a happy event, the state can place Hannah in a well-regulated Christian household where she will flourish under the influence of proper guidance.

"Consider, sirs, the two futures before Hannah, and before us as those responsible for dependent persons such as she. We may, if the jury so decides, look forward, not to the horrific sight of a child on the gallows, but to the happy day when Hannah is restored to society."

Larrabee sat down, satisfied that his moving summation had commanded the rapt attention of every juror and spectator. Nevertheless, he knew that his deft arguments would have little impact on the inevitable verdict. He could only hope that his words would encourage sympathy for Hannah. Perhaps the town would accept the idea of Hannah staying among them if they could envision her as a rehabilitated child, and the General Assembly might be more likely to consider his appeal if the community did not object.

Chapter Twenty-Three

Late Afternoon, The Courthouse, October 6, 1786

Although shadows had begun to creep into the corners of the courtroom by the time Larrabee finished his summation, Judge Law decided not to let the jury go home for the night. While he didn't like to demand so much from the tired jurors, coming to a decision in this most unusual case would be very difficult, and he didn't want to send them home and expose them to the questions and opinions of their families and friends. He quickly scribbled a note to Molly, asking her to hold the back room for the jury and to feed them dinner. After the messenger left, Judge Law instructed the jurors and adjourned court for the day.

Relieved to be freed into the crisp October evening, the members of the jury eagerly walked down Court Street toward the harbor, talking about inconsequential matters as they went. Dry leaves, their bright colors hiding in the gloom, crunched under foot, or swirled around the stocking-covered legs of the men as they hurried to their dinner at the Red Lion.

When the jurors crowded through the door of her inn, Molly ushered them all into the upper chamber, which she and her servants had been busy preparing for them. A log fire, newly laid, blazed in the large stone hearth that dominated one side of the room. Its large flames completely banished all the encroaching dampness of a fall night in a seaport town. A substantial joint of beef and a large tureen dominated the middle of the table; glistening brass candelabras at each end brightened the room.

While the jurors mingled, Bess and Lizzy carried in trays

crammed with filled tankards and set the trays down on the hearth. Bess hurried back to the kitchen. Lizzy bent down and put the tips of several iron pokers in the blaze. As she waited for the pokers to get hot, Lizzy chatted easily with the jurors standing nearby. When the iron glowed red, the young maid took up one of the pokers and plunged it into a tanker of ale, then put the iron back into the fire and took up another. The older jurors reached forward to take the steaming vessels from her hands and went to sit at the table. The younger men stood back, waiting for their drinks until all of their elders had been served.

For the next hour or so, the men ate and talked, enjoying the last minutes before they would have to begin deliberating. When he could see that the jury had finished eating, the foreman, Mr. Manwaring, got up and took a spill from the mantel and held it into the flames. When it caught fire, he held it to his pipe, then turned toward the table.

"Gentlemen, we are called to order. I suggest we commence by taking a preliminary vote."

"We can do that, Mr. Foreman," said one of the jurors, "but to my mind the question isn't really one of guilt or innocence as to the commission of the crime. The girl has confessed and never recanted during these past months. Certainly, there are cases in which persons have confessed to crimes that they did not commit, but in this case, the striking resemblance of Hannah's first crime to this one, coupled with the fact that she provided particulars that only the murderer of Eunice could have known, prove the reliability of her confession. As I see it, the issue for our consideration is whether or not she is old enough to hang for having done murder."

Mr. Manwaring scanned the jury. "Are we all agreed with this opinion?"

Murmurs of assent and nods appeared to signal a general consensus of agreement; however, one juror looked unconvinced. "Isn't the fact that the Grand Jury finally indicted Hannah Occuish evidence that she is of an age to answer for her crime?" he asked.

"Not necessarily," answered Manwaring. "We are not called

upon to approve the Grand Jury's opinion, but rather to make our own judgment."

"I suppose," temporized the juror.

"Unless there are other comments, we will address the matter of guilt or innocence from the perspective of Hannah's age."

A middle-aged man spoke first. "I've heard her called eleven by some, twelve by others. Exactly how old is Hannah?"

Once again, Manwaring scanned the room. "Does anyone know for certain?"

Most of the jurors shook their heads.

"I don't think that anyone knows for sure, including Mrs. Rogers and the girl herself," said one.

"In that case," said Mr. Manwaring, "since Mr. Larrabee refers to her as eleven or so and the prosecutor as twelve, we'll have to assume she is drawing on to twelve, but not yet that age."

"Who is she?" asked a younger juror. "Or rather," he said, "I know her name, but what is she?"

"What do you mean?" asked Mr. Manwaring.

"As far as I can make out, she's not a slave, and she's not bound. Who does she belong to?"

The foreman looked at the questioner for a second. "She belongs to the Widow. . . she lives with the Widow," he amended as the implications inherent in the question dawned on him.

"Yes, but as you say, Hannah does not belong to Mrs. Rogers. She has no contract to define a legal relationship of any kind between them. It seems, then, that the girl is not legally bound to the Widow in any way.

"And who is she actually?" he persisted. "Mr. Larrabee only says that her father is an African and her mother an Indian. Of course, we all know that her mother is Philip Occuish's daughter Sarah, which makes the child free born and part Indian, as far as I can tell. Who is her father?"

"Her father is Tuis Sharper from Groton, a mulatto Pequot. He enlisted in Stonington and fought in the Revolution," answered Mr. Manwaring.

"Then Hannah is half Nehantic and half Pequot/African, and she is the daughter of a Patriot soldier. Where is her father now?

Did he survive the war?"

Mr. Manwaring shrugged. "I don't know. If he did, he hasn't been around New London for years."

"Where is her mother?"

Mr. Manwaring shrugged again. "The Widow testified that she disappeared five years ago."

"Oh, who cares about all this roil?" another juror exclaimed in exasperated tones. "You could have heard all of this tittle tattle in the taverns for the last three months."

"And so I did hear many things, but I deemed those stories, as you so aptly call them, tittle tattle, which may or may not have been true, as is often the case of news one hears in a tavern. When I came to the trial, I expected something different in the courtroom . . . no, I suppose that I had hoped for something more. I assumed that Mr. Larrabee would separate facts from gossip about Hannah, so that we could learn who she is and perhaps be given to understand why she committed such a heinous crime. I thought that he might put her on the stand to explain herself or to express remorse, but her strange attitude . . . I had heard it spoken of during these months, as we all did, but to hear a description of the child and to see her so unmoved by all that went on and was said in the courtroom . . . Then I understood why Mr. Larrabee would not have her testify in her own defense. He knew that he could not trust her on the stand."

Another juror nodded agreement. "No he couldn't, but I also would have liked to have been given some reliable information about Hannah."

"I wonder, what is her status?" the younger juror asked thoughtfully.

"Her status? What do you mean by that?" sputtered the impatient juror.

"As we said, she's not a slave, nor even a bound girl. No, Hannah Occuish is free and comes from a propertied family, at least on her mother's side."

"So she does. What does it matter?"

The younger juror appeared annoyed by his fellow juryman's obtuseness. "What is Hannah Occuish's legal status? Like every one of us in this room, she was a free-born British subject. Now, like us, she is no longer subject to King George. We know that despite her complexion and sex, she stands to inherit property someday. What is she? Where does she belong?"

The jurors looked at one another, faces puzzled. Finally Mr. Manwaring spoke up. "She is a citizen of the State of Connecticut, and a subject to its laws. But," he added, "she is, and always will be, a dependent person. As a minor she is subject to a parent or master, and she will be subject to a male relative or a master when she grows up. That is," he added, "if she grows up."

"Yes, but if she is found not guilty by reason of her age, Hannah will grow up. She may inherit land from her grandfather and be independent."

"No," Manwaring said, shaking his head. "I don't think that will happen."

"Why not? Indians often leave land to women. And if Philip Occuish decides to put her in his will, Hannah will become an independent woman of property."

"No." Manwaring shook his head. "Her husband will have headship of her."

"But," the younger juror protested, "having property, Hannah might choose not to marry."

Mr. Manwaring smiled. "It would be a rare thing for a woman to never marry, property or not." He paused and frowned thoughtfully. "Of course, there are examples, such as Molly Coit."

"So," said the younger juror. "She would be something like Molly Coit?"

"Certainly not!" exclaimed the impatient juror. "Molly is an English woman - an American woman - and even she, despite her wealth, is a woman subject to male guardianship!"

"Which man?" the younger juror asked.

"What do you mean?"

"I am wondering: to whom is Molly Coit subject? What man has headship over her?"

The room went silent as every man in the room turned the matter over in his mind.

"Oh, this is all ridiculous!" exclaimed a juror at the far end of the table. "We are not here to discuss Hannah's distant future, but her present, nor are we bound to consider the status of women."

"Yes, gentlemen, don't let us digress upon the subject of women and the new government," requested a juror wryly. "My wife constantly awearies me on the matter. She wonders aloud if we men are fool enough to believe that we won the war without their assistance, and claims that having freed ourselves from the king's tyranny, we men intend to set up one of our own devising over the womenfolk."

The younger juror's adversary refused to be distracted by his fellow juror's half-jesting attempt to deflect conflict. "What do you two mean by these questions? And what do these details signify? All we must do is decide whether or not the girl's age acquits her of a murder she committed, and in cold blood. Murder is murder, and her status has no bearing on our decision. Molly Coit, you, I - even Judge Law himself - would be called to account if we did a murder in cold blood."

"I am only saying," the younger juror stated firmly, "that I would like to know something about the person whom I am called upon to judge and consider sending to an early death."

"I don't at all relish the idea of hanging any child, be she black or white, eleven, twelve, or fourteen," interjected an older man. "Especially one as ignorant as Hannah Occuish."

"Your last, sir, goes to the point," the younger juror rejoined. "Hannah is ignorant enough, if Sheriff Richards understands her correctly, to believe that this trial is to decide whether or not she should be whipped."

"Yes," the impatient juror sat down, drained of contentious emotions. "That *is* what she believes. That she might be whipped like her uncle."

One of the other young men spoke up. "How can we decide what to do with Hannah Occuish when the case is unique? We have no law or precedent in Connecticut to guide us."

"True, but we have precedent from England. Children have been hanged there for committing murder," offered a juror seated near Mr. Manwaring. "Even for much less," he added.

"By God, we'll not let England set the standard for us!" The startled jurors turned to gape as the agitated speaker roughly shoved his chair back and stood up. "Our men didn't die so that we could imitate the subjects of a misbegotten king!"

The angry man slapped both palms on the table and leaned forward. "Did your brothers die for such a privilege as that? How about your father?" his eyes raked down the table. "Did our fathers and brothers . . . and sons . . ." The man stopped and swallowed. "Did they all die fighting the King's men so that we can tag along like curs behind the English?"

The jurors shook their heads.

"No, they did not! Nor did any other of the thousands who perished in the war, or those of us who gave an arm, a leg, an eye! Be damned to England and its precedents and be damned to all quibbles about who this girl is or is not. The question is this: will we hang a child who has committed murder?" Once again his eyes scoured the jurors. "Well, will we?"

"No, our kin didn't die so that we could be like England and hang children." Mr. Manwaring's tone was sympathetic. "But don't you like the idea of setting Hannah loose on the community even less? That seems to be the heart of the matter. Can we, in good conscience, regardless of her lack of understanding, take the chance of allowing a person with Hannah's history of violence to remain among us? And what of the example it would set if we let her go? Wouldn't we be guilty of encouraging crime if we allow murder to go unpunished?"

The older man sat down heavily, and leaned his head in his hands. He looked up and nodded. "Maybe so."

A juror who had not yet spoken broke the tense silence. "Gentlemen, we have examined this matter from many angles. We are, as many of you have reminded us, bound by Christian principles, principles that behoove us to remember our responsibility to both the welfare of an abandoned, mulatto child and to the community. The two seem to be in irresolvable conflict. Let's consider the ramifications of the two possibilities facing us.

"If we return a not guilty verdict by reason of Hannah's age, we and we alone will share a goodly measure of guilt for any new crimes she commits, and we know she is capable of murder. Letting her go may encourage the lower elements of our population to greater degrees of disorderliness, which none of us want. All of these harrowing prospects make it impossible for me to vote for a not-guilty verdict.

"Besides, if we send back a judgment of guilty, our voice will not be the last to speak on such an important topic. If we find Hannah Occuish guilty, it falls upon Judge Law to decide whether or not to accept our verdict, and if he does, it is he who must pass sentence upon the prisoner. We all know that when Judge Law condemns Hannah, Mr. Larrabee will petition the General Assembly to commute the sentence. Only upon their negative would she be hanged. Our voting a guilty verdict, therefore, allows the questions of Hannah's age and ability to go before the General Assembly and be heard and judged by a second, and more learned, judicial body."

The jury released what amounted to a communal sigh of relief. No hands went up when Mr. Manwaring asked who thought that Hannah should be found innocent by reason of her age and/or ability. As soon as the vote had been taken, the jurors adjourned and began to make their way through the dark streets and lanes to their homes or lodgings. Within an hour, everyone in New London who wasn't too sick or young to be interested in the fate of Hannah Occuish knew that the jury had reached a verdict.

Chapter Twenty-Four

Evening, The Shaw Mansion House, New London, October 6, 1786

While Hannah slept in her cell and the jury deliberated at the Red Lion, Mrs. Shaw kept her own counsel in the small room at the top of the stairs in her stone mansion house. The light from the fire shone into the room, reflecting on the polished floorboards in front of the hearth and picking out the warm colors of the fine-napped rug in the center of the floor and of the figured paper on the walls. Two large windows, sashes closed against the cool night air, faced the river, flowing along the other side of the narrow road in front of the house. Shelves, filled with books and several carefully selected imported figurines and bowls of the finest china, lined two walls halfway up. Three well-executed oil paintings of family members hung above the shelves, each portrait flanked by slender beeswax candles standing in polished sconces attached to the walls. A few good chairs, one of which Mrs. Shaw now occupied, and a small table, all made by local craftsmen, sat in front of the fireplace.

She had chosen this room as her own when Mr. Shaw brought her to this house as a bride so many years ago. During the hectic years of her youth and middle years, she had withdrawn here for solitude whenever the demands of family and household allowed a few minutes of reprieve. Sometimes she sat in this room late at night, nursing a baby or, as the years passed, reading a book when sleep eluded her. At any time of the day or season of the year, the windows framed a panorama of the river and of the family's wharves and ships just below; a restful view that never failed to comfort Mrs. Shaw. On fine days and evenings, she threw open the sashes to the salt air and listened to the creaking ships bobbing in the tide and the gentle lapping of the waves on the small shingle dividing the river from the lane in front of the house. During inclement weather she sat, protected by the glass, watching summer thunderstorms rage over the roiling green water, or blizzards slowly burying the yard and road until she could not tell exactly where land stopped and river began.

Earlier in the evening, Mrs. Shaw had walked out of the new white courthouse without stopping to talk to anyone. She climbed into her waiting carriage and tapped the roof to signal that she wanted to leave immediately. The driver expertly gathered the reins and trotted the horses down the hill toward the river and onto Bank Street. He pulled the horses to a gentle halt at the bottom of the front steps to the Shaws' mansion house, and jumped down to hold the carriage door open for his mistress.

"Thank you." Mrs. Shaw put her hand on the driver's arm and stepped down from the carriage. "Put the horses away. I can manage the door myself."

Mrs. Shaw climbed the granite stairs briskly for someone her age and pushed the front door open. She went directly up the stairs, pausing on the landing only long enough to lean over the polished wooden banister and call softly down.

"Delia."

The slave woman's voice rose up from the cool gloom on the lower floor, where the fires had not yet been lit for the night. "Yes, Mrs. Shaw?"

"Bring my tea upstairs, please, and something to eat with it."

"Yes, ma'am. Your room is already warm. I started your fire not fifteen minutes ago, and put the kettle on when I heard the carriage. It will be ready right quick."

"Very good, Delia, thank you." Mrs. Shaw ascended the stairs to the second floor and went to her sleeping chamber to take off her hat and woolen cloak. She hung them on an iron hook on the wall, then went to the small room at the top of the stairs to wait for Delia to bring up the tea tray. Instead of reading or gazing out of the windows, as she liked to do at this time of the evening, she sat mulling over things that had been on her mind ever since the day she saw Hannah's back.

Delia came in shortly and set the small table for tea. When she finished, she turned to her mistress, waiting to see if Mrs. Shaw wanted anything else.

"Thank you, Delia, you may go, but please send Selah up to me. Tell her to bring her sewing."

Not so long ago, Mrs. Shaw's order would have taken Delia by surprise. Although she had always seemed to like the child well enough, sometimes even calling for her by name, Mrs. Shaw had always left the managing of Selah in Delia's hands. Lately, however, Mrs. Shaw insisted on personally inspecting Selah's stitches and making sure that Selah was making sufficient progress in basic reading, writing, and ciphering. She had even taken to occasionally summoning the child for no other reason than to talk to her. Now, whenever Mrs. Shaw sent for Selah, an alarm bell sounded inside Delia's head.

Wringing her hands, Delia quickly went out to the kitchen to get her daughter. "Mistress wants you. Quick, wash your hands, and get your sewing and your books. Remember, don't sit unless she invites you, and don't speak unless she asks you a question, and when she does, for the Lord's sake, just answer up and don't prattle."

"Yes ma'am." Selah jumped up, smiling.

"Remember what I've been telling you." Delia grasped her daughter's hand. "Be polite, but don't act too familiar, no matter how comfortable she makes you feel."

Selah ran to obey her mother and then quickly climbed the stairs, books and a folded apron clutched to her chest. She stopped at the threshold of the open door to Mrs. Shaw's room. Her mistress sat gazing out the window, lost in thought. Selah waited a few seconds, but when it became apparent that her mistress had not noticed her, the girl tapped gently on the doorframe.

"Oh!" Mrs. Shaw turned. "I didn't hear you come up the steps. Come in, Selah."

Selah went into the room and stood in front of her mistress.

"Did you finish hemming the sheets I gave you last week?"

"Yes, ma'am."

"And the apron?"

"Almost, ma'am."

"Here, let me see it." Mrs. Shaw held out her hand for the small bundle of material Selah was holding. The old lady put on her spectacles, unfolded the cloth, and leaned toward the light.

"Oh, yes," Mrs. Shaw said, closely examining the fine linen. "Perfect stitches, as always, Selah. I'm pleased." She took off the spectacles and laid them on the table. "When you are finished, I want you to give the apron to your mother. She needs a new one. And so does Sally. You may start on one for her as soon as this one is finished. Have your mother give you some coarse linen for Sally's."

"Yes, ma'am, I will."

"You like sewing, don't you, Selah?"

Selah hesitated. "Yes, ma'am."

"Is there something you like to do better?"

Selah nodded. "Yes, ma'am."

"And what is it?"

"I like to bake and cook."

"You do?"

Selah smiled eagerly. "Sally lets me help her, sometimes."

Mrs. Shaw put her delicate teacup to her lips, studying Selah thoughtfully over the rim. She took a sip and put the cup down.

"Did you memorize the Bible verses that I gave you last week?"

"Yes, ma'am."

"All of them?"

"Yes, ma'am."

"Well, tell them to me," said Mrs. Shaw abruptly.

Flinching slightly at the unexpected change in her mistress' tone, Selah quickly collected herself and began reciting.

Listening to Selah's innocent childish voice, Mrs. Shaw regretted snapping at the girl. She didn't intend to be short with her, but wished Selah would occasionally venture more than a 'yes, ma'am,' or a 'no, ma'am,' when she spoke to her. Although Selah had always been quiet in her presence, Mrs. Shaw had recently discovered that she found it somehow upsetting that her young servant answered very deliberately, careful never to offend, or . . . well, she couldn't quite put her finger on it. Could Selah be afraid of her? Surely not! Mrs. Shaw prided herself on being a kind mistress and a responsible one. She educated her servants and avoided the use of corporeal punishment. In Selah's case, Mrs. Shaw had always left the matter of correction to Selah's mother, Delia, Mrs. Shaw's most trustworthy slave.

"Very good," she said when Selah finished. "Now, let me see your arithmetic."

Selah sat very still while her mistress looked over her paper. When she finished, Mrs. Shaw smiled at her. "You are making excellent progress."

"Thank you, ma'am."

Mrs. Shaw picked up a piece of paper from the table and handed it to Selah. "Here is your next set of problems."

"Thank you, ma'am." Selah took the paper, and sat silently, waiting. After a few awkward moments, Mrs. Shaw, feeling a strange mixture of disappointment and uneasiness, dismissed her.

Selah stooped down and quickly gathered up her belongings. As she straightened up her eyes met Mrs. Shaw's. A spontaneous smile swept across the girl's face.

Mrs. Shaw smiled back, all of the nagging, uncomfortable feelings melting away. "Tell your mother to ask Mr. Thomas to come up, and tell her to bring more tea for us."

Shortly after Selah left, Thomas stepped into the room. "Ah, the sanctuary," he said, bending down to kiss his mother on the cheek. "Delia said that you wanted to see me."

"Yes, sit down. She is bringing more tea," his mother replied. "I have something that I want to discuss with you."

As Thomas sat down, Delia carried in a silver tray, bearing a fresh pot of tea, a small cake, and clean cups and napkins.

"What is this most important topic you wish to discuss, Mother?" Thomas' humorous tone almost concealed a niggling sense of trepidation. His mother obviously had something on her mind and she would not rest until she disposed of it to her satisfaction.

He settled in to await her pleasure.

Mrs. Shaw came quickly to the point. "I want to talk about Selah's future."

"Selah's future . . ." Thomas felt nonplused. He thought they had settled the matter of the servants last year, and could not imagine why the small slave's future would be the object of another conversation with his mother.

Delia continued to pour without the slightest indication that she had heard Mrs. Shaw, and her mistress continued as if her servant possessed no ears.

"Yes, she is eleven, and we need to consider our plans for her."

When Delia finished pouring tea, she set out cake. "Is there anything else, ma'am?"

Mrs. Shaw glanced over the small table. "No, I don't believe so. You may go."

Delia pulled the door behind her, but left it open about half an inch. She pressed her back against the wall, positioned so that she could see if anyone approached, and waited to hear what the Shaws had to say about her daughter.

Chapter Twenty-Five

Evening, The Shaw Mansion House, October 6, 1786

Delia had started eavesdropping several years earlier, listening only when she believed that the conversation had some bearing on her or, especially, on her child. Sometimes, leaning toward a cracked door or lurking in the shadows to listen to private interchanges, she felt furtive and soiled, but slavery didn't afford its victims such nice concerns. Delia knew unequivocally that she could never completely trust Mrs. Shaw - or anyone else - to protect Selah. Having been born and raised a slave herself, Delia understood that her relationship with the Shaws would never be exempt from the economic ramifications of slavery, no matter how much they might like her. When straightened circumstances threatened the welfare of their own families, even tenderhearted masters put their slaves on the block, and shed tears while pocketing the cash. That knowledge convinced Delia that the luxury of completely trusting anyone belonged to the free. Or at least Delia imagined it to be so, having no personal experience of freedom.

Though only in her late twenties, Delia did not feel optimistic about her fate. During her girlhood and teens, heady revolutionary rhetoric about freedom and equality had fired the young slave girl's hopes and imagination, but those passionate dreams gradually faded as the years passed with no sign that the fledgling government intended to free chattel slaves.

Two years previously, in 1784, the General Assembly shredded any remnant of hope. While the magistrates congratulated themselves on freeing slaves born after March 1, 1784, Delia saw the chance of freedom slip from her fingers. Even worse, her child, born a mere nine years before the cut-off date, would share her mother's fate of life-long slavery. At first, Delia could barely grasp the fact that Selah, born in 1775, and others born well after America declared its freedom from British tyranny, were in no better position than their parents and grandparents. Like generations of slaves before them, Delia and Selah would have to look to their owners for emancipation.

Pessimistic as she might feel about her own future, the young mother refused to give up hope for her daughter's. For months after learning about the emancipation law, Delia could think of nothing but escaping. But no matter how often she turned plans over in her mind, Selah's mother couldn't see how to get away with Mrs. Shaw or Mr. Thomas calling on her all day long. Delia thought of sending her daughter alone, but Selah couldn't go for at least a few more years. After many sleepless nights, Delia decided to bide her time, hoping that she and Selah would be the last servants the Shaws would ever consider selling. A thread, perhaps, but at least it gave a desperate mother something to hold onto.

From then on, Delia took special pains in all of her duties. She guarded her owners' assets as jealously as if they belonged to her, carefully keeping track of all the house and kitchen stores of supplies that came under her purview. The cook and housemaids sighed at the sound of Delia's approaching footsteps, but under her direction, well-prepared meals came to the table like clockwork and Mrs. Shaw rarely, if ever, had to call for fresh bed linens or point out slipshod cleaning. Delia also protected the Shaws' family name, never gossiping about her owners' personal or business affairs with anyone, white or black, slave or free; and she always comported herself with the utmost propriety, whether in public or in the house.

Delia knew full well that making herself so necessary to the Shaws' comfort and prosperity probably sealed her own doom. At her lowest points, Delia sadly envisioned Mrs. Shaw bequeathing Mr. Thomas to her care, so to speak. This picture of the future - sleeping in the mansion attic for the rest of her life, dancing attendance on Mr. Thomas as he grew old and even more cranky - was bleak and disheartening.

With all of these thoughts running grooves through her mind, Delia taught Selah to be quiet, polite and, with some misgivings, useful, but only useful enough to make the Shaws feel that they got their money's worth in exchange for the cost of feeding and clothing the girl. Delia taught Selah to tread the delicate balance of being always well mannered and as little noticed by her owners as possible. Delia wanted the Shaws to vaguely think well of the child before she gently slipped from their attention.

One afternoon a year or so earlier, Mrs. Shaw and Mr. Thomas closed themselves in the office for several hours with the door tightly shut. When they came out, Delia went in to tidy up. While gathering the teacups and plates scattered on the desk, Delia spied a copy of Mr. Nathaniel, Jr.'s will. After glancing around to make sure that no one else could see her, Delia set down her tray and bent over the papers. She ran her eyes quickly over the contents, hurriedly scanning for Selah's name and her own. The swift perusal did not reveal her name, but she found Selah's. Young Mr. Nathaniel, dead these three years, had directed his executor to free Selah when she turned twenty-one years of age! After indulging in a few seconds of pure happiness, Delia hastily put down the will, grabbed up the tray, and hurried out to the kitchen.

Although the contents of Mr. Nathaniel's will thrilled her, Delia knew that she would never rest easy until she held her daughter's manumission papers in her own hands. Wills could be gotten around, and slaves could be very easily transported out of the state and sold. Delia turned the matter over and over in her mind, growing increasingly agitated. She could understand the Shaws not telling Selah about Mr. Nathaniel's directive, but why had they not mentioned it to her?

Mrs. Shaw's secrecy about Selah's eventual manumission made it difficult for Delia to decide how she felt about her mistress' newfound interest in Selah and her abilities. Did Mrs. Shaw mean to try and keep Selah past the time set for her emancipation? What good would come from being a skilled baker and seamstress, Delia wondered, if those accomplishments only made her child more valuable to their mistress? Or - Delia's heart twisted with fear - enhanced her value on the auction block?

Chapter Twenty-Six

Evening, The Shaw Mansion House, October 6, 1786

While Delia anxiously waited to hear what her owners would decide about her child's future, the Shaws companionably sipped their tea and studied the flames on the hearth. Mrs. Shaw finally spoke.

"I found the trial today very disturbing."

"I think we all did, Mother," Thomas replied.

"To think of a girl so young committing such a heinous crime, and then displaying no remorse whatsoever," continued Mrs. Shaw. "I had thought that Hannah might have had a change of heart. Mr. Channing has been to see the child nearly every day since Mr. Richards arrested her."

Thomas nodded. "It is shocking."

"And Hannah Occuish is so ignorant! Mrs. Rogers had not taught her to read. What can her mistress have been thinking to allow the child to live in such darkness? Mr. Larrabee rightly put the blame on Mrs. Rogers, don't you agree?"

"Yes," Thomas nodded.

"Of course you do." Mrs. Shaw smiled fondly. "Masters and mistresses have a duty to their servants. We must teach them to read and catechize them in principles of religion, at the very least. The Widow failed on both accounts."

Mrs. Shaw looked over at her son. "And I don't hold with lashing a child, even a servant. Surely, a memorization of pertinent Bible verses or a mild whipping judiciously applied for serious misbehavior is beneficial for any child, but a lashing . . . no, it will not do."

Thomas nodded again, not bothering to comment, having experienced firsthand his mother's opinions on the correction of children. He thought himself none the worse, and probably much the better, for having had a discerning, even-handed mother. And, certainly, he reflected, he knew a great many Bible verses by heart.

"I have never had occasion to have Selah whipped," mused Mrs. Shaw. "Delia manages her so well, I hardly noticed the child until recently."

"She seems to be a good girl," Thomas responded vaguely, sensing that his mother had hoped for a different response, one that he could not yet fathom.

"Yes, very good. She reads and figures above her age and station, and is very talented with her needle. But she likes cooking better than sewing." Mrs. Shaw set down her cup. "I have been thinking, Thomas, that we should consider training Selah in fine cooking so that she can support herself when she is grown."

"If that is what you want, surely we can."

"I believe it would be the best plan. A while longer with Delia and Sally and then I'll put Selah with someone who can train her." Thomas' mother leaned back in her comfortable chair. "And there is no need to tell her about the emancipation until she is older, mature enough not to become unsettled and restless by the news. The child will be content with her lot as long as we keep her busy. Yes, and as she will undoubtedly marry when she comes of age, her family will benefit from any extra income she can earn from baking and sewing."

"And," Thomas added, "if she can support herself, she and her family will be less likely to come back to us for assistance."

Surprised by the anger that her son's comment roused, Mrs. Shaw covered her emotions by picking up a silver fork and spearing a bite of cake.

"Selah is a lovely girl," she said, wiping her lips with a linen napkin.

"A pretty enough child," murmured Thomas obligingly.

"She is of an unusually fair complexion, considering how very dark her mother is."

Thomas stared into the fire.

"Yes, she is a very lovely child. I often wonder who her father could have been. When I first noticed that Delia was with child, I ordered her to name the father, but she refused, for the first time, to obey me."

Mrs. Shaw picked up her delicate china cup and sipped her tea. While she drank, she looked toward the dark window.

"At first I felt quite angry and wanted to compel her by force, but then reconsidered. There have always been so many sailors around. Delia would not be the first young girl to be led astray by the blandishments of an unscrupulous stranger. No doubt Selah's father promised Delia marriage, perhaps even promised to buy her and free her. Poor girl, whatever he promised, he did not make good on it."

Thomas got up and put another log on the dying fire, and then sat back down. "Is there another cup in that pot, mother?"

Mrs. Shaw lifted the teapot and poured the dregs into her son's cup. "Ring for Delia to bring more."

Delia held her breath, unconsciously pushing her back harder against the wall.

"No need, this will do."

Delia let out her breath.

Mrs. Shaw waited until her son finished spooning sugar into his tea and began to drink.

"Yes, Selah will command a goodly wage with her skills, but don't you believe it would be wise to give her a bequest?"

Thomas put down his cup and looked at his mother appraisingly. "A bequest? In addition to educating her beyond her station and freeing her?"

"Yes, I think that it would be," she paused, ". . . fair of you - of us - to leave her a small legacy."

Thomas studied his mother's face. "Surely, Mother, let us hope that Selah will be long emancipated and the mistress of her own humble household on the day that I die."

"Just the same," his mother insisted.

A bequest of money! Mrs. Shaw's words literally staggered Delia. Then, her comprehension almost overcome by amazement, Delia listened to her mistress, in the most gentle of voices, extract a promise from Mr. Thomas to leave Selah an annuity of ten pounds a year. Delia put her hand to her mouth. A fortune!

"You'll add a codicil to your will, then?"

"If you like."

"No need to put it off. You'll do it within a fortnight, of course."

"Of course, if that is what you want." Thomas got up and put another log on the fire, turning his face away from his mother, remembering how blind she had always been to Nathaniel, Jr.'s faults.

"Well, Mother, if you're satisfied, I suppose I am." Thomas straightened up. "I'll leave you to your fire."

Delia moved quickly away from the door and ducked into the library to hide in the shadows by the shelves. She listened to Mr. Thomas' footsteps go down the stairs and fade down the hallway. When he firmly closed the door to his office, Delia ran her hands over her hair, collecting herself. Face serene and manner composed, she went in to clear the tea table.

Mrs. Shaw looked down at the book in her lap, apparently too engrossed to notice the cups and saucers rattling in her servant's shaking hands.

"Do you want anything, ma'am?"

"No, Delia. Go along to bed if you like, I'm going to sit here awhile. I don't feel like sleeping."

"Yes, ma'am," Delia said softly, closing the door tightly behind her.

Delia went into the empty kitchen and set down the tray. She braced a trembling hand on the scarred worktable. Two minutes or twenty minutes later, she couldn't have said which, Delia pulled back a chair and sat down. Despite all that the Shaws said, nothing, Delia struggled to remind herself, had really changed. None of it - apprenticeship, emancipation, annuity - would happen for years; years during which so much could change. While she waited, Delia could never let her guard down. And she had to make sure that Selah followed her example.

Still . . . Delia could not manage to completely quell an elation. Wearied by years of mastering her emotions and of schooling her behavior, Delia laid her head and arms on the table and sobbed until she was spent. She finally raised her head and wiped her face. Then, warmed by the red-hot embers of the kitchen fire glowing on the granite kitchen hearth, she said a prayer of thanksgiving.

As the echo of Delia's light tread died away, Mrs. Shaw rose and walked over to the window and raised the sash to the cold, fresh air. She leaned out to look at the river just below and sighed with relief, still feeling a bit surprised. She had expected Thomas to balk at the idea of leaving an annuity to Selah instead of the usual single bequest most owners left a freed slave.

Thank goodness, she thought, remembering the clattering dishes in Delia's shaking hands, *Delia knows about the annuity. If she didn't look at the will last year - and certainly I left it out in plain sight for her - at least she knows now that Selah will be emancipated and provided for. I hope that eases her mind as much as it does mine.*

While she stood by the open window, the moon broke through the heavy cover of clouds. Its bright light glinted on the river and reached deep into New London, casting the town into detailed relief for a few brief seconds. A strong wind sprang up, and the clouds rolled back over the moon as they hurried over the dark, roiling waters of Long Island Sound.

Mrs. Shaw pulled the shutter against the approaching storm, and went over to the fireplace. She bent down to put a small log on the fire and stirred up the dying embers with an ornate wrought iron poker. When the underside of the log began to glow, she pushed the fire screen into place, sat down in her chair, and picked her book up off of the delicate side table. Opening to her place, Mrs. Shaw felt happy to have put her house in order, and decided that she did not need to go to court in the morning to hear the verdict.

Chapter Twenty-Seven

Morning, The Courthouse, October 7, 1786

Shortly before nine in the morning, the clerk unlocked the front door of the new courthouse and stepped back nimbly to protect his toes from the stampede. As the people poured through the open door, the jurors came out of the back room and silently filed into the jury box. Before the crowd had time to sort itself out, Judge Law came out of his chambers and walked toward the bench. The clerk jumped up and called the court to order. As soon as everyone had taken his seat, Law called the court into session.

The Judge peered over his spectacles at the foreman. "Do you have a verdict, Mr. Manwaring?"

Taken aback by the Judge's unusual abruptness, Manwaring jumped to his feet. "We do, sir."

Mr. Larrabee tapped Hannah on the shoulder and gestured to her. She got up and stood docilely next to him, hands by her side.

"Go ahead, Mr. Foreman."

Manwaring nervously unfolded a sheet of thick paper. He cleared his throat and began reading.

We the jurors for the State of Connecticut find that Hannah Occuish, not having the fear of God, but being moved and seduced by the divil . . .

Loud groans and exclamation rose from the gallery.

. . . did attack and kill Eunice Bolles with malice aforethought . . .

The cries and weeping of the spectators surrounding Mrs. Bolles faded into the background as a hideous feeling of unreality rolled over her. It was the same terrible feeling she had felt standing in the yard, the glossy hens fighting over the feed spilled at her feet, watching James' lips move, trying to understand what he meant by saying that Eunice had been found dead.

. . . while said Eunice Bolles was in the peace of God. . .

Sobbing, Mrs. Bolles slumped forward, hands covering her face. James Bolles put his arms around his wife and pulled her close. Friends and family reached out to lay consoling hands on the Bolles' shoulders and arms.

Unsure whether or not to stop reading until the Bolles had a chance to compose themselves, Mr. Manwaring looked to the bench for guidance. Judge Law nodded for him to continue. Manwaring glanced back to Mrs. Bolles, then jerked his eyes away from the distraught parents and fastened them on the paper trembling in his hands.

. . . therefore, we find the said Hannah Occuish guilty of murder. [1]

Manwaring folded the paper and gratefully sat down.

"Thank you, Mr. Manwaring." Judge Law scanned the restless, agitated gallery, considering whether or not to take up the gavel and calling for silence. He decided to let the crowd whisper and cry among themselves for a few minutes.

While the Judge studied his courtroom, James Bolles leaned down to his wife.

"Calm yourself," he whispered. "Think of the baby."

Choking back tears, Mrs. Bolles laid a protective hand on her stomach and nodded. James shook out his damp handkerchief and wiped his wife's face while his mother patted her daughter-in-law's clammy hand.

"Look!" someone cried, pointing to Hannah.

James turned to look with everyone else. Hannah was staring down at the floor, face a blank mask, appearing completely unmoved by the verdict. The murmuring in the courtroom grew louder as jostling spectators craned their necks for a better glimpse of the defendant. A startled baby began a tearful wailing.

Without hesitating, Judge Law seized the gavel and brought it down with a loud bang. "Order!" The gavel came down a second time. "Order! Mr. Larrabee."

The courtroom went quiet as Hannah's lawyer got up out of his chair. "Your honor."

"Have your client back here on the 20th of this month for sentencing."

"Yes, sir," Larrabee answered, managing to conceal his surprise at the Judge's decision to wait a week before pronouncing an inevitable sentence. *Could he actually,* Larrabee wondered, *be considering setting aside the jury's verdict?*

Judge Law waved Larrabee over to the bench. He leaned forward. "Doesn't Hannah realize that she's been found guilty of murder?" Law asked, keeping his voice low.

"It's difficult to say, Your Honor," Larrabee replied. "Hannah doesn't pay attention to anything that happens in the courtroom."

"You mean that she isn't interested in the verdict, or that she doesn't understand?"

Larrabee shook his head. "I'm not sure. Probably both."

"But you explain everything that happens in the courtroom to her."

"Of course."

"Well, then," Law said. "She will understand about the verdict once you have a chance to talk to her."

"Maybe, if she hears me, but I don't think Hannah listens to anything I have to say."

"You will have to make her listen to you." Law gestured impatiently. "You must. And when you do, will she grasp the significance of the verdict? Will she realize that hanging is the only punishment prescribed for a person found guilty of cold-blooded murder?"

Larrabee sighed. "There's the sticking point, Judge."

Chapter Twenty-Eight

Morning, The Red Lion Inn, October 7, 1786

The second day of courtroom drama unfolded without Molly Coit. While the gallery mopped their faces with fresh handkerchiefs, Molly prepared to feed the horde that she knew would be at the Red Lion's door as soon as the judge adjourned court and Mr. Douglas secured Hannah in her cell.

Molly had thrown back the warm quilts at four that morning, a full hour before Bess was due to bring her a pitcher of hot water. Molly quickly donned her clothes in the chilly dark, and splashed cold water on her face. She bustled into the warm kitchen and began chivying the busy servants while keeping a close eye on all of the cooking and baking. She paced back and forth, stopping to peer into a large iron pot of porridge, hanging from a hook on the fireplace crane, to make sure that it hadn't burned, and to look over Lizzy's shoulder as the girl deftly plucked a dead chicken.

When she was satisfied that all was fine in the kitchen, Molly went outside to invade the stables, a sphere she almost never visited in the early morning, and unintentionally insulted the groom, who had been at the Red Lion ever since her father's day. The groom and stable boy looked at each other wonderingly as Molly quizzed them about the animals and the stocks of grain and hay on hand. Her questions suggested that she suspected both servants of negligence, at best, or thievery, at worst.

The faintly insulted faces decorating the kitchen and stables prompted Molly to ask herself why she felt the need to pry. Needing employment for her hands in order to free her mind, Molly took a large mound of bread dough from Lizzy, and ordered the girl off to tell the stable boy to stack the tankards in the common room and wipe down the tables. As her mistress put her hands into the sticky kneading box, Lizzy paused at the doorway and turned to make a cross-eyed face at Molly's back, triggering a snort of laughter, quickly stifled, from the other maid.

"Get on with you, Mistress Lizzy," smiled Molly without looking around. "There's no time to play the fool with the locusts of Egypt bound to descend upon us at noon."

As the bread dough slowly turned shiny and elastic in Molly's strong hands, the feelings that had propelled her from her warm bed moved to the fore of her consciousness, presenting themselves ripe for consideration.

Why didn't I want to go to the courtroom? she wondered, remembering all of her vast acquaintance panting with excitement to get back to Judge Law's court to feast on the proceedings.

No, she chided herself. *That's not quite true. I know that Mr. Channing and the Sheriff, and some of the others, didn't relish any of the to-do with the investigation or the trial. And James and Eunice Bolles can't be looking forward to being in the same room with Hannah.* She picked up the dough, turned it over, and slapped it down. *And surely the Widow Rogers doesn't hanker to go back.*

Well, Molly asked herself, *where's the surprise in all the curiosity?* Hadn't she seen it often enough in the tavern? Let someone walk through the Red Lion's doors with a lurid tale, and the patrons pushed around the story teller, ready to spoon up all the details. Things looked pretty much the same in the courtroom, yesterday, as they did in the common room every night, except that witnesses said their piece under oath and Judge Law made sure that questions got asked and the story told in an orderly fashion.

As Molly separated the dough into smaller mounds, her heart wrenched with pity to think of Hannah sitting silently by Mr. Larrabee's side in the courtroom. But why did she still feel as sorry for Hannah Occuish as she did for Eunice Bolles and her parents? Shouldn't she save all of her compassion for the victim and her family?

Molly tossed a large, coarsely-woven cloth over the mounds of dough and left them to rise. She wiped her hands clean on her apron, went into the larder, and came back to the kitchen carrying a large platter piled with chunks of savory cooked meat. She set the platter down on the large work table, fetched a smooth wooden board, and forked several pieces of the meat onto it. Taking up a large knife, she began chopping the meat into fine pieces.

"Are the pastry rounds rolled out?"

"Yes," Bess said. "They are in the larder. I'll bring them out."

Bess came back with a large tray, set it down on the end of the table, and went back for the second and then the third batch of pastry.

Molly counted six dozen small rounds. "The meat pies will go quickly after the court lets out. Mind you, put aside a couple of dozen for the jury and the Sheriff, and Judge Law. They'll probably come later, after the crowd has thinned out."

"Will they want the upper room?"

Molly considered for a moment. "I don't know. The jury usually mingles in the common room after a trial, but today . . . Let's wait and see. 'Tis easy enough to set up if they want privacy. No need for silver and linen today, though. Have you put the coals in the ovens?"

"Yes, the ovens should be hot enough pretty soon. I'll rake out the coals when the meat pies are ready."

"Good, they won't take long. When they're all done, you can reheat the ovens for the bread." She put down the knife and wiped her damp forehead with the hem of her long apron. "We'll be hard pressed to be finished in time. I can't imagine the court will be in session for very long. It never takes much time to read a verdict."

The servant girl sighed; they would have to make a great stir indeed to get all the baking and cooking done before court let out.

"Well, thank goodness they didn't hold the trial during the summer," Bess said. "We'd be as cooked as the pies."

Molly smiled and resumed chopping, concentrating on making the meat as fine as possible. Once again, her hands fell into the comfortable rhythm that freed her mind, allowing her thoughts to go back to the trial and the behavior of the spectators. The people's manner had struck her as . . . unseemly. Patrons in a tavern common room could be expected to lap up a sensational tale, but she believed that people ought to have a serious demeanor in a courtroom; especially when a child was on trial for her life.

Finished with chopping the meat, Molly put down the knife and went back into the larder. She brought out a huge wooden bowl, brimming with a fragrant mixture of raisins and expensive imported spices. She set the bowl on the table and scooped a mound of butter out of a rough brown-glazed pottery crock and dropped it into the spiced raisins. After thoroughly working the butter into the fruit, she spooned the fragrant concoction into the meat and stirred. When the consistency of the mixture met her exacting standards, Molly piled a heap of meat on each of the pastry rounds and deftly pulled the edges of the dough together. She pinched them closed and pierced steam holes on top of the dough. Satisfied with the look of her pies, Molly went to the open door that led to the new addition, which housed the new large brick ovens.

"Bess! The pies are ready."

Bess came into the kitchen, flushed and sweaty from raking the hot coals out of the bake ovens. Swiping a damp hand across her forehead, she picked up one of the trays and carried it into the hot kitchen lean-to.

Molly rinsed her hands in the wooden barrel of water stationed near the door to the garden and stable yard, and wiped them dry on her apron. "Keep your eyes on those pies," she instructed Bess.

"Boil or freeze," Molly grumbled to herself, stepping into the chilly hallway. Even though born and raised in New London, Molly did not like the cold. This October morning merely hinted at the winter winds and snows that would howl down the river valley pretty soon, or worse, push northeast and dump a blizzard on them. Then almost nothing would keep Molly comfortable; not even roaring fires in all the hearths. She thought of the many winter nights she had stood warming her hands at the fire while her backside froze, or sat down at her desk, shivering, to write up her accounts and found the ink frozen in the well. On frigid days, she spent as much time as possible in the kitchen and the common room, where the fire and the crowds' combined body heat kept everyone tolerably comfortable.

Molly strode quickly down the wide hall into the freezing south back room and then on to the equally cold front room, making sure that the fires had been properly laid in the stone fireplaces. As she expected, Molly found the fireplaces in order, with plenty of dry kindling and logs piled to the side.

She went back across the hall and opened the door to the common room. Hot air from a blazing fire in the huge fireplace warmed her face. Chagrined at the wastefulness of heating an empty room, Molly started to go find Lizzy to reprimand her for extravagance, but changed her mind. She was glad that Lizzy had taken it upon herself to make the innkeeper's favorite room comfortable for her. Molly chuckled to herself, knowing that Lizzy hoped her mistress would linger in the common room and leave the kitchen to the maids.

Relaxed by the enveloping warmth, Molly slowed her pace and decided that she might as well check the supply of ale. She rapped both barrels with a practiced flip of her fist. One of the wooden barrels emitted the hollow tone of a half-full keg. Although she could probably have gotten by with one half-empty keg, she decided it would be better to bring up a new one from the cellar.

Steeling herself, Molly went back out into the cold hallway. She opened the kitchen door and walked through the warm room, stepped into the almost stifling lean-to, and opened the outside door. She leaned out into a sharp wind.

"James!"

The young stable boy warily peered out of the barn door. Suppressing a groan, he jogged reluctantly across the yard in answer to Molly's beckoning wave.

"Come down to the cellar with me and bring up a keg."

James followed his mistress to the cellar door and waited obediently while Molly selected a heavy iron key from the collection she carried with her at all times. She put the key in the large wrought iron lock and opened the heavy door. Holding a candle aloft, Molly went down the steps into the pitch-black cellar, James almost treading on her skirts in his eagerness to stay in the puddle of light.

Molly stepped onto the dirt floor and walked into the dark, holding the candle up higher to throw the light farther.

"There," she said, pointing to one of the small wooden barrels stacked along the fieldstone cellar wall. "Bring up one of those barrels and put it in the common room, but don't tap it."

The boy hoisted the heavy wooden keg, balanced it on his shoulder, and followed Molly up the stairs and into the common room.

After James escaped to the barn, Molly sat down on the wooden settle in front of the common-room fire and began to mentally tick off all of the morning chores. Fires laid and wood brought in, porridge on the hob, all of the meat pies in the oven and half done by now. Bess should be shaping the dough Molly finished kneading into the loaves, which she would put into the ovens as soon as the pies came out. Plenty of ale for thirsty patrons, and the stables ready to bait their mounts. Thank goodness the day to read the verdict hadn't coincided with a wash day! Luckily, the bed linens had been changed two days ago, so no need to fire up the big iron wash pots in the yard for at least another three or four days.

Glad to relax for a moment, Molly glanced fondly around the common room, thinking how convenient it was to have sash windows with glass panes. Some of the older houses in town had old-fashioned lights, windows that did not open, or that opened on a hinge. The glass in those windows tended to be heavy and dark, and the ones that opened had to be latched. If not secured properly, the hinged windows blew back and forth in the wind, shattering the expensive glass. Inconvenient as they were, hinged windows were better than the shutters that many of the lower sort had to make do with. In the winter time, poorer people had to choose between opening the shutters to let in the sunlight or living in the winter gloom while being only marginally warmer. In the summer, things sort of evened out between those who had glass and those who didn't. Everybody had to open whatever he or she had and let in the bugs. When the insects became intolerable, as they inevitably did, people stretched cheesecloth or coarse linen over the window hole to keep them out. Light filtered through the material on bright days, but the breeze couldn't get through very well.

As she enjoyed her rare moment of solitude, Molly offered up silent prayers for the Bolles and for Hannah Occuish. She considered adding the Widow Rogers to the list, but the memory of the ribbed flesh on Hannah's back, which would never be smooth again, changed Molly's mind.

The innkeeper would never understand how the Widow could treat a servant so cruelly, no matter what Hannah had done to anger her mistress. Molly knew very well that servants could be a deal of trouble; especially the young ones. Over the years, a parade of young girls - relatives, daughters of respectable New London farmers and shopkeepers, and poor girls with no family - had cycled through the Red Lion. The girls, happy to earn a bit of cash while they waited for sweethearts to get land, welcomed a chance to hone their cookery and housewifery skills under the guidance of a woman with a reputation as an exceptional cook and household manager. Naturally, Molly had to issue the occasional stern reprimand when the high-spirited girls got up to mischief or neglected their work. One time she actually packed a defiant girl home to her parents. But she had never struck that troublesome girl, or any other servant; not even the poor girls whose parents couldn't have done anything about if she had abused their daughters.

If only Sarah Occuish had brought the child to me five years ago, Molly mourned. *It wouldn't have taken much doing to convince Father to let me have Hannah, even though she wouldn't have been much help around the tavern for the first few years. I wouldn't have minded teaching her.*

Molly loved children, and it saddened her to know that she would never have any of her own body. Getting married was too risky a business for her. While secure in the power of her charms,

Molly knew her property to be as alluring as her person. Even if a pure-hearted man fell to his knees at her feet, wanting her for herself alone, he could just as easily turn out to be a gambler or a drunkard as not. Or just a plain fool. The thought of an interfering husband made her queasy, and she didn't relish the possibility of joining the ranks of rich women made poor by a spouse's imprudence.

While Molly felt reasonably certain of being able to get along without a husband, she knew that she could not do without the Red Lion. Growing up in the tavern had cultivated a taste for associating with people of consequence - and for excitement. As a child, Molly enjoyed the game of cat and mouse played out whenever the Crown's custom man came snooping for contraband. A red-hot patriot during the war, she had relished the air of secrecy wafting through the tavern whenever the Sons of Liberty held clandestine meetings in the upper chamber. And she felt proud at the very thought that George Washington had stayed at the Red Lion - twice!

Despite all that she loved about being her own mistress, every so often Molly couldn't help feeling cheated by circumstances. Although she didn't make it a habit to dwell on unpleasant, disquieting thoughts, sometimes it didn't seem fair that she should have to choose between the Red Lion and the consolations of a family. To know that while she grieved in her secret heart for a child, the Widow Rogers, who already had grown children and grandchildren, had been allowed to have Hannah, and then she had turned around and mistreated the child! Surely the Widow could have done better by the girl! Hannah had come to Mrs. Rogers at but five years of age, no doubt a frightened and homesick child wanting her mother. Love, not the lash, Molly felt sure, would have cured the girl, or at least, she realistically amended, love would have had a better chance, and nothing lost by trying with so young a child.

Well, it was all over and done with, or as well as. Whether the jury had argued for ten hours or one, Molly knew they had to find Hannah guilty and that Larrabee would petition the General Assembly on her behalf, asking for a pardon. It would be very surprising, indeed, if the magistrates granted Hannah's petition, but there was no telling for sure what they might take it in their heads to do. Certainly, they did a good job, but . . . 'twas the magistrates' laws that gave men leave to fritter away a woman's property, and they didn't seem particularly concerned about the rights of . . .

Molly reined in her wayward mind, silently admonishing herself for traveling down that secret, but well-worn, dark path. Letting her thoughts loose in that direction would only upset and distract her, and she needed to have her wits about her today.

All she could do for Hannah now was to pray that when the girl stood before her maker, the distorted flesh on Hannah's poor back would plead for her. Christ in his wisdom and mercy, Molly firmly believed, understood it all.

Chapter Twenty-Nine

Early Afternoon, The Jail House, October 7, 1786

Hannah pressed her face against the barred window and watched Mr. Douglas walk down the hall and out of her line of sight. She wanted to look out at the harbor, but Mr. Douglas had banged down the cross bar lock on the shutters as soon as they came back from court. Sighing, Hannah stared down at the floor, idly picking at a loose thread on the hem of her skirt, waiting for Mrs. Douglas to bring her lunch. Hannah wished they would stop making such a fuss about punishing her. A few months ago, every thought of a whipping sent the child's mind swirling to the blank places of refuge, but now she almost couldn't wait for them to thrash her and get it over with. It had been very disappointing when Mr. Larrabee said that she had to stay in jail for at least another week while the Judge made up his mind about something. Hannah sighed again as the thread slowly unraveled in her restless fingers. She hoped Mrs. Douglas would bring her something good to eat.

Judge Law's House, New London, Early October of 1786

Judge Law leaned forward in the high-backed wooden settle, holding several sheets of scribbled notes, liberally festooned with heavy-inked cross-outs, closer to the firelight. As his eyes ran across the pages, the Judge grunted in satisfaction. A few more corrections, a fresh copying, and he would be finished. Law took off his spectacles and rubbed his tired eyes, wondering when he had last spent so many hours preparing for a sentencing. He couldn't remember a time, even when he was new on the bench; but, of course, he'd never had a case like this one. Now, in just a few days, the attention of the entire state - from all of the members of the General Assembly down to the New London town drunks - would be fastened upon him, evaluating his reasons for sending eleven-year-old Hannah Occuish to the gallows.

Not that Law doubted Hannah to be a fit subject for execution. It required a chilling malice aforethought to plan a murderous attack on another human being, and a horrifying ruthlessness to be capable of bashing in someone's head. Worst of all, the child had no remorse. True enough, Hannah had said the word sorry over and over again by rote during the summer, but everyone who knew her understood that, despite Reverend Channing's efforts, she had never learned to feel compassion for her victim.

Despite all of this, Law's conscience still accused him, and whenever he couldn't ignore it or beat it into submission, the Judge despairingly wondered if he should feel grateful to Larrabee or hate him. Some days, Law silently thanked Larrabee for letting New London squirm off the hook by cleverly serving up Mrs. Rogers as the villain, and a villain Hannah's scarred back proved the old woman to be. But, as the defense obligingly failed to mention, the Widow abused Hannah for years with the tacit complicity of the neighborhood, and, to a lesser extent, the town leaders, who had the responsibility to look after the welfare of orphans. If the neighbors had taken the time to report Mrs. Rogers instead of gossiping about her, or if the town officials had bothered to investigate the rumors about Mrs. Rogers and Hannah, perhaps Eunice would not be dead and Hannah would not be in jail.

As for blaming the Groton Selectmen for letting Hannah go scot-free in 1780 . . . it sounded well enough in court, but the Groton authorities couldn't have known that a five-year-old would turn into a murderess at the tender age of eleven. Besides, the Selectmen had rightly blamed Charles for instigating the assault on Mary Fish, and they *had* punished him.

As for the girl's religious education . . . the Judge ran a damp hand over his face and pushed back against the settle. In the unlikely event that Mrs. Rogers had taken a notion to give up Rog-erene ideas and provide her servant with a proper religious educa-tion, she couldn't have done it very easily. New London First Congregational Church, the state church, hadn't had a minister for years, and neither had any of the dissenting churches, for that mat-ter. During the war, and up until very recently, the members of First Church hadn't bothered to meet regularly, and when some-one did manage to organize a worship service, most of the congre-gation, including himself, whispered and talked through it. The Judge squirmed, reflecting that First Church still didn't have a set-tled minister. He hoped that the Reverend Channing would stay in New London and fill the pulpit permanently.

Regardless of whether the young minister stayed or not, Law knew that it might be too late for Hannah Occuish to benefit. Af-ter almost three months of Mr. Channing's constant attention, the child had yet to make even the most rudimentary statement of faith; and the Judge feared that she never would.

The idea of sending an unrepentant child to the gallows tor-mented the Judge, and he dreaded facing God on judgment day. After one particularly bad night, he seriously considered putting the jury's guilty verdict aside, but decided that letting Hannah go would certainly invite disaster. Having literally gotten away with murder, the girl would have no reason to control herself the next time she felt a murderous rage. And if she killed again, everyone in the state would brand the Judge her accomplice - and rightly so, in his opinion.

Law also firmly believed that releasing Hannah would send the wrong message to the restless, troublesome lower sorts, sport-ing mouths stuffed with egalitarian rhetoric. Their political fervor had been acceptable, encouraged, in fact, during the heady years of the 1770s. Back then, Americans of all ranks had gladly joined hands to rid themselves of a tyrannical King and his corrupt gov-ernment. Now, however, it seemed to Law, it was well past the time for dependent peoples - landless whites, servants, apprentic-es, Africans, and Indians - to get back to their pre-war employ-ments and trust their betters to vote and to govern.

Poor whites would eventually settle down, perhaps in the west, and better themselves, Law believed, but try as he might, he couldn't quite envision the future for people of color. Although the local Indians had thrown in their lot with the Americans and risked their lives for a modern political and social ideal, many stubbornly clung to traditional practices. Judge Law marveled that after more than a century of contact with Europeans, many Indians, some of them Christian, clung to traditional ways. He did not understand why they insisted on living in wigwams and wasting their time on seasonal migrations to hunt and fish or to make long journeys to visit relatives in upstate New York and Canada.

Law sighed to think that New London Indians gadded about enjoying themselves, leaving hundreds of prime reservation acres sitting idle while the younger sons of respectable white farmers went begging for land. Whenever Indians did settle down long enough to put in a crop, they cultivated small plots, the produce of which would never make them financially independent. The Judge shook his head, thinking it would be better if more Indians would sell their land to white families and move to Brothertown in the wilds of northern New York. They would be happier there, he reasoned.

But what about Africans? An even more troubling problem in Law's mind. During the war, revolutionary talk about rights and freedom occasionally rang somewhat hollow in his ears, especially when he looked at all of the slaves around him or thought about the Africans fighting with the Patriots against the British. Although he would never admit it aloud, such dissonant wartime experiences made the Quakers' and other churches' fulminations against slavery seem reasonable, instead of unbalanced or crazy, the way they once sounded to him.

By the latter years of the war, Judge Law knew that slavery must end. Conditions after the war proved the institution as impractical and inconvenient as it was impious. Slaves took jobs from whites, especially white people from the middling and lower sorts. On the other hand, owning slaves could be very expensive, both for the owner and the state. Masters had to support slave mothers during their lying in, and then provide for unproductive slave children, who distracted their parents from work. And even though the law required masters to shelter and feed aging and sick slaves, cagy masters found ways to dump their responsibility onto the public charge.

Soon after the war, Law and his colleague, Roger Sherman, began trying to figure out how to rid Connecticut of the pernicious institution. In all the hours they spent canvassing the topic, neither man seriously considered the idea of simply emancipating the slaves. The General Assembly would never pass the bill. Irate masters would demand compensation for their chattel property, and unconscionable owners would read the law as an invitation to abandon unproductive slaves.

Knowing that only a bill of gradual emancipation had any chance of passing, Law and Sherman proposed freeing slave children born after March 1, 1784 when they reached their twenties. The law gave masters the benefit of their young slaves' labor and forced masters to wrestle with questions of what to do about older slaves and children born before the cutoff date. Law and Sherman included a compilation of all of the old race codes in their bill. The older laws regulated the public and private conduct of all people of color, free and slave, and the inclusion of these statutes in the new bill gave the existing race code new force. After the General Assembly passed the bill at the January session of 1784, Connecticut looked forward to the day when it could forget that it had ever been a slave state.

The Judge pulled paper and pen toward him. *Everyone, no matter their race or conditions, must be made to understand that the rule of law, not unbridled passion, prevails in the new State of Connecticut.*

Chapter Thirty

Morning, The Courthouse, Mid-October of 1786

The expectant eyes of the keyed-up crowd followed Judge Law as he walked to the bench. After sitting down and arranging several papers in front of him, Law looked in Hannah's direction. The familiar detached expression on her face didn't particularly surprise him, but it did disappoint.

The Judge motioned for Mr. Larrabee to come forward. "Your client still appears unperturbed."

Hannah's lawyer nodded. "She is, usually, but her moods and reactions are unpredictable. Nobody can figure her out."

"You've explained to her what the sentence would likely be."

"I did, right after the verdict."

Judge Law raised his eyebrows in mute question.

"I also told her that we will petition the General Assembly," Larrabee said. "I've warned her not to hope too much, but she has always believed that she will somehow escape hanging and eventually be released."

The Judge shook his head. "Have you asked Mr. Channing to explain it to her?"

Larrabee nodded. "Yes, he's tried and so has Sheriff Richards. We thought that Hannah might listen to the Sheriff. She seems to like him, but he couldn't get her to pay attention, either."

"Well," the Judge picked up his gavel, "let's get it over with."

" 'Hannah, prisoner at the bar - agreeable to the laws of this land, you have been arraigned, tried, and convicted of the crime

159

of murder - a murder attended with circumstances of peculiar ag-
gravation. - You have killed, and that in a barbarous and cruel
manner, an innocent, helpless and harmless child - a child that
could not possibly, from its tender years, have injured or done
you any harm, or given you any just cause of resentment. And in
the perpetration of this shocking deed, you have discovered such
a mischievous and guileful discretion, in your attempts of con-
cealment and endeavours to make it have the appearance as
though it was the effect of accident, and not of violence; all these
circumstances have supplied the want of age, and clearly evinced
that you must have been conscious of guilt at the time of doing the
facts, and renders you a proper subject for punishment. – The
punishment annexed to your crime is death, both by the Laws of
God and man. - The law of this State by which you have been
tried, says that if any person commits any wilful murder, upon
malice, hatred, or cruelty he shall be put to death. The good and
safety of society requires that no one of such a malignant character
shall be suffered to live, and the punishment of death is but the
just demerit of your crime; - and the sparing you on account of
your age, would, as the law says, be of dangerous consequence to
the public, by holding up an idea, that children might commit
such atrocious crimes with impunity - You have not only offended
against the laws of man, but against the law of that God that made
you - that made the child whom you have killed, and that made
the whole world: - that God has commanded, "Thou shalt not kill,
- and whosoever sheddeth innocent blood, by man shall his blood
be shed." – And you must consider and realize it that after death
you must undergo another trial infinitely more solemn and awful
than what you have passed through, before God against whom you
offended - at whose bar the deceased child will appear as a swift
witness against you; - and you will be condemned and consigned
to an everlasting punishment - unless you now obtain a pardon by
confessing and sincerely repenting of your sins, and applying to
his sovereign grace through the merits of His Son Jesus Christ for
mercy, who is able and willing to save the greatest offenders that
repent and believe in him. – It is of infinite moment to you therefore, that you diligently improve the little space of time that may

*be allowed you, before your execution, to prepare for the awful
and important scenes that await you; - - and though you now appear to have but little sense thereof, God grant you may so attend
to such good instruction, advice, and direction as may be offered
you from time to time betwixt this and your execution, that by his
grace and mercy you may be prepared for the important events
that await you.' "*

The tears welling in the Judge's eyes ran down his face.

" *'And here I beg leave to remark, that the striking instance
before us, must convince us, of what necessity, of how great importance it is to society, that we early impress upon the minds of
our youth, our children, a due sense of right and wrong, good and
evil - that we early inculcate and instill into their tender minds the
great principles of humanity, morality, and religion; - for these are
the ordinary means by which restraining grace operates upon the
human mind, and keeps it back from presumptuous sins and
highhanded offenses.   And it is upon this ground, where good
impressions are early made, that the common maxims will apply,
of Nemo repente est turpissimus, that is, no one suddenly arrives
at the height of wickedness; vice as well as virtue being of a pro-
gressive nature, it generally requires an habitual course of sinful
indulgences, before those good impressions are so defaced and
obliterated as that the subject of them becomes abandoned to the
highest crimes - - - so on the other hand, where those early good
impressions are cultivated, improved, and strengthened by a
course of virtuous habits, they lead on to the highest pitch of moral excellency and perfection - - Had the unhappy prisoner now
before us, been favoured with those early good impressions, it is
not probable she would have been, at so early a period of her life,
so abandoned as to have committed the fatal deed, that has deprived an innocent child of life, involved its parents in grief and
sorrow, - - - a deed that has wounded the feelings of human nature; disturbed and injured the peace of society by so flagrant a
violation of its laws, and which brings the perpetrator to an un-
timely and ignominious death.*

" 'Nothing now remains but to pass the painful sentence of this court - - which is, that you be returned from hence to the gaol from whence you came, and from thence be carried to the place of execution - and there be hanged with a rope by the neck, between the heavens and the earth, until you are dead, dead, dead . . .' "

The chorus of cries and groans emanating from the spectators in the gallery and clustered around the courthouse windows rose to a crescendo.

" '. . . and may the Lord, of his infinite goodness and sovereign grace, have mercy on your soul.' " [5]

Judge Law's ragged voice and the sight of people crying aloud, pressing damp, wrinkled handkerchiefs to their eyes and leaning on the shoulders of friends did not perturb Hannah in the least, nor did hearing Judge Law set December 20th for her hanging. The crowd watched in open-mouthed surprise as Hannah got up and walked docilely by Mr. Douglas' side on the way back to jail.

After the Sentencing, The Jail House, October of 1786

Hannah's friend sat down on the bed next to her and put a hand on the girl's shoulder.

"Hannah," she said softly, "what can we do for you?"

The child glanced at the woman, then shrugged and looked away. "They're going to whip me."

The woman grimaced. "No, child, they aren't going to give you a whipping." She paused, searching for the right words. "You have to prepare yourself for death and to go to another world."

Hannah tuned blank eyes to her. "Another world?"

"Yes. You've been sentenced to die. They are going to hang you."

Hannah flinched, and her eyes focused. "Hang me?"

"We're sorry, but yes," said the man standing next to the

woman. "In two months' time, you will be hanged by the neck until you are dead. It's your punishment for murdering Eunice Bolles last July. Surely, you understand. You heard Judge Law sentence you today in the courtroom."

"Dead? They'll kill me?! How?" Hannah clutched the man's arm.

"Hannah, this has been explained to you many times. I know Mr. Larrabee explained the verdict to you and what your punishment would be." The man cleared his throat. "You've been sentenced to death for murdering Eunice. You will have a noose put around your neck, and you will hang by it until you are dead, just as the Judge told you this morning."

Hannah gasped and let go of the man's arm. "A rope around my neck! Kill me! Oh, no, no, no!" She began rocking back and forth on the bed, then launched herself backwards, thrashing to and fro, crying hysterically. Hannah's shocked friends tried to calm her down, but scurried back when the girl threw off their hands. The confused couple stood helplessly by until Hannah lay exhausted on the bed, dull eyes staring sightlessly at the wall. Not knowing what to do, they tiptoed out and locked the door behind them.

Mr. Douglas nodded grimly as the visitors described Hannah's fit. "She doesn't get riled up very often, but when she does, it's an explosion."

The lady wiped her eyes. "I don't like to upset the child, but she must understand her fate and have time to prepare for death."

"Don't distress yourself," advised Douglas. "Judge Law's words made no impression at all on her, and someone had to explain. Better one of you, who know her and care about her."

Feeling a bit like a man whistling as he passed a graveyard, the jailer looked in on Hannah every hour or so. Every time, he found Hannah lying on the bed, eyes riveted ahead.

★ ★ ★

"I'm glad to see you here, Mr. Larrabee," Douglas said, opening the door at the lawyer's first knock. "Perhaps you can do something for that poor child. She's been wrought up since her fate has finally been made clear to her."

"Clear to her? What do you mean?"

"Her friends managed to make her understand that Judge Law sentenced her to hang in December."

"They got her to listen to them, and now she appears to be very upset?" Larrabee asked, nonplussed.

"Hysterical for a while."

"Hysterical? Hannah?" Larrabee faltered.

"Hysterical for a while," Douglas repeated patiently. "Exhausted at the moment," he added.

Larrabee walked down the hallway and peeked into the barred room. Hannah lay collapsed on the bed, face to the wall. Thinking she must be sleeping, he turned to leave.

Before he could escape, Hannah jumped up out of bed and practically lunged at the door to grab hold of the bars. Clinging to the cold iron, she cried and begged incoherently. Shocked by Hannah's emotions and unable to understand anything she said or to convince her to calm down, Larrabee finally told his distraught client that the government would not hang a twelve-year-old child. Many repetitions of his promise later, Hannah finally stopped crying and turned away, wiping away tears with the hem of her apron. She went over to sit down on the rumpled bed, her face an odd mixture of swollen eyes, tear-streaked cheeks, and a calm, detached expression. Seeing the power of his reassurances, Larrabee couldn't help feeling a bit guilty - he hoped that he had told Hannah Occuish the truth.

Chapter Thirty-One

Morning, The Jail House, October of 1786

Mrs. Douglas put two bowls of porridge on the kitchen table. She sat down across from her husband and picked up her spoon.

"Where do you suppose Hannah's parents are, Ebenezer?"

"I have no idea," he answered, dipping into his porridge with relish.

"Hannah says that the Widow told her that Tuis Sharper probably died in the war."

The jailer nodded as he swallowed. "It's a good possibility," he said.

"Some people say Sarah Occuish was headed for Brothertown when she asked the Widow Rogers to take care of Hannah."

"I've heard that, too."

"Maybe both of them are living in Brothertown. But wouldn't you think that if Hannah's parents are up there, they would have heard about the trial and come home?" asked Mrs. Douglas.

The jailer put down his spoon. "I don't know that having Sarah Occuish or Tuis Sharper in the courtroom would have done Hannah any good. Certainly not both. As it stands, almost everyone assumes that both of them are dead. If Sarah and Tuis showed up now, a lot of people would resent them for having deserted their child, especially considering what's happened."

"But a lot of people already feel sorry for Hannah, wouldn't they pity her even more if they knew she'd been abandoned?"

"Some might, but it's easier to feel sorry for an orphan."

Mrs. Douglas looked at her husband quizzically.

"People will judge Hannah's parents for leaving her; Tuis less harshly than Sarah, but judge they will. A lot of people will assume that Hannah is like her mother. Can't you just hear them saying that the apple does not fall far from the tree?"

"I certainly can," Mrs. Douglas admitted. "But it's hardly fair of them to do."

Douglas cocked his head and raised his eyebrows sardonically. "Mrs. Douglas! Do you mean to tell me that people can be unfair?"

"Oh, eat your porridge before it gets cold."

The jailer scraped his bowl clean and handed it to his wife.

Standing, bowl in hand, Mrs. Douglas said, "I often wonder what Hannah's life was like before she came to Quaker Hill." She put the bowl into the wash tub.

The jailer leaned forward and kissed his wife's cheek. "I don't know, but I do know that Hannah will never tell us."

Evening, Poquonnock, Groton, September 1780

Tuis opened the door of the one-room house behind the Packers' house and stepped outside.

"Bring your wife and children to the lower field with you tomorrow," Mr. Packer said.

"The children?" Tuis asked. "You want us to bring Hannah?"

"Yes. I need every hand I can get with so many men off with the army or out to sea."

"But Hannah is too young to help bring in the harvest," Tuis protested.

"Have both of them out there at first light," Mr. Packer responded gruffly. "We'll find plenty for her to do."

The children shinnied down the ladder of the loft before the sun came up, dressed and ready to eat, only to find the hearth cold and their mother huddled on her pallet. Charles pushed Hannah forward.

"Wake her up."

Hannah shook her head.

Charles crept forward. "Mother."

Sarah stirred and turned over.

Charles tiptoed around the bed. "Mother, get up," he urged. "It's time to get up. Mr. Packer will be angry if we're late."

Sarah groaned. "Go away."

Charles reached out and pulled timidly on his mother's blanket. "We're hungry."

Sarah pushed the child's hand away and pulled the blanket up. "Leave me alone."

"Go feed the chickens, Charles," Tuis said, coming in the door. He thumped the bucket of water by the hearth, ignoring the water that sloshed over the iron rim onto the floor. "Take your sister with you." He picked up the small pottery jug lying next to the bed and tossed it into the cold fireplace. The children jumped as the jug shattered. "Hurry up."

While the children tossed scraps to the hungry birds crowding around their ankles, Tuis angrily scraped cold leftover cornmeal mush from the black iron pot into wooden bowls and slammed them down on the table. When Charles and Hannah came back inside, the three of them ate breakfast standing up, and as soon as the last bite disappeared down their throats, Tuis hustled the children out the door. He banged the heavy door on his way out, hoping Sarah would wake up and get to the field before Mr. Packer noticed her missing.

Half way to the lower field, Tuis stopped. "You children go back and ask Mr. Packer for an extra whetstone. Tell him that someone always forgets to bring one, and I don't want to break my scything rhythm to get mine out every time someone's blade gets dull. But for the love of God, let him think that I sent you from the fields. Don't tell him I haven't gotten there yet."

"I won't," Charles cried over his shoulder, joyfully running back toward the Packers' house, Hannah trailing along behind. At the curve of the dirt road, Charles slowed down and looked back. Satisfied that his father couldn't see them, he stopped.

"I'm not wasting a day harvesting when I can go fishing instead. You run on and ask Mr. Packer for the whetstone and take it out to Father. If he asks about me, tell him you don't know where I've gone."

Hannah laughed outright. "I'll get whipped for lying when they find out. If you're going fishing, I'm going with you."

"No, you're not. You go on and get that whetstone like I told you and take it to our father."

Hannah folded her arms across her chest and shook her head.

"Go on now, do as I say. I'm going fishing." Charles pulled a coiled fishing line out of his pocket.

"No."

Charles studied Hannah's resolute face for a few seconds. He shrugged, then turned and walked toward the Poquonnock River and went down to the narrow sand shore.

"Gather some driftwood for a fire while I catch some fish."

Half an hour later, the hungry children held spitted fish over the driftwood fire on the beach. After devouring every morsel, Charles and Hannah rambled through the woods and meadows, gathering wild grapes and stripping a few late blackberries off of the brambles.

Charles sat down on a large boulder near the dirt track meandering along the river's edge to eat his grapes and berries.

"Hannah, do you think Mother got up to the fields before Mr. Packer found out she was late?"

Hannah wiped grape juice off of her chin. "Likely not."

"I bet Father went looking for us," Charles said, pulling at a ragged cuticle. "He was probably worried about us when we didn't come back."

Hannah squatted down by a patch of sweet grass. She pinched off a slender stalk and held it to her nose.

"Mr. Packer will be pretty upset that Father came late, and by himself," Charles fretted. "Don't you think so?"

Hannah nodded.

"I reckon Father will be angry tonight." A thin stream of blood ran down Charles' thumb. "He might even get the strap."

Hannah frowned, picturing the old leather horse rein hanging on an iron nail by the door. "He might."

"Listen, Hannah, Father and Mr. Packer will only get more angry when they find out we went fishing. I've got to run away before Father gets home."

Hannah rocked back on her heels and looked up at her brother. "Where are we going to go?"

"Brothertown."

"Brothertown? What's that?"

"It's a new Indian town up north somewhere. I heard our parents talking about it. Lots of Indians are going to Brothertown to live."

"How are we going to get there?"

"I can walk, but I'll need money for food."

"Mother has some money."

Charles shook his head. Even if he managed to get his hands on the coppers Sarah kept under a floorboard near the fireplace, those few pennies wouldn't get him very far. Besides, he wasn't willing to risk going back home, even for the minutes it would take to scoop up the coins.

"Mr. Packer has lots of money," Hannah observed.

"Take money from a white man! Remember Father telling us how Mr. Rogers nailed his ears to a board when he caught him stealing money when he was a boy?"

Hannah winced. "I remember."

"Do you want the same thing to happen to me?" asked Charles scornfully.

Hannah shook her head.

"Well, then, don't get stupid ideas."

Shielding her eyes from the early morning sun, Hannah lay back, and studied the seagulls circling overhead, dodging ever closer, looking for scraps. The faint sound of children's laughter traveled down the river from the hamlet, about a quarter of a mile away.

"I know how to get some money," Charles announced.

"How?"

"I'll take Mary Fish's necklace, but you've got to help me. It'll be easy; we'll catch her on the way home from school, while she's alone, and snatch the necklace and run. By the time she gets home to tell on us, I'll be long gone."

Hannah couldn't think of any objections to Charles' simple plot. She had never particularly cared for seven-year-old Mary, and always felt vaguely resentful whenever the girl passed her by, school books cradled in her arms, laughing with her friends.

"I for sure won't be able to go back home after this," Charles warned his sister.

Hannah shrugged again. Much as she loved Poquonnock, it wouldn't be the same without Charles. Besides, she had no intention of facing their livid parents and Mr. Packer without him.

Charles looked up at the sun. "Come on, or we'll be too late to catch Mary alone."

Charles trotted toward Poquonnock. When he reached the narrow dirt lane that bisected the village, he turned west, away from the houses clustered down by the narrow bridge. He stopped in a section of the road where large trees crowded the edges, their interlaced branches forming a canopy over the narrow dirt lane.

"This is a good place," Charles said. "I'll hide behind the bushes. You stand out here and wait for Mary. Make sure she's alone, and then start talking to her, when . . ."

"What about?" interrupted Hannah.

"I don't know. You're both girls. Can't you think of anything to say to her?"

Hannah shook her head. "No."

"Do you have something that you could show her, something to make her stop for a while to study it?"

Hannah fished a small quahog shell out of her apron pocket. She turned it up on her palm and held her hand out to reveal the unusually deep, rich purple hidden on the inside.

"Is that all?" asked Charles, voice dripping contempt. "I've seen a thousand like it."

Hannah clenched her fingers over the shell and looked away.

"Oh, all right. It's not much, but if that's all you have, show it to her." Charles backed into the shadows. "I'll wait here. When she's not looking at you, grab the necklace and run. I'll jump out and hold her, if she tries to run after you. When you're gone, I'll let her go and come after you. Remember, grab the necklace and run as fast as you can."

Hannah stood patiently on the side of the road, lulled by sound of the faint breeze gently stirring the leaves arched above her, holding the shell softly in her hand, imagining the green canopy above her turning scarlet, yellow, and orange in a few weeks. Standing there, she decided that she liked Autumn the best of all the seasons.

A hiss from the bushes on the side of the road startled Hannah back to the present.

"Here she comes!" Charles whispered.

Hannah looked down the road and saw Mary strolling toward her. When the girl came abreast of Hannah and began to pass by, Hannah stepped forward. She held out her clenched hand. "Look."

Curious, Mary came over. "What is it?"

Hannah turned over her hand, uncurled her fingers, and balanced the shell on her palm. Mary stepped closer and looked down. "Oh," she looked up at Hannah. "It's beautiful."

Hannah inhaled sharply. Sarah had said the same thing when Hannah showed it to her, but Hannah had never expected this girl to see what she and her mother saw in an ordinary, small quahog shell.

As Hannah stared silently into Mary's face, Charles barreled out of the shadows. He tackled Mary full force, knocking her into his sister. Hannah stumbled backwards and fell under the large tree. Stunned, Hannah sat in the dust, watching Charles wrestle Mary to the ground.

"Run and get a stone!" Charles shouted above Mary's hysterical screams. "Hurry!"

Hannah jumped up and ran to obey. She grabbed up a rock the size of a woman's fist.

"Hit her! Hit her!"

Hannah froze, the stone clutched in her hand.

"Grab her arm! She's going to get away!" Hannah dropped

the stone and flung herself across Mary. Finally, she managed to catch one of the girl's flailing arms. Charles pinned Mary's other arm with one hand and reached for the rock with the other. He swung the stone toward Mary's head. The girl shrieked. A bright red stream flowed down her face, mixing with the dirt and tears on her cheeks. Charles swung the rock again. Mary went limp.

Charles released Mary's arm and got up. Wiping a shaking, bloody hand across his shirt front, he leaned down and inspected the child's still face.

"She's dead."

"Dead?" Hannah had seen lots of dead bodies - fish, animals at killing time, people in their coffins - but Mary's still body seemed different.

"I didn't mean to kill her," he choked. "How was I to know that she would fight so hard?" He flung the stone wildly in Hannah's direction.

Hannah dodged the rock. "She doesn't look dead."

"Well, she is! You didn't help much," he screamed. "It's all your fault, you were supposed to snatch the necklace and run, not stand there gawping at her."

Chapter Thirty-Two

Poquonnock, September of 1780

Charles knelt in the dust. He leaned forward, grasped Mary's necklace, and jerked. The gold links snapped apart, leaving a half moon of red droplets on both sides of the girl's neck. "Pull off her clothes, I can sell them."

"Is she really dead?"

"She's dead! Hurry up, before someone catches us."

Hannah knelt down by her brother and reached for Mary's apron pins with fumbling, nervous fingers. Charles quickly stripped the stockings from Mary's flaccid legs. He shoved the broken necklace into a stocking toe and tied a knot in the top, then he helped Hannah pull Mary's clothes off. Charles hastily rolled them up and tied them together with her stockings. He snatched up the clumsy bundle, and walked quickly toward the woods. Hannah hurried to keep up with him.

"Slow down! Wait for me! Where are you going?"

"I told you, up north to Brothertown. Somebody at the reservation will be able to tell me how to get there." Charles looked around at Hannah without stopping. "Go on back home. I'm not taking you."

Hannah pointed back toward Mary's body. "I'm not staying here. I'll get an awful whipping. Anyway, you said I could go if I helped you."

"No, I didn't. I never said I'd take you. Besides that was before you got Mary killed. They'll be after me for sure, and you'll just slow me down." Charles turned his back on his sister and began to jog; Hannah dogging his heels. Charles whipped around and tossed the bundle aside. He grabbed Hannah by the shoulders and threw her down on the ground. "You'd better watch it," he threatened.

As he leaned down to pick up Mary's clothes, Hannah seized a heavy stick and leaped up, brandishing it. "I'm coming," she screamed.

Charles spun around and lunged. Hannah scrambled backward, just managing to evade his grasp, but lost her footing and fell, the stick still clutched in her hand. She twisted to the side, trying to escape, but he jumped on her, pushed her flat on her back, pinned her arms with his knees, and sat on her stomach. He grabbed the stick, and viciously twisted it out of her hand, bruising her wrist. Still kneeling on his sister's arms, Charles raised up on his knees, crushing her arms into the dirt and rocks. He flung the stick away. Hannah turned her head and watched it somersault through the air and land on the edge of the road. She gasped.

"Mary's gone!"

Charles jerked his head up. He leaped and ran into the road, searching wildly for a trace of Mary. She *had* vanished. Bewildered, the children stood wondering what to do, until the creak of a wagon and laughing voices coming down the road galvanized them into action. Charles bolted into the woods and caught up the bundle, Hannah loping behind, struggling to keep up. They headed for home, all thought of running away forgotten.

The children didn't slow down until they caught sight of Mr. Packer's rooftop. Panting and sweating, they crept toward the yard and hid behind the chicken house. After he caught his breath, Charles peeked around the corner of the henhouse. He pulled his head back.

"There's no one outside," he whispered. "Go see if Mother is inside, but be quiet."

Hannah nodded. She ran across the dirt yard and eased the door open cautiously and looked inside. "She's gone."

Charles sped across the yard. Without a word, both children dashed inside and climbed the ladder to the loft.

"Here," Charles thrust the dirt-stained bundle at Hannah.

"Hide this."

Hannah looked around the almost empty loft. "Where?"

"I don't know. Under your blankets."

"Why mine? Why you don't you put them under your own?"

Charles ignored his sister's pertinent question. "I'm glad she's not dead."

Hannah threw Mary's clothes into a dark corner. "So am I."

"She'll tell on us," Charles said. "But I'm glad that I didn't kill her."

"Me, too."

Not knowing what else to do, the children lay down on their pallets.

Tuis stepped quietly inside the house and scanned the small room. He climbed the ladder and glanced quickly into the loft, climbed back down, and went outside, leaving the door open behind him.

"They're not here," he told Mr. Packer, cutting a quick look toward the door. "They're probably hiding in the woods."

"Well, you'd better find them. Mary Fish positively identified both of your children as her assailants. Captain Fish has gone to swear out a complaint. Dear God, you should see the girl! A bloody mess; the mother screaming and crying. You can expect the sheriff tomorrow morning for certain, maybe even tonight."

"What will they do to my children?" Tuis asked.

"Take them from you and bind them out."

"Bind them!" Tuis ran wet palms down the legs of his breeches.

"We're free people," Sarah exclaimed. "My father owns property. Lots of property. None of the Occuishs have been bound servants."

"That's about to change," Mr. Packer replied grimly. "After what Charles and Hannah have done to Mary Fish, I wouldn't be surprised if they take one or both of you as well. As it stands, I know the authorities will take the children, and there's nothing you can do about it. The only thing that you can do now is pick

their master before the selectmen have a chance to choose someone you might not like."

Sarah looked down at the ground, her face a mask of mingled
anger and fear.

"I'll take Charles with an indenture, and have my brother and
his wife take Hannah," said Mr. Packer. "I'll have the papers
drawn up right away."

"No." Sarah looked up. "No papers for Hannah, she's not to
blame. We'll trust you with Charles."

"You can't be serious, Sarah!" Mr. Packer exclaimed.

"No papers for Hannah, just Charles," Sarah repeated, voice
firm.

Packer looked at Tuis. "What do you say?"

"Sarah's right. Hannah is too young."

Packer shook his head. "You're making a big mistake, Tuis.
I'm telling you, if you don't bind out Hannah immediately, the
town will take the girl, and you won't have any say about where
she goes."

"Maybe," Sarah said.

"No maybe about it," Packer insisted. "The Selectmen will
take Hannah from you, and who knows where she'll end up. The
only way to keep your family together is for me to tell the Sheriff
that you're binding out the children to the Packers."

Sarah studied Mr. Packer, her face calculating. "You're right.
They will take Charles and Hannah to bind them out."

Packer nodded. "It's of a course."

"But you are willing to take Charles, and treat him well." Sarah stated rather than asked.

"Yes, I'll take the boy. The girl can go to my brother and sister, but at least she'll be in Poquonnock." Mr. Packer cleared his
throat. "We'd be willing find places for both of you, too, if it
comes to that."

"When can you have the contracts for the children ready?"
Sarah asked.

"I can have them by tomorrow afternoon."

"As quickly as that"

Packer nodded. "Easily."

Sarah's face hardened. "And you'll be here when the Sheriff comes and convince him to let you have Charles and Hannah?"

"Yes, I will," Packer promised as he opened the door to leave.

"Come down here right now."

Charles stepped hesitantly down the ladder, head turned over his shoulder to eye his parents carefully. Hannah came down after Charles and wiggled behind her brother.

"What's the matter with you?" Tuis grabbed his son by the arm and shook him. "What were you thinking?"

"I knew Mr. Packer would be upset that I didn't come to the fields, so I was going to run away," Charles sobbed.

"What does running away have to do with attacking Mary Fish?"

"I didn't want Mr. Packer to nail my ears to a board, like Mr. Rogers did to you."

"Nail your ears to a board? What are you talking about?" Tuis demanded. "Why would he do that?"

"I didn't want to take Mr. Packer's money to run away with and have him nail my ears if he caught me." Charles wiped his face with his shirt tail. "So I took Mary's clothes and necklace."

Tuis sighed with angry exasperation. "What a stupid thing to do. You could have killed that girl. Thank God you didn't. I don't know what would have happened if you had."

"What are they going to do to me?"

"You heard everything we said. You know very well that Captain Fish isn't going to let you get away with attacking his daughter," Sarah said. "If you don't want a stranger for a master, you'll do as we say and stay here with Mr. Packer."

"What about Hannah? Which one of Mr. Packer's brothers will take her?"

"So now you're worried about your sister!" Sarah exclaimed. "Well, don't bother. Mr. Packer is wrong; no one will care about her, she's too young to matter. It's you they'll blame, and rightly, too. And maybe your father and me." Sarah paused thoughtfully.

"Where are Mary Fish's things?"

"In the loft."

"Well, get up there and get them. I want that necklace."

"You do understand that I have a writ to arrest the children?" The Groton Sheriff looked across Mr. Packer's kitchen table.

"Yes," Sarah answered, laying Mary Fish's bundled clothes on the table. "We understand."

"You don't have to take the children," Mr. Packer interjected. "The Sharpers won't trouble the Fishes again. I'll take Charles, and my brother and his wife will take the girl."

The Groton Sheriff folded up the writ. "I don't know about that," he said, shaking his head doubtfully. "Mary Fish is a bloody mess, and the parents are beside themselves. The whole town wants something done about this and right quick."

Sarah took the gold necklace out of her pocket and laid it on top of the rolled clothes. She pushed Charles and Hannah forward.

"Go on."

"I'm sorry for hitting Mary Fish. I won't do it again," Charles promised.

"Me, too," Hannah whispered.

The Groton Sheriff laughed bitterly, eyes flinty. "You're sorry."

The children nodded, heads down.

"Where is the children's father? What does he have to say for himself?" the Sheriff demanded.

"I don't know." Mr. Packer looked to Sarah. "Why isn't Tuis here?"

"He went to Stonington last night to enlist in the army," Sarah answered quietly.

"He went to join the army, did he?" the Sheriff commented derisively. "I guess Tuis could see which way the wind is blowing." He looked at Mr. Packer. "Do you still want to take the responsibility for Sharper's children?"

"Yes," Mr. Packer answered, his lips a tight line. "I surely need Charles now that I'm to be short a hand for the harvest."

"I should take the boy at least, but . . . You go ahead and take them, Mr. Packer. It's likely what the court would order, anyway, if you asked for them. But you," he looked at Sarah with narrowed eyes. "You make sure to sign those contracts. And after you've done it, go on back to Niantic where you belong. Your husband managed to get away, but I can still get a writ for you."

"I'll go," Sarah answered, slapping away angry tears.

Sarah hurried the children across the yard to their house. She closed the door and turned around. "Hannah, go pack your things. Go on, don't stand there."

"Why?"

Sarah thrust the girl toward the ladder. "Don't ask questions, just hurry up and do as I say."

"Should I pack, too?'

Sarah looked at her son. "No. I'm taking Hannah with me. You stay here tonight and wait for Mr. Packer to come find you in the morning. Don't go looking for him."

Charles examined his mother through accusing eyes. "All of you will get away, except me. Why are you keeping Hannah? You don't mind giving me away."

"I've told you. The Selectmen won't let me take you," Sarah answered wearily. "They won't care about Hannah and me – they'll be glad to be rid of us and be glad to have your father fighting the British - but they would come looking you."

"We could all go to Brothertown."

"It would take months to walk there. It's too far with the cold and snow coming."

"Take me with you and hide me."

"Where? Everyone knows us, and it won't be long before all of the county hears what you did. The authorities will arrest all three of us if they have to come looking for you. What's the point in that?" Sarah put her hand on the boy's shoulder. "Don't worry, your father grew up with the Packers, and he did fine."

"If they're good enough for Father and me, why aren't they

good enough for Hannah? Why don't you leave her, too?"

"Can you really ask such as that?" Sarah took her hand off of her son's shoulder. Her voice dropped to vehement tones. "Do you think the authorities around here will feel as easy about Hannah as they will about you? Will they be as lenient with her?"

"No." Charles looked away.

"And why not? What have I explained to you?"

"I'm light skinned."

"Light skinned and you have a merry, outgoing disposition that makes friends for you wherever you go. Even if Hannah had your open, easy temper, she can't escape what they think about her every time they look at her complexion and features. And after the mischief you've gotten her into, they'll be even more suspicious of her.

"Besides," Sarah turned away, "if I leave Hannah here, what easy pickings she would be. A young mulatto servant girl, with no parents or relatives to protect her as she grows up . . . There are enough half-English babies in Poquonnock as it is."

Chapter Thirty-Three

Early Evening, The Red Lion Inn, Late October of 1786

Sheriff Richards paused reluctantly at the door of the Red Lion, remembering how he stood in this spot the day of the murder, squinting against the bright hot sun. Now he inhaled crisp salt air, tinged with the scent of wood smoke, watching the sun slowly set. The creeping twilight shadows blurred the outlines of the courthouse on the hill above and the docks in harbor just below, and the bright colors of the autumn leaves clinging to the tree branches gradually disappeared in the gloaming.

In July, Richards had come to the Red Lion to answer the Grand Jury's questions about the murder of a child; tonight he came to meet Mr. Larrabee, at the lawyer's request, to discuss a petition to save the life of another.

When the sun dropped behind Meeting House Hill, Richards pushed the tavern door open and went down the hall. This time, he climbed the back stairs and pushed open the door to the garret. He went up the stairs and knocked on the corner room door. Larrabee greeted him warmly and gestured toward the plates and tankards on the small table.

"Help yourself."

The Sheriff tossed his hat on Larrabee's bed and filled a plate. He pulled a chair up to the fireplace and sank wearily into it, thinking that a good fire was one of the finest consolations of man.

After supper, Larrabee put aside pleasant table talk and got quickly to the point of their meeting.

"I am ready to write the final draft of the petition to the General Assembly, requesting that the magistrates commute Hannah's death sentence on the grounds that she is the ignorant child of an Indian and an African. If I could only assure the authorities that Hannah would be placed in a properly governed household, I believe that the Assembly would be more inclined to grant the petition."

Richards nodded, "To be sure, it would. But not many families would be willing to take a child with her history, especially since she has refused all efforts to help her."

"Yes, I know," Larrabee said with weary disappointment. "Nevertheless, can you think of any family who might even consider taking Hannah in and training her?"

"I've thought about it many a time, but none come to mind. Respectable families would not want to risk the safety of their own children by taking Hannah in. And every household has children coming and going all the time."

"If only," Larrabee mused, "we could find her a situation in which she might be taught to be useful to someone."

"I've thought of that, too, but haven't been able to think of a place. After the example of Widow Rogers' guardianship, none of us would consider the idea of sending Hannah to live with a lone woman again, and it would be unseemly to place her under the guardianship of a single man, whatever his age."

"Of course! Not even a consideration. I mean someone who might employ her in a business, to run errands and clean up."

Richards shook his head, "It wouldn't work. Everyone knows Hannah's history as a petty thief, and no one would trust her to go about town unsupervised. In fact, that is the crux of the matter; she needs constant supervision. Who could provide that, in the unlikely event that we found someone willing to try?" Richards paused. "I had thought of Mrs. Shaw, seeing how she is training Selah . . ."

"Training whom?" interrupted Larrabee.

"Her little slave girl, Selah, about Hannah's age. A young girl of quick mind, a good cook, Mrs. Shaw says, even at her age, and a good seamstress. Mrs. Shaw is preparing the girl for freedom."

Larrabee brightened. "Have you discussed the idea with Mrs. Shaw?"

"No, she is already provided with maidservants enough, and I wouldn't like to ask her to introduce Hannah into Selah's company, seeing as the girls are of an age. If Selah were older and bigger than Hannah, I would have seriously considered seeing Mrs. Shaw about taking the girl, but as it stands, I don't want to ask her to put Selah in harm's way. Anyway, the Shaws are now well acquainted with Hannah and would have asked for her, if they wanted her."

"True enough." Larrabee picked up his ale and sipped thoughtfully. "What about Molly?"

"Molly?"

"Yes, Molly Coit. There is always plenty of work around here to do, and the servants could help Molly supervise the child. Hannah would learn useful household arts, and if Mistress Coit kept the child in the kitchen, away from the guests and their property, the girl wouldn't be tempted by their possessions."

"I suppose," Richards temporized, voice doubtful, "we could ask her."

When Molly looked in to see if they wanted more food or drink, Larrabee asked the innkeeper to spare them a moment.

"I barely have that, sir. Bess is ailing, and Lizzy is running distracted trying to keep up in the kitchen."

"Oh? I'm sorry, but perhaps we can help you. Sit down, please."

Molly pulled out a chair across from Larrabee and sank into it, eyes wary.

"We believe, Mistress Coit, that you could do a great service for the town and for yourself . . ."

Molly began shaking her head regretfully.

"Mr. Larrabee, I know that you would like me to take Hannah Occuish. I would like to oblige you, and my heart wrings for the poor child, sir, but I cannot take her."

Larrabee held up a supplicant hand. "Hear me out, please, Molly."

Molly sighed and nodded.

"I know that it's asking a lot, but your servants can help you supervise and train Hannah."

"Yes, my servants and I are always in the kitchen and the yard," Molly admitted, "but I can't promise that we would be able to keep an eye on Hannah all of the time. From having to do with this child for some time now, I know that she requires constant and diligent attention. And even then, she does not heed admonishment or correction. In any case, I could not promise to provide close supervision of her."

"But maybe being in a different home . . ."

"I doubt it," Molly smiled skeptically and clasped her chapped hands in her lap. "Also, consider her age."

"Her age?"

"Yes. Hannah is about twelve years old now. I admit, over the last few months I have often thought that if she were only younger . . ." Molly stood up, wiping her sweaty hands with her apron. "No, sir, I am sorry, but I can't take her. It's too late."

"Too late? I believed, Molly, that of all people, you might think different from the majority. Twelve is still young."

"Surely you understand what her age means."

Larrabee stared blankly at Molly.

"Hannah is a young girl, soon a young woman, who is both passionate and guileful . . . All day long, strangers come and go, not to mention half the town. Hannah might be misled into carnal sins and if so . . . No, I cannot take her at this age and be responsible for the consequences of her behavior, especially in my position. The Red Lion is a respectable inn, and I intend to protect that well-earned reputation."

Molly put her hand on Larrabee's arm sympathetically. "I'm sorry. If she had been offered to me, instead of the Widow, while still teachable, I would have welcomed her gladly." Molly dropped her hand. "But not now," she said firmly.

Larrabee studied the mingled sadness and anger in Molly's face. "Yes," he said wearily. "I understand."

Mistress Coit walked over to the door, then turned back toward the men. "If ever you hear of an orphan the town wants to bind out, even one too young to work, remember me then, Mr. Larrabee, and I will be glad to try and oblige you."

As Molly's steady footfalls descended the back stairs, Larrabee sighed and shook his head sorrowfully. "That's that," he said. "There are no more options that I know of."

The lawyer turned penetrating eyes on Richards. "Do you believe that Hannah understood - or even now - fully understands what she has done?"

Richards met Larrabee's gaze. "Not entirely, I don't."

"Nor does Mr. Channing."

"All of us who have had anything to do with Hannah," said Richards thoughtfully, "can see that she does not fully grasp her situation, and the fact that she anticipated only a whipping for attacking Eunice suggests that she did not comprehend the seriousness of her crime."

"Yes, you . . ."

"Or," he continued, "as you have mentioned yourself, she may remember that the court gave her uncle a whipping for murdering his wife, call it manslaughter if you will, and assumed she would get the same if caught. In any case, Hannah's attempts to conceal her crime prove that she knew attacking Eunice to be wrong, and despite months in jail, instruction regarding right and wrong, and a trial, she demonstrates no remorse for having done murder and dares to talk back to adults. In any case, Molly has put her finger upon the real issue. There is no place to permanently secure Hannah, and she is near the age of childbearing." Richards paused. "Think of what she is capable of doing to her own child."

"The more I consider Hannah's position," said Larrabee contemplatively, "the more it seems to me that Reverend Channing has been right from the beginning. The Widow Rogers really has done Hannah Occuish a grave disservice in failing to attend to her education and in not governing her own passions in dealing with the child. If the Widow could not manage Hannah, it would have been better to send her to someone able to handle her. Although I disputed the matter with Reverend Channing when I first took up this case, I am fully persuaded to his opinion that Mrs. Rogers is to blame."

"But you founded Hannah's defense on blaming Widow

Rogers! During the trial, as you questioned her, did you not believe the woman culpable?"

Larrabee chuckled wryly, clearly enjoying having taken Richard completely by surprise. "Not really, until now. There seemed to be other circumstances more telling."

Richards waited for Larrabee to explain, but instead, the lawyer stood up and gathered the papers scattered over his side of the table. "Well, true as I now believe Channing's theory, it's no good to think about it anymore. I'll have to fashion the best petition that I can under the circumstances."

Chapter Thirty-Four

Late Evening, The Red Lion Inn, Late October of 1786

The blackened wick flickered in a puddle of wax at the bottom of the candlestick on Larrabee's desk as he penned the last correction on his petition to the General Assembly. There was no point in repeating his defense of Hannah as a child who, having done wrong, had been gravely wronged herself. He knew the magistrates would already be familiar with his defense, and have rejected it. If he could convince the magistrates, who had never seen Hannah, that she was a tender, ignorant child, who did not understand the nature of her actions or the penalty for them, she might have a chance. Perhaps these magistrates would be able to convince New London's representatives to be lenient with a child. He knew this tactic was a long shot. The authorities tended to be skeptical about petitions made on the behalf of convicted murderers.

Larrabee laid his pen on the desk and stood, stretching weary arms over his head. Yawning loudly, he pushed a fresh candle into the candlestick and lit the wick. He sat down and held the petition close to the flame. Numerous cross-outs and additions scratched across the text, disfiguring the pages, but there was no time to make a clean copy. The captain of a Hartford-bound ship who had agreed to deliver the sealed document to the General Assembly planned to leave on the early morning tide.

Running his eye ruefully over the petition, Larrabee tiredly assured himself that his argument transcended the blotches and hatch marks marching across the pages. He adjusted his glasses and tested his hopes by reading the petition aloud.

" *'To the Honorable General Assembly of the State of Connecticut now sitting - Hannah Occuish, a prisoner now imprisoned in the Common Gaol. in the County of New London under sentence of Death for the Horrid Crime of <u>Murder</u> . . . Councill begs leave to represent that although now an infant of the age of Eleven years & six months descended of low parents viz) that her Mother is an <u>Indian Squaw</u> and her Father an <u>Affrican</u> in consequence of which she hath been Totally Deprived of Education not knowing that Christians do make a Distinction between the right hand and the Left on any Occasion.*

" *'The Counsill further states that . . . the Prisoner on being questioned about the Matter . . . made mention that she saw a Number of Boys near the Place the Child Lay Dead and thereupon search was made but no Discovery made that there had been Boys near . . . the day following . . . the Prisoner . . . Confest the same and said that she struck her with a ston by force of which Blow the child fell . . . and to prevent Discovery . . . the Prisoner seized the said Eunice by the throat and by that means Strangled her on being Questioned as to the reason of her Conduct she said a few days before the Prisoner & sd Eunice were together gathering strawberrys and that sd Eunice took from her the strawberry which she had gathered and for which she owed her a whipping but no Intention of Killing and when opportunity Presented she having a ston in her hand struck the said Eunice on the head. . . and thereupon . . . the said stons on the Dead Body in order that it might be supposed the Wall contiguous to where the Dead Body lay fell on the said Eunice and confirm her story but as Discovery was made she prays her betters not to whip her for that she would do so no more. The Councill further states that from the whole Conduct of . . . the Tryall of the Prisoner it appeared that the highest . . . Punishment First in mind of the Prisoner for Mischief don was that of whipping - and as the Prisoner is young and Tinder that Notwithstanding the Verdict of the jury who Tryed said case . . . [in] the minds of many who attended Prisoner all that from the Proofs advised against the Prisoner it did not appear at the time of doing . . . The Prisoner was of that . . . Knowledge and judgment which the Law makes necessary to Supply age to the Degree that it may be said She Could be Judged Capable of doing an act that might be deemed Felony and for the Confirmation of which the Counsill further states that at the time of doing said acts th Prisoner was of the age of Eleven year & six months and no more & wholly Void of a Christian Education Totally Ignorant of a Supreme Being that Punishes Evil & rewards the righteous having no idea of Death . . . [and] through the Whole Course of her Tryall & Condemnation no seeming sense of what was doing or might be don . . .' "[6]*

Larrabee slid his glasses off and leaned back in the chair, feeling as satisfied with his handiwork as possible, under the circumstances.

Whatever the outcome, the lawyer assured himself, *I've done all that I can do. If age alone won't suffice as a mitigating circumstance, ignorance and dependency must hope to serve.*

He carefully folded the splotched pages and wrote the direction on the front, then held a stick of sealing wax over the candle flame. When the stick began to melt, Larrabee dripped hot wax over the fold in the heavy paper. Fanning the paper to cool the seal, he went down the backstairs to the kitchen and shook the stable boy awake. As the sleepy boy ran through the darkness toward the docks, petition clutched in one hand and a small coin in the other, Hannah's lawyer climbed back to his garret chamber overlooking the harbor.

Yawning, Larrabee pulled off his shirt and draped it over the back of the chair. He padded around the room, getting ready for bed, relieved by the knowledge that he wouldn't have to start for Hartford on the morning tide. He had mulled over the idea of delivering the petition in person, but finally decided against it. There wouldn't have been much to do after handing the document to the recording secretary. He could have scurried about, trying to buttonhole busy representatives before the petition came to a vote. And what would he say to cornered magistrates? He didn't have any new evidence, and hadn't thought of a new perspective on either the case or the child. All he could do was confirm the damming evidence against Hannah and - worse - accounts of his client's strange bearing and lack of remorse. He *could* rehash popular attitudes about Indians and Africans, but he had served up that thin gruel in the petition. Better to stay in New London, hoping that Hannah's age would convince the majority of magistrates to be lenient. After all, it would be very difficult for them to condemn a child to death; especially the magistrates from other towns, who had never witnessed Hannah's lack of remorse.

As Larrabee leaned over to blow out his candle, he discovered the second candle already gutted. Glancing around the room, he realized that the diffuse glow of the moon shone into the chamber, smoothing out the sharp edges of the surrounding obstacles, allowing him to move about without stubbing toes and bruising elbows. Pulling back the bedclothes, he slid into bed, and fell to sleep in seconds.

Instead of making the day's journey home, Larrabee decided to wait at the Red Lion for news from Hartford. He didn't expect to be there long, figuring the government would deal expeditiously with such an important matter. His hopes weren't unfounded. Within two weeks, a private letter from the capitol sailed into New London, and came to the inn by the hand of a young sailor on his way home to the North Parish. Thrusting a coin into the youth's hand, Larrabee almost snatched the sealed sheets from his other. He hurried up to the garret room, pried the heavy seal open with trembling fingers, and scanned the opening lines. His eyes slowed at Hannah's name.

I hope that this communication finds you well, and it is my fondest hope that I have been of some service to you. You will be in no way astonished by the intelligence that the General Assembly voted in the negative in regards to Hannah Occuish's petition. You must not blame yourself, as you have endeavored to the utmost to plead your young client's cause, and your arguments on her behalf were much appreciated by the magistrates; however, one cannot marvel at the government's decision, in light of certain deplorable conditions. The situation in the west and in our own state is such that the magistrates clearly long to be rid of responsibility for Indians; even at the cost of extensive portions of land. I do not think you will be completely astonished to learn that Connecticut has voted to give up - here I quote from materials supplied by a friend - 'right, title, interest, & jurisdiction, & claim' to vast tracts of land in the troublesome west. Yet the matter is still not closed. Congress has called on the states to muster a thousand soldiers to send west to quell the 'Indian Nations [who] continue to commit Hostilities on the Western Frontiers of the United States . . . [and] threaten many valuable Settlements with distruction and totally to prevent the survey and Sale of the valuable Lands lying Westward of the River Ohio.' The magistrates voted to raise Connecticut's share of this army and I hope that discontented landless men, who spend their time in idleness and complaint, will take up their duty and volunteer to go to secure the west for settlement.

Larrabee pulled his desk chair back and sat down. He spread the letter on the small table and smoothed the pages before continuing to read.

Yet, I venture to suggest that had the west been in a perfect state of peace, the magistrates would have voted the same regarding your unhappy client. Tho the authorities have ever exercised leniency in matters of lesser crimes committed by Indians, you undoubtedly know that they extract the full penalty of the law for cold-blooded murder. As you feared, the magistrates would not risk pardoning Hannah Occuish without a family willing to take her; and they could not depend upon the overseers of the Indians to take her in hand. Too many of the overseers chronically neglect their duty to care for the welfare of their charges. Time and again their negligence - I will even venture in this private communication to name it criminal negligence - has forced the harassed magistrates to take up subjects touching on the welfare of the Indians better suited to local jurisdiction. You are acquainted with the is-

sue of the Warrups' difficulties, and you well know the state of turmoil in the Mohegan reservation in your own county this past decade. One imagines that the magistrates secretly miss the Crown's interference in matters pertaining to the Indians, now that they have assumed the whole of a responsibility once shared, albeit acrimoniously, between Crown and colony. It is no great thing to conceive their dread that Hannah Occuish might be brought to their attention again, especially for serious crimes. [7]

Larrabee unconsciously nodded his head as the letter slipped from his fingers and fluttered to the floor. The General Assembly's decision had not - could not - surprise him, but the sudden tide of relief washing over him did.

Chapter Thirty-Five

The Jail House, Late October, 1786

"Hannah, the General Assembly has reviewed your petition and rendered their decision." Timothy Larrabee sat down next to his client, wondering why he still looked for a reaction from her. "I'm sorry to tell you," he continued, "that the General Assembly has denied your petition for a commutation of your sentence."

The girl got up, walked to the open window to look through the bars toward the harbor. She closed her eyes and held her face up to the bracing October sea breeze.

"Hannah, don't you understand? This means that you will hang," Larrabee said, his voice tinged with frustration. "The date for your hanging is set for late December, and you must prepare yourself . . ."

Larrabee pulled out a cloth and wiped the sweat gathering on his brow. "I'm sorry, Hannah . . . sorry . . . I believed that perhaps they would consider your age." He steeled himself against a humiliating urge to cringe. "But they have rejected our petition, and there's nothing more that I can do to help you."

To the lawyer's utter astonishment, Hannah shrugged and turned her face back into the wind.

The Jail House, Late October of 1786

Hannah didn't really mind being in jail. She had plenty to eat, and no beatings. Occasionally, she wondered why everyone could not seem to decide what to do with her. First the long, tedious wait for the trial and endless sessions with Mr. Channing, then back to the courthouse two more times to sit, bored, while the adults talked round and round and everyone stared at her. After hours of this, Mr. Larrabee and the others still couldn't seem to make up their minds. Her friends said that the Judge planned to hang her, but Mr. Larrabee said that he wouldn't, because of her age. Now, as far as Hannah could make out, her lawyer had asked some other men to decide if she deserved a whipping, or else he wanted them to figure out how many lashes to give her. She wasn't exactly sure what had been decided, and she didn't care about it either way, having given up worrying about the details months ago.

It seemed silly, how much time they wasted talking and talking about it all. Hannah often wished that they would just bring out the lash and get it over with. Although she enjoyed playing with the children whose parents brought them to the jail to visit her - and especially liked being able to sass adults without fear of the lash - she wanted to escape the boredom of confinement and, most of all, people who wanted to stare at her. All day long, faces popped up at her windows, their voracious eyes enthusiastically consuming the sparse details of her room and her person. She never spoke to these peeping toms, but she often wondered why no one ever punished them. Mrs. Rogers had impressed upon her the impropriety of looking through neighbors' windows, saying nasty peekers hoped to see something titillating.

In fact, her mistress had vigorously employed a switch to impress this lesson on Hannah after she caught the girl gazing through a neighbor's window, about two years after Sarah left Hannah in Quaker Hill. Hannah hadn't exactly understood the word Mrs. Rogers used, but it seemed to her that her mistress meant to say that Hannah had been enjoying looking at her neighbors and that such pleasure was wrong. If she had understood the Widow correctly, Hannah supposed that she deserved the painful switchings. For she had been enjoying herself the night Mrs. Rogers caught her standing in the cold night air, watching Sheriff Richards' brother and his family eating and talking in their kitchen.

Quaker Hill, 1782-1786

Hannah had been sneaking out to look at the Richards and other families for many months before her mistress caught her and put an end to it. Almost a year before, one dusky summer evening, Hannah had glanced over to the Richards' house as she passed by and noticed that the first floor windows framed living, moving pictures within. She stopped, fascinated by a view into a world almost completely unknown to her. As she looked into the Richards' kitchen, faint memories of pleasant, warm kitchens in Poquonnock swam to the surface of her memory.

Hannah began finding excuses to walk past the house in the evening. She would stand in the dark road, feasting hungrily on the forbidden fruit of other peoples' lives, dimly cognizant of the fact that somehow she had lost something or had it taken from her; she didn't exactly know how or by whom.

After a few months, Hannah began creeping into the Richards' yard in order to see more clearly, and when the weather warmed and the family put the sashes up, Hannah would sit under the windows, hidden by the darkness, giving up the pleasure of seeing for the pleasure of hearing. The farm dogs never gave her away as she crept toward the windows. She knew every dog within a mile's radius, and all of them, without exception, even the most aloof and suspicious of the animals, tolerated Hannah and rarely barked at her. Instead of challenging her, most of the local dogs frisked out to the road when they saw her. Hannah always stopped to pet them, speaking gently, as they soaked up all the affection she had to give. Sometimes when Hannah lingered under windows, the dogs came over and dropped down by her side to doze. She ran her hands over their muzzles and backs as the soothing melody of voices drifted out onto the warm air, making her relaxed and drowsy.

The first time angry voices came out of the Richards' windows, Hannah's muscles tensed and she crouched, ready to sprint away into the enveloping darkness, but, to her profound astonishment, the disagreement ended quickly. After a few wary minutes, she settled back down, ears alert. During that year, she was secretly privy to other squabbles, and even overheard children being disciplined, but nothing particularly frightening happened at the sheriff's brother's house. Although she couldn't have explained why, Hannah came to prefer this family, and she began avoiding the houses where loud voices blasted out of the windows and the shadows of tipsy adults stumbled across the yard.

Only inclement weather, company in the house, illness, or the like kept Hannah indoors at night. Once in a while, it crossed her mind that the Widow Rogers might notice her missing and come looking for her. Sometimes the thought worried Hannah. She didn't know what her mistress would do if she caught her lurking around the neighbors' houses. It could be anything from a vague reprimand to a whipping, or even nothing - the Widow was always very unpredictable. Worrying didn't keep Hannah home. She waited until her mistress fell asleep, which she usually did not long after the evening meal. Then, instead of sitting alone, watching the kitchen fire slowly die in the hearth and the darkness creep in from the corners, Hannah would tiptoe out of the lonely house and fly down the dirt road. She was relatively certain that the Widow, being hard of hearing and a sound sleeper, would not wake. If her mistress did wake up, she would assume Hannah had gone upstairs to her pallet in the garret.

As Hannah watched the Richards family night after night, the almost forgotten features of her brother's face began to assemble itself in her imagination. It came bit by bit, like a puzzle, floating gently on the surface of still water, the pieces shifting and blurred. If her mind reached out to grasp the pieces, they floated down and disappeared in the depths, so she learned not to probe, not to struggle to reach them. Eventually, Hannah couldn't have said when, the pieces cohered, the water evaporated, and Charles' face came to her, vivid and alive. After she fully remembered her brother, Hannah began to feel and smell an itchy wool blanket on a pallet in a loft and the soft fabric of a small dress; she heard voices floating up from below, the words indistinct. Her heart and mind yearned toward these impressions, but like the image of Charles, they eluded when she pursued.

One night, someone inside the Richards' house lit a candle

behind a shuttered window. A warm glow suddenly flowed between the cracks, striping the ground. Suddenly, Hannah saw light coming through the wide cracks in the floor of the loft she had shared with Charles. The narrow beams of light shot through the shadowy atmosphere of the coalescing loft, randomly highlighting some details and throwing others deeper into the gloom, softening some and disguising the rest. Now Hannah began to see the rough blanket and the outline of a small cotton dress hanging from a crossbeam, a point of light revealing the bump of the iron nail under the worn cloth.

As the loft began to take shape in her mind's eye, the sounds floating up from the room below transformed into distinct words, and, for the first time in almost two years, Hannah heard her mother's voice. Not the angry voice, arguing with Tuis, or the slurred voice pouring out of the pottery jug, or the broken voice of a sick woman. Watching the play of light through the Richards' shutters, Hannah heard the cadences and tones of a mother enthralling her children with a story; a wife calling welcome to her husband as he walked toward the light of an open door at dusk; a goodwife humming as she crouched by a cooking fire on the flat, hewed stone hearth; a woman whispering in the night, trying not to wake her sleeping children in the loft above her.

For weeks after the night her memory began to awaken, Hannah could hardly wait for darkness, and as soon as the Widow went to bed, the girl sped out of the house, searching for pinpricks of lights along the deserted turnpike. As she watched and listened at the windows, the visions and sounds mingled with her memories of Poquonnock, and Charles, Sarah - even her father, Tuis, and Mr. Packer - lived and breathed again.

During that brief period of time, the fear and confusion holding Hannah's mind and spirit prisoner began to dissipate. She went about her chores more willingly, and she started getting along with the other children in the neighborhood. Mrs. Rogers could hardly believe it when she actually heard the child laugh; and she, who had found loving Hannah impossible and liking her difficult, stopped despairing of the child and finally allowed a fondness for Hannah to creep into her heart.

Chapter Thirty-Six

Quaker Hill, 1782-1786

The Widow thrashed awake in her dark, cold sleeping chamber and, in agony, threw back the heavy quilt. One hand clamped to her throbbing jaw, Mrs. Rogers staggered out of bed and stumbled along the dark hallway and down the narrow back staircase to the kitchen. Legs shaking, she made her way to the barrel by the back door and dipped a clean rag into the icy water. Holding the cold rag between her teeth, she dipped another rag into the water and held it to her hot cheek.

Still shaking, Mrs. Rogers dropped into a chair by the hearth and rocked back and forth, clinching her teeth tighter and tighter on the cloth, wits dulled by pain, unthinkingly intensifying her suffering. As the torment increased, she thought of the small glass bottle of laudanum in the larder. Bracing her hands on the arms of the chair, the Widow leaned forward to hoist herself and accidentally bit down harder. The diseased tooth cracked and crumbled in her mouth, exposing the raw nerve. Screaming, the Widow fell forward, arms out, twisting away from the stone hearth, and crashed onto the floorboards. Gulping for air, she rolled over and managed to get up on her hands and knees and pull herself up to sit on the edge of the hearth. The room spun and her heart pounded.

When her head finally cleared and her heart slowed, Mrs. Rogers took the rag out of her mouth and held it up to her lips. She spit bits of broken tooth, blood, and pus into the cloth, folded it over, and wiped the cleaner part across her lips and chin. A dull, throbbing ache told her where the tooth had been. Standing up slowly to make sure of her legs, the Widow shuffled over to the barrel, poured several dippers of water into a bowl, and laved cool water over her swollen cheek. She dipped fresh water into a tankard, took a large sip, swished the water around her mouth, and stepped to the door to spit the bloodied water outside. She stood in the dark, rinsing and spitting.

The Widow went back inside, and took up the poker. She stirred the embers in the fireplace and tossed kindling on top of them. When the sticks caught fire, she laid two logs on the small flame. Straightening up with a groan, she suddenly noticed Hannah's pallet, and remembered that it had been empty when she came down. Taking a candle, the Widow went to the bottom of the stairs. Maybe the child had gotten over wanting to sleep on a pallet in the kitchen and had gone upstairs to sleep in her bed in the garret.

"Hannah! Come downstairs!"

Cupping one hand around her mouth, she shouted again. "Hannah! Wake up!"

Angrily mindful of the candle and her sore ribs, Mrs. Rogers slowly climbed to the second floor and opened the door to the garret staircase.

"Hannah! What's the matter with you? Can't you hear me? Come downstairs right now!"

Fury overcoming pain, the Widow went up the stairs to the garret and held her candle up to illuminate the room. The light revealed an empty bed, the thin mattress bare. Mrs. Rogers walked the length of the long garret, but did not find Hannah; she went down to the second floor and looked in all of the rooms, did the same on the first, and even went down to the cellar. Nothing.

The Widow leaned out of the kitchen door and called Hannah's name. Annoyed by the silence, she blew out the candle and went outside into the bright moonlight. She walked across the yard to bang on the outhouse door, but found the door ajar, the outhouse empty. Tooth forgotten, she walked all around the house and garden, and went through the barn, calling for Hannah.

When she had searched everywhere without finding any sign

of Hannah, wild fears leapt up in her mind. Did a stranger come into the house and kidnap the girl? Had her mother or father come and taken her away? Maybe Hannah had wandered off and gotten lost in the woods or fallen into the cove!

Mrs. Rogers stood in her yard, wringing her hands, and at that moment, she realized that sometime during the last months she had learned to love Hannah. Before, she had merely been doing her duty by a deserted child, but now she wanted to take care of her.

Almost distraught, the Widow set off briskly down the road, intending to rouse out Alexander Rogers and urge him to form a search party. As she came to the bottom of the hill below her lot, Mrs. Rogers saw a form standing in a neighbor's yard at the top of the hill overlooking the cove. She quickened her pace, and as she drew closer, recognized Hannah. Relieved, Mrs. Rogers stopped to catch her breath. When her breathing returned to normal, she opened her mouth to call out to Hannah, but stopped when the girl began to walk up the sloping yard. Mrs. Rogers hurried down the road in front of the neighbor's property and stopped at the head of the dirt driveway to look up. She could see Hannah walking toward the house, looking as if some invisible force pulled her gently toward the light in the window. Wondering why the child did not go ahead up to the door and knock, the Widow looked curiously at Hannah's face for a clue.

The combination of the light emanating from the window and the moonlight streaming down revealed Hannah's features almost as well as if it were day, and Mrs. Rogers drew a quick breath at the sight; she had never seen Hannah's face like this. The child looked serene, unworried; she looked - the Widow paused to think - she looked completely happy. But no, it was more. She pondered, staring at the child. Then it dawned on her - Hannah looked pleased.

Confused, Mrs. Rogers looked from Hannah to the window. Then a thought struck her like a blow from a closed fist. She had caught Hannah in the act of spying through the window at the unsuspecting people inside; watching them do who knew what! Completely stunned by the revelation, the Widow stood transfixed, openmouthed, as frightening images careened through her bewildered mind. Hannah indulged in unspeakable behavior - practiced the type of perversion that Mrs. Rogers had always believed to be confined to men and boys! And at such a young age! Revulsion rooted the Widow to the spot, and then surging anger ripped her feet from the soil and propelled her forward without her realizing that she had moved. Mrs. Rogers charged up the slope at a half run, over the uneven ground, and headed directly for Hannah.

Hearing the heavy footfalls coming toward her, the girl turned around to see her mistress laboring up the hill, the moonlight revealing a face contorted by an anger that even Hannah had never witnessed. The child's mind did not have time to properly understand what her eyes registered before Mrs. Rogers tripped and fell heavily to her knees. Hannah impulsively dashed forward, holding out her hands to her mistress.

As she ran across the yard to Mrs. Rogers, the light in the window went out. Hannah's young eyes adjusted almost immediately, but the sudden change temporarily blinded the old lady. She groped in the dark, off balance. Seconds later, she felt Hannah's hands in her own, and heard the girl's voice, ragged with anxiety.

"Are you alright?"

Mrs. Rogers grasped the small, warm hands and pulled the child to her in a hug. Kneeling on the ground, she held Hannah close and sobbed sharply, clutching her tighter and tighter. Hannah cried with the Widow.

When they had cried themselves out, Hannah helped Mrs. Rogers to her feet. The Widow looked down at Hannah's face and smoothed the child's hair back with a gentle hand, and Hannah did not pull away.

"You frightened me going off without telling me. I ran about distracted searching for you. Why did you go out? What are you doing?"

"Looking."

"Looking? Looking for what? Did you lose something?"

"No. I just like to look at them."

"Who? The Rogers?"

"Yes. I like the Richards the best, but I like to look at lots of people."

"Lots of . . . You mean that you've done this before?"

To Hannah's eyes, Mrs. Rogers only looked very surprised, not at all angry or upset.

"How often?"

"I look lots of times. Sometimes, I listen."

Flustered, Mrs. Rogers didn't know what to think. She held out her hand.

"Come on, let's go home. We'll talk about this later."

Mrs. Rogers sent Hannah to her bed in the garret and closed the door at the bottom of the stairs. She sat down in her chair by the kitchen hearth, thinking about how to make Hannah understand that she must never again sneak around the neighborhood peeking into windows. She thanked God that she had found Hannah out before someone else had caught her lurking in yards. If she could break Hannah of this terrible habit, the child would be fine from now on.

Chapter Thirty-Seven

Quaker Hill, 1782-1786

While Mrs. Rogers brooded by the fire, Hannah climbed the stairs with a light heart, glad that her mistress seemed to understand about looking, and relieved to know that she didn't have to sneak out anymore. As she got into bed, Hannah thought about Mrs. Rogers going to the back door when they got home to rinse her mouth with water and spit blood into the yard. When she asked what was wrong, Mrs. Rogers briefly told her about the toothache and falling in the kitchen, and then sent her up to bed. The thought of Mrs. Rogers falling - twice - alone, upset Hannah, and she decided that she wouldn't go out looking for a while. She'd stay home, at least for the next few nights, in case her mistress needed her. Hannah pulled her covers up around her chin and almost immediately fell asleep.

Mrs. Rogers lifted Hannah's breakfast bowl out of the tub of hot water and handed it to the girl to dry.

"I've been thinking about last night."

Hannah dried the bowl and put it on the dresser shelf.

"Yes, Ma'am."

"I don't want you to go out at night."

Hannah held the rag in hand, waiting for the next wet dish.

"Yes, Ma'am."

"You understand, now, no more going out at night."

"Yes."

"Good," Mrs. Rogers relaxed. Perhaps Hannah wasn't as bad as she first thought.

"Yes, because of your tooth."

"My tooth?" asked the Widow, perplexed. "What has my tooth got to do with it?"

"You need me home with you while you're sick with your tooth."

"No, that's not what I meant. I mean to say that I don't want you looking into the neighbors' windows. It's wrong to do."

"Wrong?" Mrs. Rogers hadn't said anything about it being wrong last night.

"Yes, it's immoral. You must never do it again."

"Never?" Hannah's voice scaled up. "I must never see them again?"

"Never see . . . what are you talking about? You'll see all of the neighbors often enough. You don't need to peek into their windows to see them."

Hannah's face suddenly contorted, and she burst into tears. Mrs. Rogers tried to make sense of her fractured babblings about a river, a loft, her mother, a shell, but she had no idea what the child was talking about. When she heard the name Charles, Mrs. Rogers began to suspect that this "looking" was in some way connected to the child's brother. She froze when she heard Hannah mention Mary Fish. Now Mrs. Rogers thought that she understood. Charles must have been a peeping tom, and had taken his little sister along on his indecent forays. Perhaps he had been spying in on young Mary Fish when he decided to attack her, and he must have used his little sister as a decoy. That had been the problem all along: Hannah had been tainted by associating with her brother, and now she was following his example.

"Hush, hush. Listen. Listen to me," she wrapped her arms around the anguished child, and rocked her gently back and forth. "Shush, now."

Hannah relaxed into the Widow's arms. "There now. You must not go out at night any more. Someone will catch you, and I won't be able to help. You must stay home with me."

Hannah began to cry again, but the Widow told herself that

she must be firm with the child. For months, her son had been dropping hints about her inconsistent disciplining of Hannah. Heretofore, she had ignored his annoying meddling, but now she had to admit that he might have a point. She determined that she could not afford to be indecisive when Hannah's very soul hung in the balance.

"No more of this, now. No more tears, and you will stay in nights," she said briskly, steeling herself against the mute pleading in the child's face.

"None of those big eyes, Hannah. You have chores to do, miss, and you get about them."

Hannah stood immobile, and dropped her gaze to the floor.

"Did you hear me, Hannah?"

When Hannah didn't answer, Mrs. Rogers raised her voice. "Did you hear me? Look at me!"

Hannah turned up vacant eyes, and nodded woodenly. The Widow's heart sank. The new face, the open look that had softened Hannah's features for the last month or so was gone, and the withdrawn expression that Mrs. Rogers knew so well was back. She smothered a soft cry, desperately wanting to reach across the unseen void that had reopened between them to grasp the child and pull her to safety. Mrs. Rogers opened her mouth to give in - to allow Hannah to go out at night and peek into windows. She pulled herself up short. What an appalling thought! If she relented, what would become of the both of them?

Mrs. Rogers sat down, hands tightly gripping the arms of the chair. Pain radiated from her sore, aching jaw.

"Get me a cold, wet rag for my tooth."

Hannah dully obeyed, and throughout the day, she did everything else that her mistress told her to do without comment or hesitation. That night, when the Widow sent her up to the garret to sleep, Hannah wordlessly dragged herself up the narrow stairs. Mrs. Rogers stationed herself in the kitchen.

She caught Hannah trying to sneak out later that night. After taking a switch to the girl's legs, Mrs. Rogers sent the child back to the bed in the lonely, dark garret. The punishment did not work. The next night, Mrs. Rogers caught Hannah trying to leave the house and whipped her again. She caught her the next evening and the one after that. Every time Mrs. Rogers caught Hannah attempting to sneak out, she switched the girl harder, drawing more shrieks and blood.

After a couple of weeks of whippings, Hannah stayed in her garret bed at night, nursing her raw legs. Believing that she had broken Hannah of a disgusting, lewd habit, Mrs. Rogers decided that she could trust her away from the house and yard, and sent Hannah on an errand that took her past Alexander Rogers' house.

As Hannah approached the house, their dogs rushed out to greet her. Tongues lolling, they frisked happily, glad to see her after such a long absence. Hannah swooped down, picked up a stone, and shied it at the nearest dog, hitting him a sharp blow on the chest. The dog yelped more in surprise than in pain, and dashed away. The others paused, unsure what to do. Hannah stomped her foot and yelled at them, until they retreated toward the house. They stood in a pack, looking confusedly at Hannah as she walked past. When she disappeared up the road, the dogs turned and trotted away.

Chapter Thirty-Eight

Quaker Hill, The Widow's House, December 19, 1786

Mrs. Rogers spent the night before Hannah's execution alone in the house overlooking the cove. She had been living by herself since the morning Hannah rode away behind Sheriff Richards. The Widow's son had offered his home to her, but she brusquely refused his offer, saying that she preferred her independence and planned to live in her own house until death took her from it. She would not let anyone come to live with her, but she did promise her son that if the day ever came when she couldn't take care of herself, then she would consider it. Secretly, Mrs. Rogers thought that day would never come. Like everybody else in the world, the Widow planned to stay vigorous until she died peacefully in her sleep.

That wish seemed to be coming true, so far. At the advanced age of sixty-eight, she could walk for miles without tiring, lift heavy buckets of water out of the well, go up and down the stairs, and do all of her own cooking, baking, and washing. Of course, doing for one instead of a household didn't take as much energy, but she knew plenty of people her age who spent the winters in a chair by the fire, supervising the children and grandchildren hustling around the house and farm.

Mrs. Rogers pointed out all of these salient facts to her son whenever he broached the topic of her coming to live with him, forcing him to eventually concede the truth of what she said. Nevertheless, he could not resist mentioning his spare room at the end of every visit to her. Tonight had been no different.

"Before you sing the litany of your powers, Mother, which we all know full well," he assured her, "let me ask you this. What if you get ill? It could be hours, even a day or two until someone found you."

"It could happen so, yes, but your wife could get sick when you are gone on business and not be found for hours or days. What's the difference? Besides, I never ail, and accidents . . . Well, no use to worry. Anyone can have an accident."

Once again, her son had to give in to his mother's superior logic. "As you wish," he said. "But remember the room is yours for the asking."

Smiling at the memory, Mrs. Rogers walked over to the window to look out at the white caps tossing on the cove. She had always loved this view, and had often, during the past months of sleepless nights, sat by the window, watching the softly undulating water until lulled to sleep in her chair. The December sky looked like it might bring snow in the next day or two, and the Widow decided to keep her chickens in the coop tomorrow.

She snapped the curtain over the glass and walked restlessly into the front hall. She pulled on the door. Finding it secure, she prowled the first floor, stopping to examine every window, and then went and did the same on the second story. Worrying that the garret window hadn't been properly latched, she opened the narrow garret door and put her foot on the first step.

Oh, that window is fine, I know it. She closed the door and hurried down the back stairs to the kitchen to make a pot of tea.

Mrs. Rogers sat at the kitchen table, sipping her tea, and listening to the wind blowing in from the river. Shivering, she got up to put more wood on the fire, and discovered that she had forgotten to bring more in. Tossing a shawl over her shoulders, she went out into the cold yard and made several trips back and forth to the woodpile, chastising herself. Because of her neglect, the fire would burn pretty low before the wood spread out on the sides of the wide hearth would be dry enough to burn without smoking.

As the Widow bent down to hold cold hands closer to the dwindling flames, Hannah's face popped into her mind. She jerked upright and turned abruptly toward the table to pour another cup of tea, then grabbed Mr. Greene's newspaper, shook it open, and sat down. A few minutes later, she cast the newspaper aside and got up. She started toward the front hall, intending to check the front door lock, but remembered that she had already done that job.

Seeing as she was on her feet, Mrs. Rogers selected the least damp log and put it on the fire. When the log began to smoke, she adjusted the damper, but the wind pushed the smoke back down into the house. Coughing and sputtering, Mrs. Rogers hurried across the kitchen and flung the door open. A draft of cold night air flowed into the room and pushed the warm air and smoke up the chimney. When the air finally cleared, she closed the door and readjusted the damper.

The log began to burn cleanly. Mrs. Rogers fetched her mending bag and pulled her chair close to the glowing fire. As the needle pulled together the jagged edges of a tear in her best dress, the Widow reviewed her latest conversation with her son, congratulating herself for arguing her case so well. Just before he had left tonight, she reminded him again about her excellent health, and, once again, he had to concede her point.

No, I am never sick, the Widow repeated triumphantly to herself, *except for my teeth.*

Casting her mending aside, she got up and stood indecisively for a few seconds. She looked down at her hands, surprised to see them wringing, and felt even more surprised at the tears splashing down on them. The Widow almost never cried.

Of course, she had shed copious tears when her parents and husband died and sobbed heart-wrenchingly the day they buried her twin, Hannah. She missed Hannah so much! Mrs. Rogers ran the back of her hand across her wet face, finally admitting to herself that Hannah Occuish was the Hannah she missed. She missed her, despite the fact that the child had grown increasingly remote and difficult. No matter how hard she tried during the past year, the Widow had not been able to reclaim her original indifference.

Mrs. Rogers sat down in the chair by the hearth, and she did not get back up, except to throw a log on the fire, for the rest of the night.

* * *

A myriad of thoughts scrambled through Mrs. Rogers' mind while she kept vigil for Hannah Occuish through the night. She thought about the small child that Sarah had brought to her. Although Hannah didn't put herself forward, anyone could see that the child had a quick mind. A discerning person, as Mrs. Rogers had always considered herself to be, could see that the problems of the parents had already exacted a toll on the daughter. Sarah Occuish seemed too indulgent and irritable by turns, a practice the Widow condemned in a parent. She thought it no wonder that the child startled too easily and cried and clung to her mother more than most girls her age.

When Hannah's mother asked the older woman to take care of her small daughter for a spell, Mrs. Rogers never hesitated to take on the responsibility. She felt confident that she could do the child a world of good in just a few weeks.

After Sarah left, Hannah often cried during the day for her mother and brother, but Mrs. Rogers told her that it was useless to cry. Her mother had gone away on business and would be back sooner or later. If Hannah asked which she thought it might be, the Widow admitted that she did not know, but guessed that they would see Sarah within the year. As for Charles - Mrs. Rogers instructed Hannah to wait for her mother or father to come and take her to Groton to see him and then gave the weeping child a small chore to do.

Disappointed by the results, Hannah stopped asking about Charles and her parents and rarely cried for them during the day. If she did and couldn't offer a reasonable explanation for her tears - a bump, a stomachache, or some such childish ailment - Mrs. Rogers always fell back on the remedy of work as a cure for sorrow. A sound sleeper, Mrs. Rogers never knew how often in the first six months Hannah awoke in the dark garret to cry for hours, frightened and alone in her bed.

After months of no word from Sarah, the Widow knew that the job of raising Hannah had fallen to her. She didn't relish the idea. After a year of Mrs. Rogers' careful childrearing methods,

Hannah showed no signs of turning into the girl her mistress had once envisioned her becoming. Instead of being tractable and grateful, Hannah disobeyed Mrs. Rogers, went about with a morose face, and quarreled with the neighborhood children.

The Widow considered herself a kind person and marveled that after a year of living in her house, Hannah didn't seem the least bit fond of her. Mrs. Rogers attributed the child's unappreciative attitude, lack of emotion, and stubbornness to her Indian and African blood and vowed to overcome the unfortunate aspects of Hannah's nature by educating her. The spark of interest in the girl's eyes gratified her mistress the first time she opened the speller on the table in front Hannah.

Believing that a mulatto child was bound to have trouble learning, Mrs. Rogers decided to go slowly, and set a goal of teaching Hannah two letters a month. They spent an hour each day during the first week of lessons reviewing the letter A, followed by a week of studying B and two weeks of reviewing both letters. Three months later, when they had barely finished with G and H, Hannah had become quite adept at manufacturing excuses to avoid study time. As weary of the classroom as her pupil, the Widow stopped the lessons. Shaking her head, her mistress had to admit that her suspicions that dark-skinned people did not take well to reading had been correct. Even so, she had always believed that she, Mrs. Rogers, could succeed where others might fail, and she resented Hannah for not trying harder.

If Hannah could not learn to read, she must be read to. At first the Widow read aloud at night before bed, but instead of being enthralled by the beautiful language of the King James Bible, Hannah fell asleep. She tried reading to the child in the morning or afternoon, but Hannah's attention wandered, and Mrs. Rogers usually ended up slamming the book closed and ordering Hannah off to work.

During Hannah's second year in Quaker Hill, Mrs. Rogers began sending her small servant on errands around the neighborhood. Hannah seemed happier after that. Then came the dreadful night when Mrs. Rogers caught Hannah peeking into Alexander Rogers' windows. Even now, it amazed her to think that she did not drop down in the Rogers' yard in a fit of stroke. Instead, when others might have given up on the child, she'd taken Hannah home and tried to teach her better, tried to protect her. She even sat up of nights to guard the child from her own depraved impulses, and had finally made Hannah see reason and stop trying to sneak out of the house at night.

Of course, the Widow didn't blame Hannah, certain that Charles had taught his wicked habit to his innocent sister. But the habit was so ingrained, Hannah refused to stay home at night until Mrs. Rogers applied the switch quite firmly.

Hannah's remote attitude came back ten-fold, and nothing Mrs. Rogers did reached the child. One day, the Widow discovered a small item of hers, nothing of any real value, secreted under Hannah's bed clothes in the garret. When questioned, Hannah stared at the floor and shrugged. After a few more objects turned up missing around the house, Mrs. Rogers had to admit that Hannah had taken up stealing. Hoping to break her of taking things that did not belong to her, Mrs. Rogers kept the child's hands busy with even more work, and she stayed on top of Hannah to make sure that she did her chores. No matter what the Widow did, Hannah stole whenever the opportunity presented itself, seeming to take some kind of pleasure in the act.

Her initial success with the switch in mind, the Widow cut a supple branch from a bush in the yard and kept it handy by the kitchen door. After that, communication between mistress and servant degenerated into the Widow's reactions to Hannah's misdeeds. As the battle of wills between the two escalated, Mrs. Rogers began to feel herself the loser. She threw away the switch and got out the lash.

With each whipping, Hannah retreated deeper into her interior world, and the Widow became more obsessed with the idea of reforming her. The struggle between mistress and servant spilled out of Mrs. Rogers' house and into the neighborhood when Hannah began to steal from the neighbors and pick on smaller children.

Once in a while, Mrs. Rogers had a sneaking suspicion that she might be too hard on Hannah, but she angrily refused to entertain such a notion for long. When her own son ventured to suggest that she ease up on the child, the Widow snapped that Hannah forced her hand and briskly advised him to mind his own business.

Now Hannah would die in a few short hours. Too tired to obey the impulse to jump up and find something useful to do, the Widow sat, mind reeling, until the pink glow of sunrise on the water brightened the window.

Rocking back and forth by the cold hearth, tears began to run down the Widow's face.

"Hannah, oh, Hannah!" Frightened, she tried to get a hold of herself, to stop these foolish useless tears, to tell herself that Hannah had brought the hanging upon herself, that if she had only listened, had only obeyed she would be asleep in her bed in the garret. Loud, racking sobs tore the Widow's chest, and her eyes swelled to mere slits. Trembling hands ineffectively wiping the tears and mucus running down her face and chin, she struggled to draw breath, and almost slid out of her chair, but pulled back and slumped forward. Head curled to her knees, the Widow cried herself to utter exhaustion.

Disturbed by the feeble afternoon sunlight coming through the kitchen window, the Widow stirred. Slowly fighting her way to consciousness, she rubbed her hands across her face, and bracing her stiff back with two hands, got up out of the chair. She hobbled over to the table to rest her palms on it for support and squinted at the clock on the mantel. Hannah was dead.

During the many years left to her, Mrs. Rogers attempted to soothe her conscience by imagining that she had cried that long, terrible night through for Hannah Occuish - but in her heart, she always knew better.

Chapter Thirty-Nine

The Red Lion Inn, December 20, 1786

Molly snapped the curtains over the front windows of the Red Lion, obliterating Main Street from view, unable to stomach the thought - never mind the sight - of people sporting their best clothes to an execution.

"Mistress Coit, we're going now."

Molly turned and ran an impassive eye over Bess' finery. "Make sure to come back early. The inn will be crowded tonight, and I'll need your help."

"We will," Bess promised.

The stable boy trailed down the front steps behind Bess and the stableman. He stopped and stood forlornly in the front yard, enviously watching them hurry up Main Street without him. Blowing a gusty sigh as the excited couple disappeared around the corner of Main and Court Street, James cut his gaze across the Parade, hoping to enjoy at least a glimpse of Hannah Occuish being carted from the jail to the church. Seeing no one, he glumly assumed that he'd missed that excitement, too. It wasn't fair. Everybody - at least almost everybody - would be at the hanging without him.

"Someone has to stay back and mind the horses," Molly had replied, turning a deaf ear to James' eager pleas for permission to watch the execution. "And a hanging is no place for a child," she added, lips pursed sardonically.

"But I've heard it said that servants should go and see . . ."

"Not by me, you haven't, and you, sir, will not go. 'Tis better

214

for all of us that you stay here, where you belong. I don't want you having nightmares and waking the house with your screaming."

"But the sermon," James wheedled, "surely the sermon will do me good."

Molly cocked an eyebrow. "If I know Mr. Channing's mind as well as I think I do, he will not be looking for you in the pews."

Now, while his friends enjoyed a holiday, James had a day of work to look forward to. A whole day with only Mistress Coit and Lizzy for company.

He sighed again.

"James!" Lizzy's face popped into the open doorway. "What are you doing out front? I've been calling out back for you these past five minutes! Run and fill the kitchen water barrel."

Casting a final longing glance at the throng headed up Court Street to the Congregational Church, James turned and dragged his feet toward the well at the back of the inn.

Lizzy closed the door and walked slowly toward the kitchen, wearing a puzzled face. She'd slipped on her work gown that morning and gone downstairs to her usual tasks in deference to Molly, even though she didn't understand Mistress Coit's unusual decision to stay home. As far as Lizzy could see, a murder had been done, and the murderer must answer for it. Although she didn't particularly want to see the hanging, the young woman had looked forward to hearing Mr. Channing make sense of it all.

Oh, well, the maid thought, dipping water out of the replenished kitchen barrel, *I'll just have to wait for the sermon pamphlet to know what he really said.*

Lizzy crouched down and reached over the hot flames with a long iron hook and pulled the fireplace crane toward her. She poured the water into the large iron kettle hanging on the crane and pushed it back over the fire.

Molly came into the room. "I see you found James."

The maid straightened up. "Yes, he was out front enjoying the commotion and his own misery in equal measures."

Smiling to herself, Molly unwrapped a new sugarloaf, folded the paper, and put it aside to use later for dying cloth. She snipped off a large chunk of the hard sugar and handed it to Lizzy.

"I want me some shortcakes with our tea."

Wondering at her mistress' unusual hankering, Lizzy broke up the sugar and pounded it fine. Molly dumped the sugar into a bowl and mixed in the rest of the ingredients. She rolled out the dough, cut twelve large rounds, sprinkled them liberally with sugar, and put them on the reflector. She pushed the reflector next to the fire, gauging the heat with an out-held hand.

When the shortcakes turned golden brown, Molly slipped them onto a blue-willow platter and put the platter on the kitchen table. She measured loose tea into a squat teapot, poured hot water over the fragrant leaves, and covered the pot with a cozy.

"Sit, Lizzy, and have your tea."

Lizzy shook dish water from her hands and sat down opposite Molly. Cradling the warm cups in their hands, maid and mistress drank their tea and ate shortcakes in companionable silence.

Molly carried her second cup of tea to the small room adjoining the kitchen. She sat down in her father's chair and flipped open the heavy inn ledgers. Relishing the current of warm air from the kitchen fire swirling around her feet, Molly dipped her quill into the inkwell and went to work with a calm mind.

Like her friend, Mrs. Douglas, Molly had resigned herself long ago to the fact that Hannah would end up on the gallows. As she had said to Mrs. Shaw and Mrs. Douglas last summer, the men would do what they had to do, and the women would do what they could. Sitting in the office, Molly felt confident that everyone had done just that. Although she felt a jumble of pity, anger, and sorrow, she did not feel guilty or remorseful about Hannah. Like her friends, Molly Coit had never even heard of Hannah until the day Richards rode into town with her clinging on behind him. After that, Molly had done all that she could for the girl.

Reckoning finished, Molly slapped the ledger closed with a satisfying thump. She got up and went out to the kitchen lean-to to whisk the straw broom over the smooth brick floor. Sweeping the dirt into neat piles, Molly thought about a conversation she had with Sheriff Richards shortly after the trial in October. Eyes averted, he confessed that he had known something about Hannah's wretched life before she murdered Eunice Bolles.

Richards' admission of guilt earned him a small portion of Molly's pity - but only a very small one. She saved the lion's share for Eunice and Hannah, and Molly naturally felt very sorry for the Bolles. After all, they had lost a child, but even they, in her opinion, shared culpability for their daughter's death. If they hadn't stood by with all the rest of Quaker Hill and let Mrs. Rogers abuse Hannah, maybe Eunice would still be alive. Instead of remonstrating with Mrs. Rogers, the Bolles probably told themselves that the way the Widow treated her servant was none of their concern. Well, Hannah Occuish had certainly made it their business.

Molly swept the small piles of dirt onto an old newspaper, twisted the paper into a small bundle, and put it in the old basket by the door, which James emptied every night before he went to bed. She took the dirty broom outside and smacked it against the back of the house to knock the dirt off of the bristles. Seeing dust still clinging to them, she gave the broom another vigorous wallop. After a second inspection revealed clean bristles, Molly went inside and upended the broom in a corner. She wiped her hands clean on her apron.

Wrapping her shawl tighter around her shoulders, Molly stepped back into the December cold and went outside to look for James. She found him in the gloomy stable, dutifully mucking the stalls, a pouting countenance giving eloquent expression to his feelings.

"James!" Molly called, hand over her mouth to conceal a smile.

The boy looked up. "Ma'am?"

"Come in for your tea when you've finished. We have shortcakes with sprinkled sugar."

James' face lit up. "Yes, Mistress."

Chapter Forty

The Jail House, December 20, 1786

Although she still felt compassion for Hannah, Mrs. Douglas had given up hope that the girl would shake off her lethargy and do something to save herself. Mrs. Douglas also knew that her husband had either not come to the same realization, or had been unable to admit it to himself. Only last night, standing by the blazing kitchen fire to warm his hands, Ebenezer said that he hoped Hannah would ask God's forgiveness before the execution the following day.

"Maybe tonight or tomorrow morning she'll be penitent. It wouldn't be too late even on the gallows."

Mrs. Douglas studied her husband pityingly, unable to fashion a reply to such an unrealistic comment.

"You think I'm being notional," he continued, "but a minister's words have been known to move even the most hardened criminal at the last hour."

"True enough, Ebenezer, but nothing seems to stir this child. She lives deep within herself, and words don't seem to reach her."

"If Mr. Channing's sermon doesn't touch her, maybe the sight of the gallows will jar Hannah awake."

Mrs. Douglas looked doubtful. "Perhaps, Ebenezer. I certainly hope so." She paused, choosing her words carefully. "Whether or not Hannah repents, you have certainly done all that you could to comfort her." She walked over and put protective arms around him. "You have no cause to reproach yourself, whatever happens."

The jailer sank down into his favorite chair. "It's not me, exactly, that I'm thinking about, or at least it is and it isn't. I didn't know that the Widow was mistreating Hannah. I leave it to her neighbors to ponder in their hearts what they knew and did nothing about. I don't fault myself, but I do tremble when I think that this could have happened to one of my children . . ."

"What, being murdered?" Mrs. Douglas asked.

Douglas shook his head. "No. Being in Hannah's position."

"Mr. Douglas! How can you say such a thing?!" Mrs. Douglas drew back in amazement. "One of our children a murderer! Has worry robbed you of your senses?"

"No, no. Not a murderer. I mean orphaned. I hate to think what might become of our children if we both die while they are still young."

"How can a man, well-provided with kin left and right, even think about such a thing? We could trust one or more of them to take care of our children."

"Hannah's mother trusted her to others. She did the right thing by leaving Hannah with people she believed better able than she to raise her daughter. All of them - the Widow, her family, and neighbors - all of them failed Sarah. And Hannah."

"Our kin wouldn't act like the Widow! They're all kind people."

"I would have said the same thing not long ago, but, now I'm not so sure. If by some mischance our children ended up with Uncle . . ."

"Uncle!" Mrs. Douglas gasped. "I never considered . . . No."

"You never know what can happen."

"But even so, surely the rest of the family would . . ."

"Would have to know he mistreated the children before they could do anything to help them, and frightened children don't tell tales for fear of reprisal."

Mrs. Douglas nodded mutely, stricken to the very core of her being. She couldn't bear to think of her children sequestered on their irascible, moody uncle's remote farm, with no one to gainsay him. "Yes . . . " she whispered.

"I'm sorry. I shouldn't have brought this up." Douglas looked at his wife remorsefully. "Don't fret. We're well enough and I plan to speak to my brothers and sisters and yours this week. I'll ask them to make sure that if something happens to both of us, they won't let the children go to Uncle." He paused. "But in Hannah, I can see the possible fate of any friendless young orphan who falls into unkind hands." He paused. "And the very thought haunts me."

Mrs. Douglas stood at Hannah's cell door window, breakfast tray in hand. Instead of taking the food in to the girl, she went back to the kitchen and put the tray on the table.

"Hannah is still crying and pacing," she told her husband.

"I know," he replied. "I can't understand the change in her. After months of indifference, she has suddenly taken to clinging to every visitor and counting off the days until her execution. Her feet have been wearing a groove in the floorboards and she's been crying for days. She claims to be worried about her soul, but still won't call on God."

Mrs. Douglas shook her head sadly. "It's not so mysterious."

Douglas drew back in a gesture of surprise. "It's not? It's certainly a mystery to me."

"Hannah has a great deal of first-hand experience with being punished, so she can easily imagine an angry, chastising God. She hasn't experienced much love or tenderness in her life, so how can she conceive of a loving, forgiving God? I believe she thinks asking him for mercy is as useless as expecting the neighbors or someone else to rescue her from the Widow."

The jailer looked away, literally squirming in his chair. "And so now she'll go to hell."

"Maybe."

Douglas' eyes shot up. "Of course, she'll go to hell! She's an unrepentant murderer! If that doesn't qualify her for hell, what does?"

"Having done murder qualifies her for execution, but hell . . . I don't know," said Mrs. Douglas hesitatingly. "I don't presume to tell God how to manage his business, but it seems to me that

Hannah is so damaged by abuse, she can't be expected to . . ."

"Careful!" Douglas warned. "You're treading on dangerous ground. I hope you haven't expressed these notions to anyone else."

"Just to Mr. Channing."

"*Just* to Mr. Channing you say!" Douglas croaked, thunderstruck. "What did he tell you?"

"He heard me out, and said my questions would bear thinking about."

The jailer's mouth fell open.

"What should we do, Ebenezer?"

"What should we do?" The jailer shook his head like a dazed man recovering his senses. "What do you mean? There's nothing we can do."

"I believe there is. Hannah's terrified now. She'll be even more so during the sermon and the . . . the execution preliminaries. We have to do something to help her," Mrs. Douglas insisted.

"Such as?"

"'Tis cruel, how frightened she is."

"Some would say 'twas cruel to bash in a child's head with a stone," the jailer reminded his wife. "Eunice must have been as terrified when Hannah rained blows down on her. You do remember the Sheriff saying she quoted Eunice's pleas for mercy when confessing."

Mrs. Douglas cast an impatient look at her husband. "Of course, I remember. Who could forget such as that? But that's not the point at this moment, as you know very well."

Douglas threw up his hands in a gesture of surrender. "What is the point, then? The child is scared, a normal state of affairs for someone about to be hanged."

"You pipe a different tune from the one you played last night!"

"Not really." The jailer said, voice weary. "I'm just hunting for the right key."

"What we have today is an eleven-year-old . . ."

"Twelve."

"Twelve, if that number is more comforting to you. What we

have is a twelve-year-old girl who is to be executed this morning, and before that happens, she will be frightened out of her wits for several hours. That's an unnecessary cruelty. We can only be grateful that she doesn't know what it means to be hanged, or she would be in screaming hysteria from now until the noose stops her voice."

"What do you want of me?"

"Permission to give her a large dose of laudanum."

"Give her . . ." Douglas stared at his wife. "You can't be serious."

"Why not? Prisoners go to the gallows in England floating on a sea of ale and beer."

"This isn't England."

"And you will tell me that condemned prisoners in America are never given the comfort of a drink before they're led to the gallows?"

"A tankard or two of ale is not the same as laudanum."

"What does it matter? Tell me, who hasn't taken a dose of laudanum for a toothache, a broken bone, or for some other dreadful pain? Are those conditions worse than Hannah's is now, and will be, today?"

Douglas winced, unwilling spectator to a vision of the rope cutting into Hannah's neck. "Give her a drink or two, but, mind you, don't let her get so drunk that everyone will notice." He got up. "It won't help with the hanging, though, she'll be sober by then."

Mrs. Douglas maintained a steady gaze at her husband's face. "Laudanum."

"No, the same as the rest, a drink or two."

"She's not the same as the rest; she is a child."

The couple stared each other down. Mrs. Douglas' eyes dropped first. "Two drinks. One now and one just before she leaves."

The jailer nodded.

***

Reverend Channing knocked on the kitchen door, just as Mrs. Douglas set a large tankard of ale on the table.

"Come in, sir," she said, wiping her hands nervously on her apron, turning to stand in front of the table. "My husband took you in to see Hannah?"

"Yes." The minister stood in the hall doorway, hat in hand.

"Did she say anything?"

Channing shook his head.

"I'm sorry, Mr. Channing, but it's not your fault. You did everything you could for Hannah."

"Did I?" he asked. "I pray that I did."

"What else could you have done?"

"That's what I've been wondering for weeks, Mrs. Douglas. . . Is that for Hannah?" he asked, looking behind her.

Spine stiffening, Mrs. Douglas nodded her head guardedly.

"A good plan, I think, though there are those who wouldn't agree with me."

Mrs. Douglas relaxed. "They need never know."

"No," said Channing, a ghost of a smile on his lips. "No, they don't."

"I suppose those who would object think Hannah should have her wits about her until the end," said Mrs. Douglas, "but I don't think it's important for her to be alert to the end. Few of us are."

"Probably not," the minister said, turning his face away. "I prepared two sermons, and it grieves me to say that I will have to give the one that I had hoped to toss into the fire."

"This is a hard day for you, too." Mrs. Douglas put a sympathetic hand on the young man's forearm.

"Your husband is outside with the Sheriff, getting the cart ready to take Hannah to the church," Channing said, abruptly changing the subject. "I need to speak to him. I imagine it will be a while before he'll be in to get her." Channing put on his hat. "Goodbye, Mrs. Douglas."

Before Mr. Channing had pulled the door fully closed, the jailer's wife grabbed the ale and hurried down the hallway to let herself into Hannah's cell.

"Stop that pacing and come over here and drink this," she held the tankard out toward the girl, but Hannah didn't seem to have registered the woman's presence.

"Hannah," Mrs. Douglas commanded, voice firm. "Come over here and drink this."

Hannah flinched and looked over.

"Come here and drink," she repeated.

The girl walked over.

"Take it, child."

Hannah reached out both hands.

"Go ahead," urged Mrs. Douglas. "Hurry and drink it all down."

Hannah put the rim to her lips. She sipped slowly at first, then began to gulp, mouth dry from hours of crying. Hannah leaned her head back and drank to the dregs. She stumbled over and sat on the edge of the bed.

Mrs. Douglas picked up the white dress she'd laid over the chair that morning. "Put this on, Hannah."

The girl stared at her, face befuddled.

"Here, stand up so I can help you."

Before she finished changing Hannah, Mrs. Douglas heard her husband and Sheriff Richards come inside from the yard. She walked quickly to the door and called down the hall. "Hannah's changing her dress. Wait there, and I'll bring her out to you in a few minutes."

Mrs. Douglas turned her back to the closed door. Walking quickly toward Hannah, she took a bundle out of her apron pocket. She unwrapped a small glass bottle and a silver spoon and tipped the bottle to pour a brimming spoonful of thick, syrupy liquid.

"Quick, open up your mouth and take this." Mrs. Douglas whispered, holding the full spoon to the girl's lips. "Hurry."

Hannah tasted the syrup and frowned. "I don't have a tooth-ache."

"Don't fret, 'tis good for more than just a bad tooth. Take it now," Mrs. Douglas urged.

Hannah swallowed the laudanum.

"Good. That's a good girl, Hannah."

Mrs. Douglas pulled the small bundle out of her pocket and put it on the tray with Hannah's uneaten breakfast and went to the kitchen. She took the empty tankard off of the tray, filled it to the brim with ale, and leaning her head back, drank it to the bottom. She wiped her mouth with her apron and got up. After putting the bottle of laudanum on a high shelf, she went to her sleeping chamber to change into her best dress.

Chapter Forty-One

The First Congregational Church, New London, December 20, 1786

Squatting down, Henry Channing threw several sheets of paper into the fire burning on the small hearth in his study. He stood up and meditatively watched as the thick paper curled in the heat, and wisps of smoke spiraled up from the edges. The paper caught fire and flamed brightly for a few seconds, then turned to ash.

Channing picked up the papers lying on his desk. He pushed open the study door and walked into the church. An expectant hush fell over the crowd, and all eyes followed the young minister as he climbed the stairs to the high pulpit of the First Congregational Church and took out his sermon notes.

Below him, a sea of humanity overflowed the pews and spilled into the side aisles and out of the doorway into the yard and around the new building. Hannah Occuish sat in the front pew, with Mr. Douglas on one side of her and Sheriff Richards on the other.

Hands smoothing the pages before him, Channing looked out at the crowd. He knew that the people expected to hear an execution sermon along the lines of the published ones that everyone had read: a chronicle of a life of hardhearted sin, escalating into crime, and culminating in a hanging. They did not, however, anticipate a recounting of Hannah's repentance. Instead, they expected the minister to plead with Hannah to repent before the hanging. If she did, the execution sermon appendix would then contain the usual description of the criminal's public confession on the gallows.

But Channing didn't plan to deliver what New London wanted from him. He had decided to tell them the truth that had become quite evident to him back in July, just hours after Eunice Bolles had been laid in her grave.

The Red Lion Inn, July of 1786

"Mr. Channing!" Larrabee opened the garret door wide and stepped aside. "Come in. What brings you out in this foul storm?"

"Mr. Larrabee, I've been told that Hannah Occuish has been badly beaten by the Widow."

Larrabee nodded. "I've heard about it."

"And I've heard that you are to be her counsel."

"Yes, Judge Law spoke to me this morning," Larrabee admitted.

"Good. That's good," said Channing, sitting down in the chair Larrabee had pulled out for him. "I spent the morning with Hannah Occuish." The minister leaned forward. "When I spoke to her about God, she said that she has never heard of him!"

"You don't believe that, do you?" Larrabee smiled at the young man. "I've heard that Mrs. Rogers keeps a Bible in her front room. Hannah could have read it whenever she had time."

"Hannah cannot read," Channing stated tersely. "Her mistress lays the blame on her race."

"Well, perhaps she is right, Mr. Channing. Hannah is the product of two ignorant peoples, and I plan to build my defense of her upon that fact."

"I can't agree with you. Many persons of her complexion read well. Either the Widow is not a good teacher, or she did not give Hannah time to study her letters."

"You are too precipitate in forming a negative judgment of Mrs. Rogers. The child must work as her mistress commands her, and if Hannah cannot read, for whatever reason, she can learn about God in church."

Mr. Channing raised his eyebrows. "You have forgotten, Mr. Larrabee, the Widow does not attend any church. And none of the churches in New London have had a minister for . . ."

"Yes, yes, I know," Larrabee said quickly, holding up a hand.

"You also know that Mrs. Rogers punishes the child far too harshly. Hannah has lived for years in fear of whippings."

Larrabee nodded. "Yes, I have heard all about Hannah's wounded back and legs; but surely you do not question Mrs. Rogers' right to correct her servant?"

"No, it's a master's job to train and correct his dependents, but discipline must be based on moral principles in order to teach those same principles. If we terrorize our children and servants with harsh punishment, we don't teach them right from wrong, we only teach them to avoid being caught."

"Yes, it is true that's the only lesson Hannah seems to have learned from Mrs. Rogers." Larrabee hitched his chair closer to the table. "But are you suggesting that the Widow, that any master, should spare the rod?"

"I do not question any master's right to administer reasonable discipline."

Larrabee smiled. "Come now, what constitutes reasonable, Mr. Channing?"

"I admit that question has long been a matter of debate; however, I believe that our society must make a finer determination than it has done to date."

Larrabee shook his head doubtfully. "What would happen to us if masters could not discipline their servants as they see fit without fear of interference or rebuke?"

Reverend Channing leaned forward. "What has happened to us when they can?"

Morning, First Congregational Church, December 20, 1786

Reverend Channing glanced down at his notes and then began to speak. [8]

" 'The cry of innocent blood hath entered into the ears of the Lord . . . but this day will silence its claims . . . justice forbids that [Hannah] should live out half of her days . . . Yes; in a few hours [she] will be executed . . . one who had never learned to live . . .' "

A grave silence, punctuated by soft sobs, reigned as the congregation waited for the minister to chronicle Hannah Occuish's descent into to a life of sin that had culminated in murder and, shortly, her own death on the gallows standing just a stone's throw away.

" '[In light of the] . . . impracticability of adapting a Discourse . . . To the improvement of one who, until within a few weeks ignorant of the first principals of Religion, having been left to heathenish darkness in a Christian land . . . she hath repeatedly declared to me, that she did not know that there was a GOD, before she was told it after her imprisonment.' "

Men and women dabbed their eyes with handkerchiefs kept easy to hand.

" 'Principally then to my Auditory let the present opportunity be devoted.' "

Mr. Channing's auditory stirred uneasily, glancing sideways at each other.

" 'Are there any in this assembly whose consciences reproach them with . . . cruel inattention to their Children & Servants? Such are this day called to their duty . . . May every spectator of this day's painful scene, learn the importance of faithfulness in relations of Parent & Master.' "

Scattered gasps of dismay rose from the congregation as the minister skewered them for failing to take their servants to church and for inconsistency in disciplining their charges.

" 'Shameful & unpardonable, my brethern, is the almost universal neglect of family Instruction & Government. One of the truly unhappy consequences of this neglect, we behold in the ignominious end of this poor girl . . .

" '. . . some of those duties [to instruct]; to the discharge of which you are obligated as <u>Parents</u> & <u>Master</u>; & to the neglect of which the melancholy scene at this day is in a great measure to be charged.' "

"What does he mean by that?" someone's loud whisper reverberated through the church.

" 'Children & Servants should early be taught to read . . . But are not our servants, my brethern, too often forgotten? Most of those who have, instead of being spurred to that application, without which there can be no proficiency, are constantly interrupted by our many calls. At length ambition flags, and, being discouraged, they trifle away the little time allotted them. Their consequent little progress is now imputed to a want of genius peculiar to the complexion . . . highly favored will be that servant, who is not left, either to heathenish darkness in a <u>Christian Land</u>, or to spell out unassisted the principals of Religion . . .

" 'I would here anticipate another objection [that] Servants bought with our money are our absolute property . . . in a word; . . . they are not your own: for they <u>are bought with a price</u>. If you alienate them from his service who hath <u>bought them even with his own blood</u>, the debt contracted on your part will, I fear, render you insolvent, & continue you to that prison whence there is no discharge . . .' "

A gasp rose from the congregation.

" '. . . lighter offences are passed with a gentle rebuke; more heinous crimes call for great severity. A light reproof in the latter case wold countenance rather than correct the offence: and, let me add, the parent or master would not be guiltless.' "

Chapter Forty-Two

Late Morning, Meeting House Hill, New London, December 20, 1786

"Step back! Step back!" an officer barked. "Move away." The people pressing up against the rectangle of soldiers surrounding the small wagon backed slowly, impeded by the forward push from behind. "Farther! Keeping moving!"

The mass stumbled raggedly backwards.

"Farther! Let us pass."

The officer walked back and forth, shouting until the soldiers no longer felt the crowd's breath on their necks.

"Carry on, Sheriff."

The horse obediently leaned into the traces, and began pulling the small cart slowly up Court Street. Richards pulled the right rein at the courthouse, and walked the horse toward a clearing at the top of the hill overlooking the harbor. He stopped the wagon parallel to the front of the gallows.

"Form a walkway!" the officer shouted.

The soldiers nervously repositioned themselves to form a guarded path from the back of the small wagon to the gallows.

Carefully ignoring the gallows to his left, Richards rubbed his damp hands dry on his breeches. He leaned down and looped the reins around a small iron spike protruding from the wagon headboard. "How should we do this?" he asked.

Douglas answered softly. "We'd better walk on either side of her and hold her arms to keep her steady."

Richards nodded. "When we get up there, you stay with her, and I'll, uh," he cleared his throat.

Douglas jumped down without waiting for Richards to finish and went to the back of the cart. Richards came up behind him.

"Hannah."

The girl raised her head, her glassy eyes level with theirs.

"It's time to get down." Richards picked up the coil of rope lying in Hannah's lap and looped it over one shoulder.

"It's time to get down," Douglas repeated, taking her nearest arm; Richards took the other.

"You have to get out of the cart."

Hannah looked around them, scrutinizing the crowd hopefully.

"We'll have to lift her out," said Douglas. "On three."

The Sheriff and jailer lifted Hannah off the end of her coffin. As her feet touched the ground, Hannah lurched to one side, jerking the coil of rope around Richards' shoulder and the noose around her own neck. The men grasped her arms tightly and held her up between them. Keeping one hand firmly on the girl's upper arm, Richards shrugged off a loop of the rope, easing the tension on his shoulder and Hannah's neck. He and Mr. Douglas walked forward. Hannah stumbled along, torso twisting and turning to look over the line of soldiers, the loop of rope swinging back and forth between herself and Sheriff Richards.

As they passed, the soldiers fell in behind, slowly moving forward and forming a line in front of the gallows. Richards and Douglas stopped and turned Hannah toward the crowd. Judge Law, Colonel Halsey, Mr. Hempstead, and other leading citizens stood in a group to their right, at the end of the line of soldiers.

"Hold her."

Douglas tightened his steadying grip and nodded. "I've got her."

Richards released Hannah's arm and pulled a sheet of parchment from his pocket. He unfolded the crisp paper and read aloud.

Hannah Occuish, you have been convicted of murdering Eunice Bolles, a six-year-old child in the peace of God, with malice aforethought. Let it be known that all who commit heinous crimes will be called to account, regardless of age or circumstance, as prescribed by the law of the State of Connecticut.

Richards refolded the parchment and shoved it back into his pocket. He took hold of Hannah's arm and nodded to Douglas. As if mystified, Hannah turned unresistingly to face the gallows.

Douglas cleared his throat. "Step up."

"What?" Hannah asked confusedly.

"Step up on the gallows."

Comprehension dawned on Hannah's face. "No! No!" She jerked her arms back and forth, screaming and twisting to look behind her.

"Poor child!" someone cried out. "Poor child! She's terrified."

"Poor Eunice!" another voice shouted.

"Let's carry her," Richards said, glancing back at the line of tense soldiers. "The crowd is pushing forward."

"Only for a better look," Douglas spat, struggling to keep his grip on Hannah's arm. "We can't get her up there until we bind her." He looked over to the group with the Judge. "Mr. Hempstead, the other rope!"

The sharp winter wind snatched Hempstead's hat from his head as he hurried over to the gallows, rope in hand.

"Her legs, get her legs."

Bareheaded, Hempstead bent down and wound the rope around Hannah's legs. He made a hasty knot by her ankles and stood up, resisting the urge to clamp his hands over his ears to muffle Hannah's piercing shrieks. Heads turned away from the writhing, screaming prisoner, Richards and Douglas pushed Hannah's arms together and held them tightly. Hempstead tied her wrists quickly and backed away even more quickly, ears ringing. Richards and Douglas lifted Hannah's body and set her feet onto the gallows.

One hand on Hannah's upper arm, Richards dipped his shoulder and dropped the coil of rope. Mr. Hempstead picked it up and paid out a length of it.

"Shall I . . ."

"Yes," Douglas interrupted, gesturing for him to go ahead.

Hempstead threw the coil of rope over the crossbeam of the gallows. The hangman picked up the coil and drew up the slack.

Richards tightened his grip on Hannah's arm. "Stop, you're pulling the noose tighter."

To his surprise, Hannah stopped struggling and looked him in the face. "Thank you for being kind to me."

"Kind?" Richard flinched. "Did you say I've been kind?" He crouched down.

Hannah's unbound, long hair whipped across Richards' face. He turned reflexively, one hand clawing the strands from his eyes. When he looked back at her, Hannah was intently examining the crowd.

"Come on, Sheriff. It's a terrible pity, but there's nothing else we can do." Douglas put a consoling hand on Richards' arm. "May God have mercy on us all."

At Douglas' nod, the hangman pulled the rope swiftly hand over hand, quickly lifting Hannah's feet off of the platform. Legs bound, the child's body writhed and bucked, pulling the noose tighter. Hannah's face and features turned red, then to swollen purple, and her tongue began to protrude between puffy, blue lips.

"Give me a hand!" a man cried, struggling to hold up a fainting woman. A bystander elbowed forward, shouting, "Move back! Move back, I say, and give her room!"

Together, the men eased the woman to the frozen ground, amidst a forest of legs and blowing skirts. While they patted the unconscious woman's hands and face, cries and groans rose from the undulating sea of surrounding humanity. Some people shielded their eyes with sweaty palms and creased handkerchiefs or looked away, wondering what had possessed them to want to see someone hang. Other spectators locked their eyes on Hannah, their faces masks of disassociated shock or stoic determination to see justice done; a few stared slack-faced, their features stamped by morbid fascination. More than a few would-be spectators pushed through the crowd to make their escape, like young Larrabee had done so many years ago.

Flinching at the sound of loud retching just behind them, Thomas Shaw slipped a hand under his mother's elbow. "Shall we go home?"

Mrs. Shaw looked over at Judge Law's level profile; his expression exuded grim resolve. She shook her head. "No, Thomas, we have to stay. If we leave now, the rabble will take it as a condemnation of the government."

Thomas looked askance at his mother. "Are you sure? No one would expect a woman your age to stand in the cold for so long."

"Yes." Mrs. Shaw nodded. "It can't take much longer."

Thomas shook his head doubtfully. "I hope you're right."

Ten minutes later, Hannah's body hung limply at the end of the rope, spasmodically twitching; her face grotesquely mottled and swollen beyond recognition. When the twitching finally stopped, the hangman slowly lowered Hannah's body into Douglas' and Richards' upheld arms. The jailer and sheriff laid Hannah on the ground in front of the scaffold and knelt beside her. The doctor came forward and stooped down with them. He put two fingers on Hannah's neck.

"She's dead."

"You're sure she's dead?"

The doctor looked at Richards sadly. "As dead as Eunice Bolles."

Chapter Forty-Three

Late Morning, The Gallows, Meeting House Hill, December 20, 1786

"Are they still planning to take her?" Richards asked Douglas. "Yes, they are."

"Well, call them over. Let's get this over with." Richards ran a hand over his face. "Let's get this over with," he repeated, getting to his feet.

"To be sure, Will." Douglas stood up and waved to several Indian men, standing in a small copse of trees at the edge of the field.

All heads twisted to see who Douglas was gesturing to, and then, murmuring and staring, moved back to make a path to the gallows for Joseph Occuish and his companions. Joseph walked slowly, clutching the lead reins of a horse, hitched to a small wagon. He stopped the cart alongside Hannah's body and waited for an Indian woman to climb down from the seat. The woman, her skirts blowing in the cold wind, silently watched the men slide the coffin out of the back of Richards' cart, and put it on the ground next to Hannah's body.

After Joseph and the others lifted Hannah into the coffin, the woman knelt down. With gentle hands, she composed Hannah's limbs and straightened her clothes. Finished, the woman stood up and stepped back to let Joseph nail down the coffin lid. Without saying a word, the men lifted the casket into the bed of their wagon. The woman climbed into the wagon and sat down next to the casket. She leaned back against the cart, rested her hand on top of the coffin, and closed her eyes. Joseph grasped the horse's bridle and turned the cart toward Niantic.

As the Nehantics and their cart disappeared into the woods, Thomas Shaw handed his mother and Mrs. Law up the step of the Shaws' elegant closed carriage. Judge Law climbed in after them, followed by the younger man.

"It's finally over," said the Judge, sitting down next to his wife.

Mrs. Shaw turned her head away from the window and studied the Judge's face for a few seconds. "Yes, well, I'm not sure that it is over," she remarked.

Law's eyebrows went up. "Oh?"

"This part is over, but . . ." Mrs. Shaw gestured toward the gallows. "It's not over."

Judge Law grimaced. "Oh, the people will talk about the hanging for a while, but that's all it will be, talk. Besides, what can be said now that has not already been thrashed out during the past few months? No, it's all over, and it's best for the town that we put all of this behind us."

"Yes," Thomas Shaw agreed. "That is the best that we can do, now. And pray that nothing like this happens again."

"Happens again? A murder like this?" Mrs. Law's voice rose in dismay. "Nothing like this can happen again, now that Hannah Occuish is dead."

"It is unlikely that someone will commit murder any time soon, especially since those with a taste for violence have seen that the state will not tolerate the murder of its citizens," Thomas rejoined. "But that's not all this case was about."

"Oh, certainly," said Mrs. Law. "You're referring to the Widow. That's not likely to happen again, either. Surely the people have listened to Mr. Channing and will be more careful about how they correct their servants and children."

Mrs. Shaw turned her head and looked out of the window, not overly concerned about giving offense. Ann Prentis Law's powers of perception had never been impressive in their schooldays, and they seemed even less so now.

Thomas stepped into the breach. "Yes, some will," he said in soothing tones. "No doubt Reverend Channing's sermon moved the hearts of masters and parents, or at least, of some of them. But others, I fear, are not so easily persuaded, and they will not heed his advice until . . ."

"Until the law compels them," Mrs. Shaw finished for her son, looking back into the carriage.

"Yes, that's so," the Judge agreed. "People are naturally corrupt, and the government must enforce the rule of law to protect its citizens. Without law as the basis for a civil society, we are all lost."

Mrs. Shaw gazed at the Judge. "If only we could agree on the definition of a civil society."

The Shaws' driver slowly negotiated a path through the thousands of people making their way back to town, the mob coalescing into small, chattering groups, shaking off the gallows mood as they walked.

"What a frightful sight!" a woman commented. "I have never seen anything so terrible, and you'll never catch me at such a gruesome spectacle again."

"It's not likely you'll have the opportunity of attending another; the hanging of a murderer being such a rare thing," her companion sagely remarked.

An older man shook his head sadly. "What a terrible thing, to hang a child."

"Oh, we all knew that it had to be done. Hannah was a murderess, like Kate Garrett before her."

"Who?"

"The Indian girl hanged for killing her infant, oh, fifty years ago."

"Speaking of Indians, where was Hannah's mother today? I didn't see her with the other Indians," a young woman asked, tightening her grip on her small daughter's hand.

"Neither did I. I didn't see Mrs. Bolles or the Widow Rogers, either."

"Of course not! You wouldn't expect Mrs. Bolles to come to an execution and risk marking the baby. As for the Widow . . . I'm not surprised that she didn't dare to show her face today. Even her own kind are angry with her."

The older man nodded. "My wife always said that no good could come from those zealots. They are a law unto themselves in matters of doctrine, and this is what comes of their ideas."

"Oh, they aren't all of the Widow's stamp," opined the young mother. "Besides, I lean toward the Baptists myself, and I have a sister who married a Quaker. Though I don't pretend to like all of his ideas, he's a good husband to my sister."

"It's true, the Widow is to blame. Think of what Mrs. Rogers did to that poor girl! Mr. Channing said it right, a spring wound too tight will rebound."

"She may have been too harsh on the child, but 'twas the girl who accomplished murder all by herself."

"Maybe so . . ."

"It is so, yet Mr. Channing put the blame for this coil upon us all. I tell you, my blood ran cold to hear him accuse us! How can I be held accountable for the abuse of Hannah Occuish? I didn't know anything about it."

"Nor did I."

"What do you say, sir?" The older man asked the man who happened to be walking beside him.

The man shook his head. "I'm so lately come from Scotland to this town - and to this country - that I'm unfit to form an opinion," he answered politely.

"True, true," said the older man with approval. "Best not to judge your new neighbors."

The newcomer nodded pleasantly. *To hear this babble,* he thought, *you'd believe that no one knew anything at all about Hannah Occuish and the Widow.* He smiled to himself. *Odd, considering how everyone seems to know everybody else's business well enough. Ach, why should I fret?* he chided himself, picking up his pace. *I'd never do anything like that; besides, I'm new here, so that girl is no fault of mine.*

Chapter Forty-Four

Evening, The Red Lion Inn, December 20, 1786

"We need another cask of ale in the common room."

"Here." Molly held out her ring of keys to Lizzy. "Take James and bring up another."

"Oh!"

"Better bring up two while you're at it." Molly jingled the ring of keys in front of Lizzy. "Go ahead, take them, else you won't be able to get into the cellar."

"Yes, ma'am." Lizzy smiled and reached out tentatively. "Thank you, but are you sure? The keys? What if I lose them?"

"You won't. I know that I can rely on you, and I'll need your help even more now. With Bess leaving us you'll have to help train the new girl." Molly folded the keys into Lizzy's hands. "Go on now, there's no time to waste. I imagine a hanging makes for as much thirst as everything else seems to do."

Molly went over to the hearth. "Bess, how is that chowder?"

The maid dipped the serving spoon into the big black iron pot and took a sip. She shook her head. "It's not right."

Molly took the spoon from Bess' hand and sipped from it. "No, it's not. What do you think it needs?"

"A bit more nutmeg."

Molly smiled. "Your husband will be a lucky man."

Flushed with pleasure, Bess got a small flat grinder and grated the nutmeg over the bubbling chowder.

"James!" Molly waylaid the stable boy as he trailed behind Lizzy on the way to the cellar.

"Did the wagon of marsh hay arrive?"

"No, ma'am. But Mrs. Shaw's servant came by with a note for you." James dug a grimy hand into his pocket and handed over a folded, sealed sheet of heavy paper.

Molly took the note. "When did this come?"

James shrugged. "A while ago."

"A while ago . . . how long a while?"

James shrugged again. "Not so long ago. I was getting the chickens into the coop when he came, so I thought I'd better finish that before I came in."

"Normally, that would be the thing to do, but a message from an important person deserves better attention. From now on, bring all notes directly to me, no matter who sends them or what you are doing."

James nodded. "I will, mistress."

"Make sure that you do. Now go along and help Lizzy."

Molly sat down by the hearth and broke the wax seal on the note. She ran her eyes over the single heavy white page. Snorting in amusement, Molly refolded the note and thrust it into her apron pocket. "Bess, I'll watch the kitchen. You go up and put a pallet on the floor in your room."

Bess banged a tray of dirty tankards down on the kitchen table and wiped her damp face with her apron. "Don't any of them hanker for an evening by their own firesides?"

"Let's hope no such rage takes hold," Molly laughed. "A full common room means a full purse."

"And a full cellar," added Lizzy happily, her hand unconsciously feeling for the ring of keys strung on a cord tied securely around her waist.

"Mistress!" James burst through the kitchen door. "Mrs. Shaw's man has come back. He's just outside, but he doesn't have a note. He has somebody with him."

Molly grinned. "Well, tell them to come in."

With an air of excitement, James stood back, holding the door wide to admit a middle-aged manservant and a young girl.

The girl carried a small bundle under one arm.

"Mrs. Shaw said you would be expecting us." The man gestured toward the girl. "Here she is, ma'am."

The girl curtsied. "How do you do, Mistress Coit?"

"I do well, and I hope you do, too."

Selah smiled. "I do."

"Would you like chowder before you go back into the cold?" Molly looked at the manservant.

"Yes, ma'am, I would."

"And you?" she looked at Selah. "Do you like chowder?"

Selah nodded. "Yes, ma'am."

"Bess, get down four bowls. I know without asking that our James is hungry."

While Bess ladled out the chowder, Molly threw her cloak around her shoulders and went out to the stable.

"Go inside," she said to the stableman. "Bess has a bowl of chowder for you."

Molly stood in the stable doorway, puffs of frozen breath wreathing her head, watching the stablemen hasten to the warm kitchen. When the door closed behind him, she took the note out of her pocket and held it up to catch the bright starlight and re-read the neatly penned lines.

Dear Mistress Coit:

I know that you will not mind my sending Selah to you this evening, instead of next month, as we agreed, to begin her training in domestic economy under your most excellent oversight. I am entirely sensible of your kindness in taking Selah under liberal terms, and though you take her without benefit of a contract of indenture to protect your rights as mistress, I trust you will not be sorry to have Selah as a member of your respectable household. Her present state of training in basic cooking and sewing will amply compensate for the trouble of teaching her the art of fine cookery and baking, and I know that you will do as well by her as you have done by other young girls of diverse stations entrusted to your diligent care.

Again, I ask your forgiveness that you find Selah at your door before time - and without more than a few hours of notice. But it seems to me fitting to send her on to you today. Since we have so sadly disposed of one girl's fate this morning, we would do our souls well to more happily dispose of another's before this day ends.

Respectfully yours,

Smiling to herself, Molly folded Mrs. Shaw's note and slipped it back in her pocket.

"Indeed, we must not forget to look to the good of our own souls this day." Molly rubbed her hands together to warm them and chuckled. "Oh, well, let it never be said that the lady Shaw lacks a flair for the dramatic."

Leaning her head against the stable doorframe, Molly gazed fondly at the Red Lion. Three stories of windows sparkled with flickering candles and hearth fires, showcasing the animated figures within. From her vantage point by the stables, Molly watched her guests eating and talking in the side dining room on one side of the hall and her servants bustling around the kitchen on the other. And, she knew, the common room and front dining room were even more crowded. She could plainly see the jurors seated at the end of the table nearest the back window of the private chamber on the second floor and a mother walking a fretful baby to and fro in the women's sleeping chamber across the hall. Only Molly's room off of the kitchen and the maids' shared chamber on the third floor had dark windows, and they would stay dark until the early hours of the morning.

Shivering from the cold, Molly wrapped her cloak tightly around herself and walked purposefully across the stable yard, an anticipatory smile on her lips. She pushed the kitchen door wide, and stepped eagerly into the Red Lion's warm embrace.

The End

Afterwards

Sarah Occuish dropped out of the records after leaving Hannah in Quaker Hill, and Tuis Sharper disappeared after joining the army in Stonington in 1780. Charles ran away from Mr. Edward Packer in 1792 and was living in Stonington in 1810.

The Shaws emancipated Selah in 1795, at the age of 21. She married Jack Almy, a slave, in February of 1800, who was emancipated four years later. Mr. and Mrs. Almy owned a house near the courthouse. In 1814, Jack Almy was charged with running a brothel. Only one of the Almy's six children survived infancy. Selah died October 29, 1817 at the age of 43.

Five months after the Reverend Henry Channing verbally scourged the town, the New London Congregational Church ordained the young preaching candidate, and a "revival of religion in the congregation, followed . . ." Channing's subsequent writings suggest that Hannah's execution had a deep impact on his thought. He left New London in 1806.

Sheriff Richards remained in his office until his death in 1812.

Judge Richard Law, son of Governor Jonathan Law, first mayor of New London, and a former member of Congress and an elector to the state constitutional convention, continued his distinguished career as a judge and Chief Justice of the Superior Court. He died in 1806.

Colonel Halsey's unusual ship made its first voyage in January of 1787, and was still in service when the Colonel died thirty-two years later.

The Shaw family expanded their trading business, and grew increasingly wealthy. They also continued to free their slaves. In 1787, Thomas gave the Congregational Church two houses and plots of land for the minister and the church sexton and served on the town school committee.

Sixty-eight years old when Hannah went to the gallows, the Widow Rogers lived to the great age of ninety. Mrs. Rogers is buried with her husband, Ichabod, in the Rogerene cemetery, now on the grounds of Connecticut College, in Quaker Hill.

Many of the Indians from New London County, including

some of the Occuishs, moved to Brothertown.

Mrs. Bolles gave birth a few months after Hannah's execution. The Bolles named their new daughter Eunice.

The courthouse is still in use. Shaw's Mansion, Stephen Hempstead's family home, Fort Griswold, and Fort Trumbull are open to the public. Timothy Greene's building houses a restaurant on State Street, formerly Court Street. What I believe to be the Widow Rogers' house and a number of other structures from the period are still standing in New London, Quaker Hill, Groton, and Poquonnock Bridge. The Parade still functions as New London's downtown center and was renovated in 2010 and 2011.

Molly Coit expanded the Red Lion's services to include gourmet meals. Her good food, combined with the Red Lion's reputation for respectability, attracted local townswomen, as well as townsmen and travelers, to the Red Lion's dining rooms.

After sheltering George Washington, surviving the British invasion and burning of the town in 1781, and providing Molly Coit with independence, the Red Lion succumbed to the ravages of urban redevelopment in the 1960s.[9]

Appendix

Questions For the Author

Why did Hannah murder Eunice Bolles?

Everyone asks that question, despite Hannah's own explanation: she meant to give Eunice a whipping for telling on her, but lost control of herself. When Hannah realized what she had done, she pulled Eunice over to the wall and pushed the stones down on her to make it look like an accident. Hannah never recanted her confession.

Although rage at being whipped precipitated the attack, Henry Channing's sociological indictment of New London rings true. His analysis of Hannah's life anticipated modern physiological explanations, such as fetal alcohol syndrome, and psychological explanations, such as post-traumatic stress disorder or fury at the racial and social injustice that circumscribed her life.

Who was Hannah Occuish and how old was she?

The court records of 1780 call her Hannah Sharper, daughter of Sarah Sharper. The appendix to Channing's published sermon identifies her as Hannah Occuish, noting that she assaulted Mary Fish in Groton. Although the sources describe Hannah as a Pequot mulatto or as a Negro, Occuish is a Nehantic Indian name. Hannah's mother, Sarah Occuish, was probably the daughter of Baptist minister Philip Occuish and his wife, Sarah.

Tuis Sharper of Stonington, a mulatto man, was probably Hannah's father.[10] Persons named Tuis and Sharper seem to have been associated with the Packer family of Groton.[11] The fact that Sarah, Hannah, and Charles were sometimes called Sharper and were associated with the Packers of Groton strongly suggests a blood relationship between Tuis Sharper and Hannah.

Contemporary newspapers, Timothy Larrabee's petition, and Henry Channing's sermon give various ages for Hannah.[12] Larrabee and Channing are probably the most reliable sources for

Hannah's age; therefore, Hannah stepped onto the gallows at the age of eleven years and about nine months.

Why didn't you focus more on the influence of race in Hannah's life?

Throughout the novel, I attempted to illuminate the angry hum of racism that permeated every aspect of Hannah's life, while also exploring how gender, status, age, and condition shaped perceptions of her. I also wanted to consider how the memory of the John Stoddard and Jacob Occuish cases may have influenced the authorities, and to examine the influence of religious beliefs on conflicts between their notions about duty and their own self-interest.[13]

Hannah's story is interesting, but what does it tell us about American history?

The Occuish case is difficult to place in historiographical context.[14] The paucity of court records — a docket entry, list of names and court costs, and Larrabee's petition - precludes making positive statements about important legal aspects of the case.[15] And we cannot compare Hannah with other young children who committed murder, because there are none of any race in the records until much later.[16]

Seeing Hannah's life in a rich historical context, however, provides a fresh perspective on the troubling inconsistencies between revolutionary ideals and the legal status of people of color and of women. Deciding what to do with Hannah raised questions about the definition of citizenship[17] and about the role of religion in maintaining the precarious balance between personal freedom and civil stability.

Finally, Hannah's case certainly raised a question in 1786 that we face with alarming frequency in the twenty-first century: what does a democratic society do with children who commit murder?

How did you pick the case of Hannah Occuish for a first novel?

I came across the case in 1993 while doing research in the Indian Papers, held in the State Archives in the Connecticut State Library, for Christopher Collier, professor and State Historian. The following semester, I submitted a research paper on Hannah Occuish. I considered doing my Ph.D. dissertation on her case, but as there didn't seem to be enough material, I moved on to the Rogerenes.

While researching the Rogerenes, under the direction of Richard D. Brown at the University of Connecticut, I found links between the dissenters and Hannah Occuish. After completing my Ph.D., I returned to the Occuish case, and began to think that Hannah's story would be better told as a fleshed-out novel. I started writing it in 1999.

Jan Schenk Grosskopf

Separating Fact From Fiction

Did you make up the stories about the Rogerenes, Sharper's ears, Kate Garret, Sarah Bramble, Jacob Occuish, Betty Shaw, Sally Brooks, and John Stoddard and the murder of the Bolles?

No. The stories come from primary and secondary sources. Whether or not Timothy Larrabee was influenced by the execution of Shaw, however, I can't say.

In the novel, Sarah Occuish takes Hannah away from Groton, remarking that there are enough mixed-race babies in Poquonnock. Did she actually say that?

I put those words in Sarah's mouth, but she had to have been well aware of what could happen to her daughter.

Was Hannah sexually molested?

I don't know. Helping Charles attack Mary Fish and fighting with him over the spoils while Mary lay unconscious and bleeding in the dust, and killing Eunice while she cried for mercy suggest that Hannah was unable to sympathize with the suffering of others. We also know that losing her family and being forced to live with and work for a cruel and demanding mistress had to be traumatizing.

Thinking about Hannah's vulnerability reminds us about the millions of children who are potential - or are already - prisoners of the international sex slave industry. I hope that learning about Hannah will encourage readers to contact the International Justice Mission to find out what they can do to combat the exploitation and abuse of children and women.

Factual Details of Hannah Occuish's Life

In 1780, Hannah and Charles, children of Sarah, attacked seven-year-old Mary Fish on her way to or from school and stripped her unconscious body. While the children argued over a gold necklace and clothing, Mary revived and ran home. The Groton sheriff read a writ for both children to Sarah at Mr. Packer's house. The town bound out Charles, but Sarah Occuish slipped away to Quaker Hill with Hannah. Sarah, an alcoholic, left Hannah with neighbors in Quaker Hill and never returned. Hannah ended up with the Widow Rogers.

In June of 1786, the Widow viciously lashed Hannah for taking strawberries from Eunice Bolles and Mary Rogers. Hannah, a child with the reputation of being a bully and petty thief, publicly vowed to whip Eunice. After Eunice was found dead the morning of July 21, 1786, Hannah told the investigators that on her way to the well, she saw four boys throwing rocks and heard the stone wall fall. A search revealed no evidence of the boys. At a meeting that evening, the authorities decided to re-question Hannah the next morning. After that questioning at the Widow's, the investigators took Hannah to the Bolles' and showed her Eunice's body - a common investigative practice of the time.

Standing by the coffin, Hannah confessed. She said that she saw Eunice on her way to school, ran back to the house, set down the water pail, secreted a rock in her hand, ran out into the road, and called Eunice over to look at some patchwork. While Eunice was looking down, Hannah hit her on the head with the rock and, losing control of herself, kept beating Eunice, despite the girl's pleas for mercy, until Eunice was unconscious. When she began to come around, Hannah strangled Eunice and dragged her over to the stone wall and pushed it down on the body, hoping it would appear that Eunice had tried to climb the wall.

The mood in town changed from somewhat ugly to sympathetic after word got out that the Widow abused and neglected Hannah. Nevertheless, her remote attitude in court, lack of remorse, and disrespectful behavior to adults while she was in jail perplexed and upset everyone.

The Superior Court, Judge Richard Law presiding, heard Hannah's case on October 6, 1786. (There are no transcriptions of the court testimony.) The jury found her guilty on October 7th, and Law sentenced her on October 20ᵗʰ. Hannah showed no interest in her trial or the sentencing, thinking it was about whether or not to whip her. She was briefly upset when someone explained the sentence, but calmed down when assured that the state would not hang a child.

Timothy Larrabee's petition for pardon was submitted and denied in late October. Hannah was upset for a few weeks before the execution; however, she sat quietly in church while Mr. Channing preached her execution sermon on December 20ᵗʰ. She was frightened on the way to Meeting House Hill and screamed and struggling while being put on the scaffold. After having thanked Richards, Hannah was hanged in front of thousands of spectators.

The Nehantics

The scourge of debt - whether contracted to pay doctors' fees or to purchase the English goods that signaled respectability - undermined the Nehantics' efforts to remain independent.[18] By the mid-1700s, many Indians began leaving Connecticut. The exodus to Brothertown in Oneida, New York swelled from a trickle into a stream from the 1780s onward.[19]

By 1868, the Nehantics were in severe financial crises. Interest from the tribe's invested funds and income from renting out 400 prime acres amounted to the ridiculously low sum of about $150.00. The General Assembly allowed a judge to keep up to $125.00 - almost all of the tribe's cash - for the ostensible purpose of maintaining the Nehantics' half-acre cemetery, containing six gravestones. Not long afterwards, relatives of former Indian overseers snapped up about 160 reservation acres for about $4000.00. In September of 1870, the Superior Court ordered the sale of the remaining 240 acres, and had a stone placed in the tribal cemetery, inscribed: "Niantic Indian Burying Ground, Tribe Extinct, 1870." This was done despite the fact that Nehantics still lived in the area.[20]

Although declared extinct in 1870, the Nehantics received some money during the following decades. It's not clear if this included the $125.00 put aside to keep up the burial ground.[21] James Luce bought the cemetery in 1886, and the state used the money to move the Nehantics' remains, including Hannah's grandparents, to the Niantic Cemetery.[22]

Endnotes

[1] Used at the time to mean part Indian and part African.

[2] Used to mean mentally ill or senile.

[3] Indictment Against Hannah Occuish, 1786, New London Superior Court Files, September 1786, State Archives, Connecticut State Library (CSL), Hartford, New London Superior Court Files. The indictment is quoted in full.

[4] There is no record of what the foreman actually said.

[5] *The Connecticut Courant*, October 30, 1786. All newspapers can be found in many archives and on-line sources.

[6] Quotation from Petition to General Assembly for Hannah Occuish, October 1786, Crimes and Misdemeanors, Vol. 6, Reel 24, 306a and b, CSL.

[7] The letter is fiction, the facts and quotation in the letter are not (Leonard Woods Labaree, compiled, *Public Records of the State of Connecticut, May 1785-January 1789* (Hartford) 232-33, 255-56, 568-69.)

[8] I have excerpted Mr. Channing's sermon. See Henry Trevett Channing, *God Admonishing his People as Parents and Masters* (New London, 1787), Early American Prints, Series 1, No. 199547, Readex, web.

[9] The New London County Historical Society (NLCHS), headquartered in the Shaw Mansion, New London, Connecticut, has a picture of the Red Lion, taken in the 1960s.

Information about New London town leaders can be found in many local historical societies and in histories, genealogies, court records, and the state and colony records. For examples, see Barbara W. Brown and James M. Rose, James, *Black Roots in Southeastern Connecticut 1650-1900* (New London, 1980, reprint 2001) 5, 275-6, 368, 369; Francis Manwaring Caulkins, *History of New London* (New London, 1896, reprint 1985) quotation, 589; 364, 476, 506 (ft 2), 532, 576, 588, 619, 667, and "Town Officers -New London" (Unpub. manuscript) M201; Denise

Schenk Grosskopf, "The Limits of Religious Dissent in Seventeenth-Century Connecticut: The Rogerene Heresy," (Doctoral Dissertation, University of Connecticut, 1999); Jan Schenk Grosskopf, "Family, Religion, and Disorder: The Rogerenes of New London, 1675-1726, *Connecticut History*, Vol. 40, No. 2, Fall 2001, 203-224; Paul F. Laubenstein, ed., *The First Church of Christ in New London Three Hundredth Anniversary May 10, 17, 31 and October 11, 1942* (New London, CT, 1946) NLCHS, 285.8 F519a; *Records and Papers of the New London County Historical Society*, Part IV, Volume I. (New London, 1893) 79, 80-1; James Swift Rogers, *James Rogers of New London, CT., and His* Descendants (Boston, 1902) 97 and entire.

For a discussion of the connections between revolutionary rhetoric and ideas about women's rights see Kate Davies, *Catharine Maccaulay and Mercy Otis Warren The Revolutionary Atlantic and the Politics of Gender* (Oxford, Eng,: Oxford University Press, 2005).

For the New London and Groton battles, see Rufus Avery and Stephen Hempstead, *Narrative of Jonathan Rathbun, with Accurate Accounts of the Capture of Groton Fort, The Massacre that Followed, and the Sacking and Burning of New London, September 6, 1781, by the British Forces, under the command of the Traitor Benedict Arnold* (1840) *NLCHS, .973.3377R188.* Also see Caulkins, *History of New London*, Chapter XXXII, 545-572.

[10] Early on, Sharper and Tuis seem to have been used as a slave's or servant's first name. In 1726, James Harris of Colchester bought a male named Sharper, who lived in New London. On November 23, 1740, a Sharper, presumably male, joined the First Congregational Church in Groton. This Sharper may have been the Sharper and his wife Sylvia, mentioned in the Groton town records of 1780, deserted by Obadiah Bailey when they grew too old to work. Bailey's servants may have been the parents of Tuis and grandparents of Hannah. It's interesting that Bailey deserted them the same year Tuis Sharper joined the army and Sarah took Hannah to Quaker Hill. The only other Sharper mentioned before the late 1700s lived in Lebanon in 1759. There were also six persons with the last name of Tuis, sometimes spelled Tewis or Tewit.

Sharper as a last name enters the record in 1770. Stonington officials arrested Tuis Sharper, an Indian, for breach of peace in 1770. This Tuis Sharper, described as a mulatto Indian, is probably the Tuis Sharper arrested in Stonington in 1773 on suspicion of theft, and the Tuis

Sharper who enlisted from Stonington in 1780. This Tuis Sharper would have been old enough to have fathered Hannah in the mid-1770s and certainly old enough to go to war in 1780 (*First Book of First Church of Christ, Groton, Connecticut* (no date or place) 285.8 F519gr v 1, NLCHS, 5; Receipt for Tues Sharper, Black; Stoddard Papers, CT Army Receipts, Ledyard Historical Society, Bill Memorial Library, Ledyard, CT; Brown and Rose, *Black Roots*, 275-6, 454, 516, 574-5; Vital Statistics (East Lyme), Birth and Marriage Record (CSL).

[11] In 1765, James Packer mentioned a Tuis in his will, commending the faithfulness of his aged servant. Perhaps this is the Tuis, an Indian man, arrested in Groton in 1731 for stealing corn. As already noted, authorities read the writ against Hannah and her brother in the home of Joseph Packer of Groton in 1780. In 1792, Hannah's brother Charles, aged twenty, ran away from his master, Edward Packer of Groton (Connecticut Superior Court Records, State of Ct v. Charles Aves and Hannah Sharper, September 1780, CSL; Brown and Rose, *Black Roots*, 564).

[12] Timothy Larrabee told the General Assembly Hannah was eleven years and six months when she committed murder in July of 1786. On December 20, 1786, Channing said that Hannah was eleven years and nine months. A hostile article in the July issue of the Norwich newspaper described Hannah as a Negro, aged fourteen, who murdered Eunice Bolles, aged seven. In July of 1786, the *Connecticut Courant* gave Hannah's age as twelve years and four months and Eunice's as six years, six months. The *Connecticut Gazette* recorded Hannah's age as twelve years and nine months on the day of her execution. (Caulkins appears to have followed the lead of the newspapers when she noted Hannah's age as twelve years and nine months, *History of New London*, 576-77.)

[13] The murder of the Bolles family in 1676 by teenaged John Stoddard had to be on the investigators' minds in 1786. It could hardly have been otherwise, considering the close relationship between the victims of both crimes and the location of both murders, as well as the involvement in both cases of local Indians, the Rogerenes, and the authorities' own ancestors. Knowledge of their forebears' careful investigation in 1676, combined with the knowledge of having failed in their duty to an abused orphan, no doubt influenced the investigation of Eunice's murder and

the disposition of Hannah's case, despite important changes in the law. For a discussion of changes in law, see Cornelia Hughes Dayton, *Women before the Bar, Gender, Law, & Society in Connecticut, 1639-1789* (Chapel Hill and London, 1995). For discussions of ideas about duty, see Lisa Wilson, *Life After Death: Widows in Pennsylvania, 1750*-1850 (Philadelphia, 1992) and Ye *Heart of a Man, The Domestic Life of Men in Colonial New England* (New Haven and London, 1999).

[14] In his study of execution sermons, Daniel Cohen has shown that Mr. Channing's sermon is an illustrative example of the trend to prescribe education as a hedge against crime and as a means of producing good citizens (Daniel Cohen, *Pillars of Salt, Monuments of Grace* (New York, 1993).

[15] It has been suggested that Hannah did not have a guardian present during questioning; however, she was first questioned as a witness, not as a suspect, at the Widow's house on the morning of the murder. We don't know who was present then or the next day when authorities questioned Hannah at the Widow's house and the Bolles' house. In light of the fact that Hannah was an abandoned orphan and not bound out, the authorities who questioned her were ultimately responsible for her.

[16] For a discussion of children and the law, see Holly Brewer, *By Birth or Consent, Children, Law, and the Anglo-American Revolution in Authority* (Omohundro Institute of Early American History and Culture and UNC, 2005). To read about another interesting court case, see Richard D. Brown and Irene Quenzler Brown, *The Hanging of Ephraim Wheeler: A Study of Rape, Incest, and Justice in Early America* (Cambridge, MA, 2000). Hannah does not fit the profile of female murderers. Females who killed usually murdered children in their care, often their own (see Peter C. Hoffer and N.E.H Hull, *Murdering Mothers* (New York, 1981).

[17] Brewer, *By Birth or Consent,* Chpt. 4; Joanne Pope Melish, *Disowning Slavery, Gradual Emancipation and "Race" in New England, 1780-1860* (Ithaca and London, 1998) 79.

[18] The Nehantics' experience was much like the Narragansetts and Na-

ticks of Rhode Island and Massachusetts, who attempted to use English notions about social status and adopted English ways in order to protect their land. The Narragansetts' and Naticks' efforts were often sabotaged by white neighbors, who tore down their fences, destroyed their crops, and scattered their livestock. Appeals to authority produced little protection, forcing Indians to sell their land to support themselves (Stuart Banner, *How the Indians Lost Their Land; Law and Power on the Frontier* (Cambridge, 2005) entire; Jean M. O'Brien, *Dispossession by Degrees: Indian Land and Identity in Natick, Massachusetts, 1650-1790* (New York, 1997) entire; Lawrence M. Hauptman and James D. Wherry, eds., *The Pequots in Southern New England* (London 1990) 121, 123-4; Daniel R. Mandell, *Behind the Frontier, Indians in Eighteenth-century Eastern Massachusetts*, (Lincoln and London, 2000) entire; David. J. Silverman, *Faith and Boundaries: Colonists, Christianity, and community among the Wampanoag Indians of Martha's Vineyard, 1600-1871* (New York, 2005) entire).

[19] Although the records are very incomplete, Brown and Rose traced the permanent movement of Abraham, Philip, Jr. and Rhoda (Hannah's first cousin) to Brothertown with, presumably, at least a few unlisted family members. For example, Rhoda married a member of the Pequot Charles family. Her husband and/or children (if they had any) may have moved north with her. Smith records that some of the great-grandchildren eventually moved to Wisconsin and notes that Occuish descendants attempted to assert their right to reservation lands, but the government refused to recognize their claims.

Brown and Rose also noted at least seven other named individuals, which included Samuel Occom, who moved north from 1786 onward. According to Smith, the Nehantics numbered 104 in 1774, but by 1830, only seventeen remained. The statistics, however, apparently included only those deemed "full-blooded," whatever that meant (Brown and Rose, *Black Roots*, 73, 275-6; Smith, Jane T. (Hills), *Last of the Nehantics*, (Hartford, 1916) entire.)

[20] Smith, entire, quotation, 12.

[21] If not, it wouldn't be surprising; designated funds had a habit of going missing in New London (Denise J. Grosskopf, *They Will Make Mer-*

chandize of You (manuscript in progress) Chapter 3. "The Politics of Authority and Resistance in Connecticut and New London, 1676-1721" and Chapter 4. "Stolen Estates, Burdensome Taxes, and the Rights of Englishmen."

[22] Smith, entire.

CPSIA information can be obtained at www.ICGtesting.com
Printed in the USA
LVOW121924260613

340384LV00001B/12/P